JORDON GREENE

Great meeting you at Scuppernong Books in Greensboro! Enjoy the read!

TO WATCH YOU
BLEED

ARRAY()BOOKS
CONCORD, NORTH CAROLINA

Published by Array Books
213 Franklin Avenue NW | Concord, North Carolina 28025
1.704.659.3915

Edited by Chelly Peeler
Cover design © 2017 by Paramita Bhattacharjee. All rights reserved.
Interior design by Jordon Greene

Published in the United States of America

First Edition

ISBN-10: 0-9983913-0-1
ISBN-13: 978-0-9983913-0-4
1. Fiction: Psychological Thriller
2. Fiction: Psychological Horror
3. Fiction: Mystery & Suspense

To my brother, Jared Greene
for not murdering me in my sleep
while I wrote this story.

ACKNOWLEDGMENTS

First, I'd like to thank my editor, Chelly Peeler. Beyond the fact that you have great taste in music, your edits and recommendations have made all the difference in this story. You're easy to work with and have a great eye for my mistakes.

As usual my family had a large role in the process as well. Thanks to my brother, Jared, and my mother, Kim. Both helped in almost every stage of the book's development but were particularly instrumental in crafting the outline.

A big thank you goes out to Nichole Appleby for helping me with the psychology behind the characters, and to Paul Lorenz for guiding me through my main character's occupation as an Architect. Thanks to Mike Wagner and Kristina Sanger Love for critiquing my initial outline before I began writing.

Thank you to Michael Wienhold and Mike Wager for beta reading the book before it went to the editor. Your notes and corrections were critical to the story. I'd also like to thank KD Delk, Lauren Gragg, Kevin Enloe, Angela Willis and Lisa Hoyle for your help as well. Whether you helped me find the right synonym, described a location, helped with the synopsis or gave input on the book's title, I truly appreciate it.

To you, the reader, thank you for picking up a copy of my newest story. I hope you enjoy it.

CHAPTER 1

A burst of brilliant white danced across the night sky just beyond my vantage outside the rear passenger window. I flinched as thunder shook the car a second later.

"Ah!" Dusty yelped from the seat in front of me.

"Calm your tits," my dad chided him dismissively. "You're not a little girl, or a baby, now are you?"

"No," Dusty tried, his voice was quiet and hurt. "I'm not."

With my lips pursed, I groaned and let my gaze escape to the heavy raindrops pelting my window. It was a cold November rain. It saturated every inch of the bare-limbed sycamores along the roadway, their branches swaying boisterously in the roiling wind.

Dad refused to slow the car despite how hard the wipers were working, and failing, to clear the front windshield. I'm positive the tires had lost traction at least twice since we exited the elementary school parking lot from Dusty's basketball game. I gripped my seatbelt tightly as another lightning bolt streaked the sky, followed a second later by a deafening thunderclap. My pale blue Marvel Comics t-shirt, the one with Captain America and Iron Man facing each other in an epic staring competition, clung to my shoulders, moistened from the short trip to the car.

"You're not?" Dad asked with a hint of a slur. The ever present bottle of cheap Smirnoff vodka was stowed neatly between his hip and the center console. It was Dad's drink of choice. It did the job without the telltale odor. He had taken several generous swigs during the car ride and it was beginning to show.

"No!" Dusty urged with a frown.

I couldn't see his eyes in the dark, but I could imagine the tears taking root at the corners of my little brother's eyes. I wished Dad would stop. Stop badgering him, stop drinking. All of it. Hell, maybe I wished he would just die. I don't know…no. I didn't mean it. I just wanted him to stop being such a douche.

"Then why do you still squeal like a girl then?" Dad asked, taking his eyes off the road to look at my brother. "I mean your brother here doesn't squeal and whine every time a little bit of lightning strikes."

I felt the anger building, but I kept my mouth shut. Dusty didn't answer, he just sat there trying to find the words to say.

"You're what, nine? Your brother's only thirteen, and he doesn't do that shit," Dad continued, waving his arms, his eyes no longer on the road. "I mean for God's sake, you cannot even dribble a damned basketba—"

The car jolted as a tire left the pavement and met gravel a few inches below. I threw my hand against the plastic armrest on my door and clamped my lips shut even though my insides wanted to scream. Once I forced my eyes to open again, I saw Dad fighting with the steering wheel, slowed by the vodka. The car bounced again and jumped back onto the small two-lane road. I let out a breath I had not realized I was holding.

"Ha ha, well wasn't that exciting," Dad whooped. I'm not sure if it was him or the alcohol talking, but the important thing was that we were back on the road. At least we were not on the side of the road wrapped around a tree.

"So Dusty, like I was saying," Dad continued as he paused to take another gulp of his clear companion, "we've really got to work on your dribbling. I bet y'all could have won if you didn't suck at it so badly."

"Why do you have to be so mean to him?" I asked, my voice an octave higher than I had intended. My face felt warm despite the cold outside and it was growing warmer. Why could he not leave Dusty alone? It was just a stupid school game, it didn't even count for anything. It was supposed to be fun, it's not like he was trying out for the NBA.

"Shut up, Chase, I'm talking to your brother." His slur was more pronounced now and the car jerked back and forth at random intervals as Dad tried to compensate the car's trajectory over and over again.

Heat burning in my face, I pushed myself back into my seat and kept my mouth shut. It was either stay quiet or dodge Dad's hand as it shot back aimlessly, trying to connect with anything fleshy. I chose the safer route.

"I'll try harder," Dusty whispered.

"You'll do what?" Dad asked, cupping his ear. "What will you do?"

"I'll try harder!" This time Dusty nearly yelled it.

"Damn right you will!" Dad retorted. "I'm going to wear the hide of that skinny butt until you do."

At that my little brother broke down. It started as a whimper. I begged him silently to stop, but it was no use.

"You're not crying now are you, boy?" Dad asked. He took his eyes off the road again. I wanted to close my eyes, but I couldn't.

Dusty failed to answer and finally the whimper turned into a sob. I finally managed to close my eyes, not wanting to be here, not wanting to witness what was sure to come.

I heard a thump above the sound of the rain popping against the windows. I refused to watch. I had enough images seared into memory to know what was happening. I imagined Dad shoving Dusty against the passenger door, probably pushing harder than he realized.

"Ouch," Dusty yelped again. His sobs became full on crying. I knew the tears were pouring just like the rain outside. I kept my eyes closed.

"Oh come on, you're being such a little girl," Dad complained. "Stop crying or I'll give you something to cry about you little pansy."

I opened my eyes as Dusty tried to contain the emotions that burned inside him. I empathized with him. I knew all too well how he felt right then. The desire to please my dad, the fear of an alcohol in-duced beating, the feeling of knuckles against my cheek, the hope that he just wouldn't get drunk again. Useless. It was all useless.

"Well, well, the little pansy decided to be a big boy," my dad jeered.

That brought Dusty down again and he burst into sobs. His hands went up just as the back of Dad's free hand made contact with Dusty's mouth. He squealed in pain. Quickly the hand retracted and made another swatting motion, this time meeting Dusty's arm instead.

"Stop!" I cried. "You're hurting him!"

I unbuckled my seatbelt and wedged myself between my brother and Dad on top of the center console. I had to stop him. I needed to.

A sudden jolt of pain pierced up my nose as a hand meant for my little brother slammed into me. I extended my hands out, shoving back at my dad and guarding Dusty at the same time. *Not again! Not Dusty!*

The car jerked hazardously from side-to-side but I couldn't stop. He had to stop. I could not let him do this again.

"Move it, Chase, I have to deal with your brother!"

"No! Stop," I screamed as another flash of light shone through the windows. Yet, this time it remained steady. It did not blink out as quickly as it appeared and there was no booming thunder. I looked out the windshield and saw the source of the light. Another car jerked back and forth along the pavement.

"Dad!" was all I could get out. He saw it, too, but his reactions were slow and overemphasized as he yanked the steering wheel. Suddenly the sounds of tires screeching echoed in my head and I felt a harsh bang as the undercarriage met the pavement and the car jerked up onto two wheels. Dad jerked the steering wheel the opposite direction as I tried to get back to my seat and the car wrenched back to the right. My body was slung against the door.

The sound of metal crunching and Dusty screaming began to melt together in my mind as the tires caught the ground again. I tried to hold my body still and attach my safety belt, but the momentum of the car kept me from my seat. Then abruptly the car jolted to a stop, slamming against the door as the opposite side of the car began to rise off the ground.

Everything moved so fast as the car began to flip. Unbelted, my body slammed against the passenger door window and then against the ceiling. I reached out and tried to grab the headrest as my body was thrown like a rag doll. As the car continued to roll, my knee jammed into the driver's side door with a crack accompanied by a sudden searing pain. I let out a high-pitched scream. My body slammed against the door, then the seat and once against the passenger window, which was nothing but shards of sharp glass. I felt the slivers cut through my skin as I was thrown helplessly. The car made another revolution and then the ceiling suddenly caved in just before my chest slammed against it.

I felt all the oxygen in my lungs rush out just as I was thrown against the driver's side door again. Finally, I let out a scream as the car's motion began to slow, teetering on its side before it rolled back onto the roof. My body lay awkwardly along the ceiling, my back bent up toward the floor where the roof had caved in.

"Ugh," I groaned. Pain seared up my back and intensified as my head began to throb. I opened my mouth to a familiar coppery smell and the salty iron taste of blood on my lips. Each breath hurt and my mind spun in no particular direction, dazed by only God knew how many head on impacts with all parts of the cabin.

Outside came another flash of light and a thunderclap that rocked the ground underneath me. My mind snapped back to reality.

Dusty! Dad!

I jerked up, at once regretting the decision. A splitting sensation ran up my side and sent me back to the ceiling, panting.

Come on, Chase!

Then I heard a soft whimper, a stutter almost. *Dusty!*

More carefully this time, I willed myself to get to my hands and knees. *OH!* I let my right knee go slack as the pain overwhelmed my senses. I took a deep breath and pulled myself forward between the small opening that separated the front seats. The roof was buried into the headrests. I squirmed my way through, my eyes scared to look at what I might find.

First, I saw Dad. His mouth was hanging wide open, his arms and hands slack at his side. A stream of blood etched a trail down his forehead, past his blank eyes. It dripped over his lips and then fell to the ceiling below where it mingled with the gathering storm water. A shiver ran down my spine as I realized he was dead.

"Cha…" came Dusty's tiny strained voice. "Chase."

I snatched my gaze away from my dad's lifeless body and turned to Dusty, ignoring the shooting pain in my side. My lips began to tremble as my gaze settled on him. I did my best to smile.

"Hey, Dusty," I said carefully, trying to sound happy. "It's okay."

Ungluing my eyes from his, I examined the ceiling bearing down on Dusty's head. There was that same stream of blood trailing down his face past those scared brown eyes. His chest labored under each breath. I checked him over. It was easy to see that his door had bent inward, pinning him tightly between itself and the center console.

My mind replayed the rolling and tumbling of the car and inside I felt the jolting pain of the door slamming against my brother's small frame. I winced and a tear ran down my cheek. *What do I do?*

"It's going to be all right, buddy," I told him, hoping it not to be a lie. I leaned across him, trying not to touch him, not wanting to introduce any new pain, and reached for his door handle. I yanked and pulled, nothing. Dusty whimpered at the sudden movement.

"Sorry, Dusty," I said. "I've got to get the door open."

With a grimace I tried again, but it refused to budge. My heart sank as Dusty sobbed sporadically through the pain. A sharp white flash permeated the car, giving the blood on Dusty's face a more immediate presence. His face shouldn't have looked like that. He should've been smiling and laughing, not that.

I searched the car for something, anything to unpin Dusty. Finally, it hit me. It should have been an easy thought, but my mind was still a fog. If I could get out of the car, maybe I could wrench the door open from the outside.

As quickly as the throbbing in my head and the jolting pain in my side would allow me, I pulled myself back into the backseat. Forgetting about my knee, I placed it firmly against the ceiling. I immediately wished I could take it back. My body fell limp to the ground under the pain. I clenched my teeth and squinted my eyes, trying to stave off the pain.

Finally, I got back up to one knee and both hands and tried my door. *Darn it!* I thought. It wouldn't budge. I tried again anyway. Nothing. I turned, careful to mind my likely broken knee, and tried the opposite door. I yanked and reeled. It would not budge. It was no good; it too was stuck in place, squashed solid between the roof and undercarriage.

Defeated, I wedged my body back between the front seats and put on my best smile for Dusty. I reached out and placed my hand on his, giving it a good squeeze.

"It's all good, Dusty," I lied. "We're going to be just fine."

He nodded. I couldn't tell if he believed me or not. I'm not sure which hurt worse, lying to my little brother or thinking he didn't believe me.

Dad's cell phone! I can call 9-1-1. Quickly I turned to my dad's lifeless form in the driver's seat and after apologizing, I reached aimlessly around his body. He always kept the phone in his left pocket. I reached around his waist, my face nearly nose-to-nose with my dad's lifeless expression. His eyes were open, staring coldly into my being. I shivered, the sudden realization that he would never say "Hey, Chase" again rung through my head. I froze in place, staring back into his eyes. Then a memory of his thick leather belt chaotically ripping across my legs and shoulders jolted me from my shock.

I diverted my eyes and my hand finally found its way into the corpse's pocket. There it was. I gripped the phone and pulled back as I caught another noise in the thumping rain outside. It was a light *splat, splat*. I looked up, craning my neck beneath Dusty's body to look out what was left of the window, guarding my eyes from the rain. I squinted in disbelief. There was someone coming.

"Help!" I yelled, a jolt of hope coursing through my veins. "Help!"

The footsteps stopped and then began again. In seconds the feet were just next to the window and then knees crouched down in the mud.

"Hurry," I pleaded.

Finally, a face appeared in the opening. Rain slapped against the shadowy figure. I squinted to make out more details, but it was too dark. They had short hair at least. A man. I think.

"Please help!" I begged. "The door won't open. My brother's hurt."

The man began to yank on the door. It would not budge. He tried again. Finally, I caught a glimpse of detail as lightning illuminated his face. A wide jaw, slightly prominent but flat nose and bloodshot eyes. His hair was matted to his head from the downpour and he wore an unbuttoned collared shirt.

He yanked at the door again before stopping to scan the cabin. Suddenly he froze, his gaze fixed behind me.

"Is he alive?" the man spoke. His tenor voice held a familiar slur to it as his eyes went wide.

"No," I found the word, hating myself for how little sympathy I found behind it.

"Oh no!" The man's eyes opened wide. In the dark I couldn't see, but I could imagine his face had gone white. "No, no, no, no."

He kept repeating the same word over and over again as he began to back away from the door, sliding on his butt in the mud.

"Wait!" I yelled. "Don't leave. My brother needs help!"

"No, no, no, no," was all that exited his lips. Finally, he stumbled up to his feet and bolted away.

"No! Please! Help us!" I screamed as loud as I could.

In the distance the faint sound of an engine roaring to life and screeching tires sank back to me.

"Please," I begged, but I knew he was gone.

"Ch…" Dusty tried

"Yeah, Dusty," I replied. "I'm right here. It's going to be okay."

"Cha…" he tried again. This time blood bubbled from his lips, and he choked on the red liquid.

"Dusty!" I urged him, squeezing his hand tight. I cupped my other hand against his cheek. Blood dribbled onto my hand as he tried to speak again. "No, Dusty! You're going to be all right."

9-1-1.

I raised the phone and began to swipe the screen open.

"It…hurts," Dusty said between spats of blood and labored breaths.

I fumbled out the numbers *9-1-1* and hit send.

"I know," I cried. The tears ran down my face unhindered as I stared into my little brother's eyes. "It's going to be all ri…"

Dusty's hand went limp in my own. I looked into his eyes, searching for the brother I knew. There was nothing there anymore, just those brilliant green eyes with a sudden emptiness behind them. Empty.

"Dusty?" I whispered, dropping the phone. "Dusty?"

I shook his hand. Nothing.

"Dusty?" It started as a whisper and grew into a scream. "Dusty? No! You can't leave me here. No, Dusty, you cannot leave me!"

I beat the ceiling with my spare hand, refusing to let go of his limp hand.

"No," I whispered between sobs. "No."

THREE YEARS LATER

CHAPTER 2

Beep! Beep! Beep!

Dalton Summers slapped the *Snooze* button on the alarm clock and sighed gently as the noise stopped. Lying flat on his back, he stared up into the dark where he knew a rich maple wood striped ceiling and steadily rotating fan blades resided.

He had been up the past half hour. Real sleep, deep REM sleep, had refused to darken his eyes as it so easily did on most nights. Instead, Dalton resigned himself early on to letting his vision roam aimlessly in the black. Today was the big day, at least he hoped it would be, and that possibility had kept his mind active throughout the night.

Careful not to wake Lenore, he pull the thick comforter back and slipped out of bed. In the dark, Dalton got to his feet and made his way to the bathroom door with his right hand out to be sure he did not slam his face into a wall or picture frame. The last thing he needed this early in the morning was his wife breathing down his throat over one of her precious frames shattered all over the floor.

He reached out where he expected the doorknob to be and his hand made contact with the cold brushed metal handle. Inside he shut the door and flipped the light switch. Light filled the room. It stung for a few moments before his sky blue eyes adjusted to the light.

Dalton twisted the cold and hot knobs and waited for the water to regulate to a decent temperature. He looked into the mirror, pushing down several stray fluffs of hair as he grimaced at the extra weight he was putting on. The six-pack abs he had never had were beginning to take form, just not in the nice shapely fashion one might appreciate. He'd have to start frequenting the treadmill again.

He stepped into the shower and the let warm water cascade gently over his head and shoulders. He could feel his body waking up now, becoming more cognizant than he had been even in his sleepless state in bed.

Since starting his career at Ryker+Michaels Architecture right out of college, Dalton's dream had been to be the next Frank Lloyd Wright or Paolo Soleri, just like every eager student of architecture. To break the molds and design something new, something modern and at one with the landscape around it, that's what he had always wanted. His unwillingness to move and his usual clientele had other plans for him, though. They always preferred something more classical or Victorian.

A few, a very few, appreciated a little flare of the modern or organic. Most, however, came into the office with a clipping file of cookie cutter homes or pictures from a magazine of some quaint living room or baby's room.

A year ago, a client had seemed excited about a design that would have set the house around the natural landscape, a large oak tree in particular. After fighting Dalton at nearly every angle, they had eventually settled on a traditional home with a Victorian bent.

Today, however, he was meeting with a new client who happened to share first names with Dalton's little brother. Gavin Bostian was an up-and-coming NASCAR driver who, to Dalton's pleasure, appreciated the arts. Gavin had come to contact Dalton through a series of unrelated cocktail parties and meet-and-greets as he worked to establish his race team in the Concord area near the Charlotte Motor Speedway.

Dalton's eye for the modern had been exactly what Gavin was searching for and Dalton hoped it was the opportunity he had been dreaming of. Today was the first day of the property search and while no one was committed to anything yet, Dalton had a swarm of ideas that he hoped would please Gavin. They pleased Dalton, that much was certain.

Dalton cut the water to the shower nozzle and grabbed a towel to dry off. No longer drenched, he donned the clothes he had placed on the bathroom clothes rack the night before, brushed his teeth and combed his hair into submission. Aided by the mirror, Dalton straightened his pale yellow tie and clipped it into place with a simple brushed metal bar pin.

Cutting the bathroom light, Dalton tip-toed through the bedroom and out into the main hallway. Passing the staircase up to Aiden and Mara's rooms, the guest room and what now served as a storage room, Dalton entered the kitchen. He retrieved a clean glass from a cabinet. He placed the glass down on the black marble countertops and filled it half-full with Dr. Pepper, his coffee substitute, and headed back down the hall to his study.

In the study, he plopped down in a cushy swivel chair and rolled up to his desk. He activated the power on his desktop computer in one fluid memorized motion. He laid back, examining his large collection of books. The collection of paperbacks lined each wall from floor to ceiling with the exception of two symmetrical windows looking out onto the lake and boat dock.

The monitor finally came to life and Dalton logged in and navigated to a set of rough sketches. Each showed a radically different low-detail house concept. Dalton scanned the lines he had laid out, memorizing the structure and computing a more solid visual in his head, something he could vocalize to Gavin out at the potential properties.

Outside in the hallway, he heard the faint patting of feet pass the study door. *Lenore*, Dalton thought dismissively and went back to his task.

Returning his attention to the screen, Dalton swiped to the next concept and scrutinized the layout. There was something that nagged at him. He stared at the digital pencil strokes, trying to find what disquieted him about the image.

"Aiden! Mara! Time to get up!" his wife yelled from the kitchen. Dalton could imagine her standing at the bottom of the staircase as she did every morning. Chocolate brown hair up in a quick ponytail, a bathrobe sashed at the waist and no makeup. "Breakfast will be ready in about ten minutes."

It also meant he only had a few more minutes before he needed to be walking out the door and on his way to the office. Dalton fingered through two more concepts before he stood up and grabbed his briefcase, walking back out into the hallway.

Like clockwork, the sound of Mara dragging her feet down the stairs reached Dalton. He stepped lightly into the kitchen just before the staircase. Lenore was still facing the stove, working on some bacon and eggs. He could hear the sound of Mara's usual morning groans getting closer.

As Mara's foot left the last stair and she came into sight, Dalton jumped toward her with a gruff scream. She jerked back and screeched, nearly tumbling back to the stairs before Dalton caught her.

"Dad!" Mara complained with a grin. Her brilliant blue eyes, the one physical characteristic Dalton could claim she got from him, shined back even through the film of morning. "Stop it! You're going to kill me of fright."

Dalton grinned.

"Dalton! Do you really have to do that?" Lenore asked, her voice reeking of irritation. "I almost threw the eggs all over the counter!"

Looking at Mara, Dalton shrugged and rolled his eyes. He ruffled his hand through the curls in her dirty blond hair before letting her loose from a hug. Mara grinned back and poured a glass of orange juice before taking a seat on a stool lining the bar counter.

"Okay, sorry," Dalton apologized before taking one last sip from his cup and depositing the glass in the sink.

"Where is Aiden?" Lenore asked as she finally turned away from the stove, looking at Mara.

Mara put her hands in the air, palms out, with a quizzical look on her face. "Why are you asking me? He's not my responsibility."

Lenore cocked her head and glared at Mara.

"Aiden! Get down here or you're going to be late!" Lenore yelled. Despite the gulf that had grown between her and Dalton, he always admired her sea green eyes. Those beautiful eyes had been the first thing he had noticed so many years ago when they first met. They were still mesmerizing.

Seconds later, the youngest member of the Summers household came barging down the stairs. Aiden pursed his lips and tiredly glared his honey brown eyes at his mother as he propped himself up against the bar next to Dalton.

"I was on my way when you hollered, Mom," Aiden claimed, though Dalton had serious doubts. Two years his sister's junior, at sixteen, the boy was smart but his internal clock was lacking. His smartphone's many reminders helped to a point, but not nearly enough.

"Sure you were," Mara jested, rolling her eyes.

Aiden gave her a sideways glance and his middle finger below the bar top, out of Lenore's sight. Mara grinned, shaking her head. Dalton urged Aiden's arm down a few inches to be certain Lenore did not catch sight of the middle digit, a sideways grin painted across his face.

Aiden grabbed a pop tart from the cupboard and tore the wrapper off.

"Aiden! I'm making breakfast," Lenore complained.

"I know. I thought I'd have a pop tart, too, though," Aiden defended himself.

"It's not like it's going to hurt him, Lenore," Dalton interjected. "I mean it's not like he needs to go on a diet."

Aiden was short for his age, not by much but enough. He still had a few years to grow, but Dalton hoped he hurried. Despite his short stature, his youngest child was just as fit as his father had ever been as a teenager. That was one of the few things the boy shared with his sister. They both had inherited their parents' high metabolisms and slim frames. Yet, whereas Aiden had managed to get his natural tan from Lenore, Mara's tan came from frequent tanning bed sessions, courtesy of Dalton's genes.

"Okay," Lenore gave in as she shoveled a scoop of eggs and a helping of bacon onto each plate. "You just better eat all of this."

"I will," Aiden said. "Oh, and don't forget that I won't be home tonight during trick-or-treating, I'm going to Zed's."

Before Lenore or Dalton could respond, Mara huffed.

"If the nerd gets to go, so should I!" Mara whined. "It's my senior year, it'll be my last Halloween party. Plus, he needs someone to take care of him." Mara patted Aiden's face, then pushed him away with a shove, "Look at him, he's so vulnerable."

"Get off," Aiden swatted her hand away.

"We've already discussed this, Mara. You're not going," Lenore asserted.

"But Mom!" she tried, and then turned her attention to Dalton, "Dad! Come on!"

"Mara," Dalton begun, "You know good and well why you're not going. It's off the table, it's done. You have yourself to thank for that, honey. Two more months."

"It was just one time," Mara tried again. She had repeated the statement multiple times since punishment had been handed down a week ago.

"One time?" Aiden sneered. "Sure it was. I'm *sure* it was the first time you had your mouth shoved between Nath—"

"Aiden!" Lenore raised her voice. "That's enough."

"Okay. I was just saying it wasn't the—" Aiden tried again.

"Aiden." Dalton shook his head slowly, hiding a grin.

"In the Target parking lot," Aiden said as quickly as he could.

"Aiden, stop!" Lenore yelled.

Aiden grinned from ear to ear.

"You're just mad cause you can't get Mason to do you," Mara jeered back.

"Oh," Aiden huffed. "Disgusting, but good."

Dalton grinned, but quickly replaced the expression with a grimace as his wife scowled at him.

"Really, you two. We're at the table, please." Lenore tried uselessly to bring order to the bar table.

"All right, guys, let's calm it down for your mom," Dalton told them. "I'm heading out. Can't be late for today's client. I think this is the one."

Lenore smiled and took a sip from her coffee cup. "I hope so. You've been waiting for this for years."

"Yep," Dalton agreed as he picked up his briefcase. He patted Aiden on the head with a grin and gave Mara a quick hug as he made his way to the garage. "See you this evening."

"Oh, Dalton!" Lenore stopped him just as he was turning the doorknob leading to the garage.

"Yeah?"

"Can you please be home by six or seven? Just before the trick-or-treaters come by at least?" Lenore asked. "You know I don't like being here by myself."

"You'll have Mara," Dalton reminded her with a nod in Mara's direction. Mara frowned and took another bite of from her bacon.

"I just feel safer when you're here," Lenore explained. "Junk happens all the time during trick-or-treating."

"Whatever, Lenore, I'll try to be here by seven."

Twenty minutes later, Dalton killed the ignition on the year-old BMW M4, terminating the excuse for a debate he'd been listening to on *SiriusXM's Progress* station. It was not his usual morning companion, definitely not the soaring guitar riffs and hard-hitting bass of *Octane*, but it had held his attention. It had featured the one thing in politics he loathed more than Republicans. A libertarian.

Retrieving his briefcase from the passenger seat, Dalton slid out of the BMW and took a second to straighten his tie again with his reflection in the driver's side window. His favorite line from the radio show played through his head as he passed by the large front window of his practice. *Cage/Summers Architecture* was plastered across the large front windowpane in slim modern letters.

"You're worse than the Republicans," Walter Daniels, the Democratic Senator from New York, had explained. "At least the Republicans realize that there are some sensible regulations that need to be placed on gun ownership."

Dalton had quietly rooted Daniels on and was surprised to hear the Republican vocalize his agreement. The Libertarian, some obscure city councilman out of Wisconsin, had went on with some witty, but irrelevant rebuttal. Dalton had glazed over as the man kept talking. Fortunately, before he could go on for long, Dalton had pulled into the office parking lot.

Inside, Dalton made his way past the empty receptionist desk and back to his office. He took a quick glance at one of his earlier designs hanging on the wall in the waiting room above a forty-two inch flat-screen LED television. Ideas sparked in his brain. He could see a slanting roof-line disappearing slowly and naturally into a neighboring rock bed. A wall lined with glass overlooking crystal blue water edged by white-washed stone.

Dalton unlocked the door to his office and stepped in. It was a generous space, spartan and functional. The front and rear walls were lined with onyx shelves reaching toward the ceiling every twelve inches, stacked from edge-to-edge with periodicals, sketch books, and old textbooks along with a few utilitarian decorations sporadically placed between the literature. A silver orb atop a bed of rock. A black picture frame with a photo of his family during better days. Among it all sat a large glass desk, a comfy leather swivel chair and two minimalistic black cushioned chairs for his guests.

After placing his coat on the hook next to the door, Dalton deposited his briefcase on the desk and took a seat. He opened the case and began to pull out its contents. He placed his favorite ball point pen next to a black metal meshed paper bin and a set of envelopes he had brought from home just next to the pen. Then he pulled out his large tablet and docked it on the center of the desk.

As the computer screen flickered to life, Dalton heard the front door open with a gentle beep. Feet shuffled in the neighboring room. Dalton leaned to his right and peered out into the waiting room, spotting Jenna Hansen as she settled in at the receptionist's desk.

He took the stack of mail and began to sort through the envelopes. The usual invitations to the next big architecture gala in Chicago, one in Los Angeles. A phone bill he had mistakenly placed in his briefcase and one last envelope, marked from *Williams, Salyer & Hunt: Attorneys at Law.*

Dalton stared at the last envelope, a slight grimace on his lips.

"Morning, Mr. Wayne."

Dalton jumped in his chair, his focus broken. His eyes caught sight of his slender assistant standing in the doorway, back leaned up against the doorframe.

"Mr. Wayne," Dalton whispered with a grin, looking down on his desk as he shook his head.

It was an office joke. Ever since he had misguidedly revealed his middle name to the auburn beauty, she rarely failed to miss an opportunity. She loved Batman, a comic geek generally, and having a boss with the middle name Wayne was just too much to resist apparently.

"Good morning, Jenna," Dalton said through his grin.

"So today's the big client, right?" she asked, her eyes showing how excited she was to call her boss *Mr. Wayne* still.

"Yes," Dalton swiped the screen, moving to another set of rough sketches. "I'm meeting Mr. Bostian in a few hours. Let's just hope that it goes well."

"I'm sure it will," said Jenna. "You two seem to have everything going quite well so far."

Dalton nodded and looked back up to Jenna, "I think we do. I think this piece of land fits his requirements well. Just enough open space, not too flat and it's lake front like he wanted. Pricey, but he said to find the best."

"See, you got it. Well, I'm going to leave you to it. Let me know if you need anything," Jenna said as she swiveled on her high heels and made her way out of his office, but not before Dalton stole a glance at her fine specimen of a buttocks behind her form fitting white skirt. Nice and curvy. Not too much, but just enough for a good grasp.

With a satisfied grin, Dalton returned his attention back to his computer. On top of his keyboard laid the envelopes he had been looking through. Suddenly his mood shifted, becoming dreary.

No use in that. Not now, you have a client to prepare for.

He picked up the envelopes and tossed them into his still open briefcase and snapped the lid shut.

CHAPTER 3

Aiden's face was a blur in the rear view mirror as a heavy drum so-lo laid waste to the Camaro's sound system. He bobbed his head light-ly and sang along.

"It's never enough, no it's never enough", Aiden whispered, qui-eter than he would have done if he'd been on the road rather than the school parking lot. "I'll never be what you want me to be. I'm do…"

Aiden clamped his lips as a pack of students traversed past him on the sidewalk. It was a group of five, a large crowd for the early morning trek from the student parking lot to the long corridors of North West Cabarrus High School. Two broad-shouldered senior jocks with overly-decorated juniors attached at the hip led the pack with a fifth wheel tagging along. She looked like she could use another meal, or five.

Football players and their cheerleaders. Classic, Aiden thought.

Before he could start to belt out the next line, an older bronze-and-bondo Chevy truck whined into the space across the dividing lane. It was followed immediately by an early nineties Firebird complete with hood flares and faded dual grey stripes from hood to trunk. Aiden turned his attention back to his music as a slim boy with bright red hair and skinny jeans stepped out of the Firebird.

"Where are you, Mason?" he asked, picking up his phone to

check his messages and the time. *7:47am.* "You're pushing it, man."

Aiden looked up as two girls passed by. He smirked. It was his sister, Mara, and her ditsy dark-skinned friend, Chloe. Mara flipped him a middle digit with a grin, followed by a chuckle from Chloe, which Aiden was grateful he couldn't hear over the music. It was an annoying noise, whiny.

"You hoe," Aiden laughed. She couldn't hear him, but he didn't care as he returned the gesture, jutting his middle finger up under the windshield. Mara raised an eyebrow and grinned before disappearing behind the line of cars.

"All right, Mason," Aiden said, picking up his phone again and tapping Mason's name on the screen. The rhythmic ring of an outgoing call replaced the thump coming from the Camaro's speakers. After two rings, the line picked up.

"What, man?" Mason's gruff voice came on the line.

"Where are you?" Aiden asked. "It's ten till, and you're not even here yet. You're...we're going to be late for first period."

"If you're so worried, why don't you go on," Mason argued. "Or do you need me to hold your hand?"

Aiden pursed his lips and shook his head, looking out at the field of cars. There were plenty of older vehicles with a peppering of gleaming new autos. "No, douche bag. You're just not usually late."

"Oh, so you're worried? Thanks, Mother," Mason jeered lightly across the digital line. "Well, have no fear, I'm pulling in now."

Looking across the half-full lot, Aiden spotted Mason's silver Mustang making the turn into the lot. He parked about ten spaces away from Aiden on the same aisle by a white sedan.

"Well hurry then," Aiden said. "I'd like to not be late for class, if that's all right with you."

"Yeah, yeah," Mason fussed.

Aiden switched off his Camaro and transferred the call to his phone as he got out of the car. Aiden's best friend since third-grade, a thin teenager with dirty blond hair, exited the Mustang. He wore a size-too-small plain gray t-shirt that highlighted the boy's athletic form. Mason saw Aiden about ten yards ahead and pocketed his phone.

"Let's go," Aiden urged.

Without a hurry in his step, Mason reached Aiden, who turned and made for the school at a fast walk. Reluctantly, Mason matched his pace and the two soon passed through the large maroon-painted metal doors into the school lobby. The large space echoed with quick footsteps and the chatter of hundreds of students as they crisscrossed the open space, trying to finish up last minute conversations before rushing to class.

"You are going to Zed's party tonight, right?" Mason asked. Aiden let a slight grin cross his lips as Mason's attention drifted. His brown eyes glued to the lowest point of the low-cut v-necks that passed as shirts on a group of girls passing by. One of them giggled as they passed.

"Yes, I already told you I was," Aiden grunted. "That's why I'm coming by your house this evening, remember?"

"Yeah, I just wanted to be sure you weren't ditching me to go trick-or-treating tonight instead."

Aiden rolled his eyes. He angled around the corner and sidestepped to his right to avoid of a couple leaning against the wall, hands slithering over and *under* clothes.

"I grew out of that last year," Aiden joked. It had been at least three years since he had donned a costume for Halloween, but Mason caught the sarcasm.

"Well, I hope not too much," Mason said. "It is a costume party you know. And, of course you know that Faith will be there, too. Who knows how kinky she'll be dressed."

Against his teenage pride, Aiden had agreed to dress up for to-night's party at Zed's. It had taken some convincing, not the least of which had been Faith Moreno would be there, in costume as well. He wouldn't dare speak to the girl. He wanted to, but he wouldn't. He couldn't. They had been friends since kindergarten, until it had become awkward a few years ago.

"You are going to ask her to the party, right?" Mason asked.

"Why do I have to ask her?" Aiden retorted, "She's going already."

"That's not the point, Aiden," Mason sighed. "You should still ask her to go with *you*."

"But I thought you were my date," Aiden cocked his head and pooched his lips at Mason.

"Eff off," Mason gasped and then snickered.

Aiden chuckled loudly and punched Mason playfully on the shoulder.

"See you in second period, man," Aiden said before slipping into class.

Lenore turned the hot water knob a few more degrees to warm up the sink water. She delved her hands back down into the water to pick up another dish, a glass cup from the morning's breakfast.

After the kids had shuffled out the door for school, she had taken her usual morning nap. An hour later, she woke from her slumber and began tending to the dishes. Then she would soon be in her office writing. It was a consistent routine that she attributed equally to being a mom for nearly two decades and her penchants as a former scientist.

Lenore had studied astronomy back at UC Berkley before moving into an Associate Professor position at Embry-Riddle closer to her hometown in Pensacola. The years of precise, rigid research and experimentation had proven useful in developing a consistent routine. She no longer studied the stars much these days, but the discipline remained.

Wiping the grease and small egg fragments from the last glass plate, Lenore placed it into the dishwasher and closed the door. She pulled the metal cork in the sink and let the soapy water spiral down into the pipes. As she pulled her hands from the water, Lenore noted her pruned fingers, transformed in the minutes of total emersion. She frowned.

It won't be long until they always look like that.

At forty-three, Lenore's skin was taut and smooth and she even managed to hold on to a natural tan. Combined with high cheekbones and, as her husband claimed on their second date over twenty years ago, "the most adorable nose among women," Lenore was an attractive woman. Yet, the older she got, the more the little changes bothered her.

Her eyes drifted to the one-and-a-half carat diamond on her left hand. She spread her fingers and entertained one of her first memories of Dalton. She was still teaching at Embry-Riddle, but her passion for the written word had taken hold already. They were at an arts conference in Atlanta, Georgia. She was attending to promote her first novel, a sci-fi horror story that had largely been a flop. Dalton had attended as a representative for his former employer's firm.

The first words out of Dalton's mouth had been, "I hate horror, but…" It ended there for a few moments while his mind caught up with his poor word choice. Lenore remembered the conflicting emotions she had fostered. She felt defensive. His comment was abrupt and she *was* selling a horror book. Yet, she found herself attracted to his otherwise desirable demeanor. Thick brown hair that was just enough neat and just enough messy. A rigid jawline and the most gorgeous sky blue eyes. Instead of talking again, he picked up a free bookmark and made his way off. Eventually Dalton got the nerve back up to approach her again on the last day of the conference and so their long-distance relationship had begun. The good days.

Lenore broke her concentration from the diamond and wiped her hands dry on a nearby cloth before walking barefooted down the hall to her office. She took a seat behind a large mahogany desk at the edge of the room. She leaned back, trying to purge thoughts of earlier years from her mind and replace them with Keira's lonely world in outer space. Keira was the leading lady of her most recent novel, a sequel to her bestselling young adult sci-fi novel.

The astronomer in her had begged for years to be let out on the page while the horrific bloody tales of her previous five books had taken precedence. She had finally let it out and she could not figure out why she had waited so long. They had been the most successful of her books to date, selling well and above her expectations. There was even the occasional rumor of a possible movie deal coming down the chute. Her publisher had been eager to capitalize on the success and signed her on for a sequel.

For the past two weeks, though, Lenore had struggled with the story's climax. She had the perfect idea, but the words to explain it eluded her. Keira's battle for survival was to hit a pinnacle, one that would define the future of humanity. After four rewrites and endless editing, Lenore felt it did not do the story justice. For the eleventh day in a row, she stared blankly at the same words on the computer screen, searching for the right words to fill the page.

Bump, bump.

Lenore jerked from her stupor and looked around the room. She waited a few seconds before dismissing the sound and returning her attention to the screen.

"All right, come on, Keira, give me something," Lenore talked to herself, attempting to prompt her imagination through her character.

Bump.

Again, Lenore's eyes went up, scanning the ceiling.

Bump. Bump.

Her stare shot to the right, into the corner. It was coming from upstairs. She cocked her head sideways, waiting for the sound as she rose from her seat cautiously. It did not take long for it to come again.

Bump. Bump.

"Dalton?" she said more than yelled. She maneuvered about the desk and peeked around the door frame. The hall was empty so she stepped out but unconsciously kept close to the off-white wall. For a minute it seemed the noise had stopped, but it quickly picked up again. Her muscles tensed and her breathing became more deliberate as she tip-toed back down the hallway toward the kitchen. She stopped at the opening to the staircase and gradually peeked around the corner.

A louder bang sounded down the stairs just before she could manage a glimpse. She swung back around, her back flat against the wall. Her breathing quickened along with her heartbeat. She swallowed hard. Quicker this time, she chanced a look around the corner. Nothing. Just the hardwood stairs leading up into the dark hallway.

In the corner of her eye, she caught sight of the knife block as she flattened her back against the wall once more. Lenore glanced back at the opening to the staircase to her left once more. She shrugged and jogged into the kitchen, snagging the largest knife from the block. She gripped the handle tight, letting its presence send a few waves of courage up her arm and through her body.

"Aiden?" she called out. "Mara? Dalton? If you're here, you need to say something."

The noise came down the stairs again, reaching her more abruptly this time, or at least it seemed to at her heightened state. Her hand twitched as she raised the knife and took a step forward. No one answered her calls. She took another step, then another, and finally mounted the stairs.

Why would either of her kids, or Dalton, be home? It was only ten in the morning. Both Aiden and Mara would be at school, stuck in some classroom, and Dalton should be about to meet his client. No, it wasn't them. Still she called out again as she reached the top of the stairs and peered through the dark. She reached for the light switch and flipped the light on. The dark hall erupted in light. Empty.

"Mara? Aiden?" she called out, her voice shaking. She took a deep breath to calm her shaking hand to no avail. "This isn't funny."

Bump, bump.

There it was again. It sounded like it was just down the hall on the left. Aiden's room. The large knife gleamed in the hall light as Lenore raised it to chest level. Her feet perched ready with each step down the carpeted hallway. The noise came again, louder this time.

"Aiden?" Her voice quivered, quieter than she had expected. Another thudding noise sounded ahead. It *was* coming from Aiden's room.

Lenore stole a glance back down the hall as she maneuvered up to Aiden's bedroom door and placed her hand on the silver door knob. In futility, she attempted to calm her breathing.

"Aiden, if you're in there you need to say something *now*," Lenore tried one last time.

Half a minute passed and there was no reply. She took in a slow, careful breath. Then in one quick motion, she twisted the knob and pushed the door in. It swung wide. Her eyes darted fitfully about the room, hand ready to come down hard on whoever was in the room. She crinkled her brow. It was empty.

Carefully, Lenore stepped into the room. Strategically she placed her bare feet on the hardwood floor, mindful of the junk littering the room. Ahead the closet door stood partially ajar, a three-inch black gap staring her down. She met its gaze and approached, pulling the blade closer to her shoulder.

Reaching the closet, she braced her feet and extended her arm, but paused. Adrenaline pumped through her veins. She steadied her hand holding the large knife. Like a viper on the attack, she reached forward and reeled the door back. Light flooded into the walk-in closet. She jumped forward, involuntarily yelling at…nothing.

The closet was empty, just like the room. She shook and let out the breath she had been holding. Turning around, she exited the closet and took a seat on the only spot on Aiden's bed uncluttered with clean clothes.

"I must be losing it," she told herself. She laid the knife on top of the clutter and cupped her face in the palm of her hands. "Well, I about killed Aiden's clothes."

Meow.

"Ah! Dammit," Lenore yelled in fright, jumping off the bed and back to her feet. She reeled around at the grey short-haired fur ball that had decided to reveal himself from under the bed.

"Smokey, you shouldn't sneak up on me like that."

Unaffected by the admonishment, Smokey sauntered over to the desk where the mouse to Aiden's computer hung from the edge of the desk. It swayed like the pendulum on one of those big old clocks. Lenore shook her head and watched the old cat. Reaching the mouse, Smokey pawed at it playfully. It swayed back more violently and abruptly slapped against the metal desk leg. The same thudding noise that had scared the hell out of her moments ago.

"Well, I'll be damned," Lenore grinned at the cat. "It was all your fault. Did Aiden lock you in here this morning, Smokey?"

As Lenore turned to walk out of the room, she remembered the knife she had brought with her. It still laid on the bed. She went back and retrieved the knife and gave the cat a sideways glance as she walked back out of the room.

"If you only knew how close you just came to being Chinese

food."

"Who can tell me what the Articles of Confederation are?" Mr. Navarro asked the class, tapping the dry erase board with his favorite red marker. He had scribbled *ARTICLES OF CONFEDERATION* in all capital letters up high on the board.

Mara rolled her eyes and withheld a sigh. The usual suspects popped their hands in the air, almost waving them in excitement. The same nerds that seemed to jump at every opportunity no matter the class subject.

She was no fool, but obtaining the highest GPA at the end of her senior year was not on the forefront of her mind. No, Mara let her mind drift to better thoughts. Mr. Navarro's full tanned lips, and everything below them. It was obvious that the history teacher worked out regularly, no wonder he was the constant talk of his female students.

The fact that she would get to look at him for a solid forty-five minutes every day was the sole motivating factor for Mara to beg to be switched to his U.S. History I class. It was a far cry better than the elderly, bad-breathed Mr. Jacobs. Not all of it had been lies. Yet, her desire to learn about her history was without doubt a bald-faced, albeit advantageous, lie.

One of the nerds finished rattling off a much too long explanation that must have pleased Mr. Navarro. Mara had blocked the words out, especially when he turned to write a list of points on the board.

"Hey, Mara," Lillian Lane whispered across the aisle from the yellow, plastic-topped desk to her left.

Pulled from her trance, Mara discreetly turned her attention to her short friend from middle school. Lilly's brown eyes and gently raised cheekbones complemented her naturally soft tanned skin. The blond highlights in her chestnut curls reached all the way down to her shoulders.

"Yeah," Mara replied. She shifted her brilliant blues back to the front of the room, hoping Mr. Navarro had not noticed her diversion. Then she quickly retrained them on Lilly.

"So are you still in jail?" Lilly asked, squinting in anticipation.

Behind Lilly, Chloe Godfrey giggled a little louder than she ought and Mara gave her a wide-eyed stare, hoping she'd get the message. After a quizzical expression creased Chloe's mocha brow, the girl finally got the idea and closed her bright cherry red painted lips. Mara could not help but smile back at her Latina friend. Her cheeks were plump, her wavy deep auburn hair a near perfect match to Mara's own locks if it weren't for the blond dyes Mara kept in place.

"Yes, still in jail," Mara admitted with a huff. "I'm not going to make it to the party tonight. How many times are you going to ask me that?"

"Until it stops amusing me," Lilly joked. "I mean you were just having a little fun. What's a little fun from time-to-time going to hurt?"

Mara grinned mischievously back at Lilly, "Try telling that to my parents."

"You mean your prison guards?" Chloe chimed in from behind, giggling quietly.

"Yeah, I guess," Mara smiled and shook her head. Her grin intensified as she continued, "Well, it should be a good night either way. Nathan's coming over."

"How do you plan on that? I thought you were not allowed to see each other except at school," Chloe asked, bewildered.

"I've got a window in my…"

"Ladies, do you have something you'd like to discuss with the class?" Mr. Navarro interrupted, clearing his throat to make a point. "Or maybe you'd like to explain one of the problems with the Articles of Confederation."

"Uh…" Mara stuttered. "I…uh…"

"Lillian?" Mr. Navarro tried with a raised brow.

She stared blankly at him, mouth trying to form words, but not knowing what to say.

"No?" he asked. "How about you ladies try and pay a little more attention. I'm sure whatever you're so determined to talk about can wait until class is over."

"Yes, Mr. Navarro," Mara grinned, happy to be noticed by the man, even if not for the best of reasons.

Mr. Navarro shook his head lightly and returned to lecturing the class on the virtues and shortcomings of America's first constitution. For a few minutes, Mara maintained her attention ahead on the teacher. It wasn't too difficult. Then her thoughts moved to her plans tonight. She smiled. She may not get to party at Zed's, but she had something better planned.

The party was coming to her.

CHAPTER 4

The cool fall breeze whipped around Dalton's slacks and tousled his hair. He fastened the two middle buttons on his light leather jacket.

It had shaped up to be a cooler than usual autumn in the region. The temperature was no higher than fifty, maybe fifty-five, degrees and it was only an hour past noon. The wind chill had to be well under that. As unpredictable as North Carolina weather could be, shifting through all four seasons in a matter days and then back again, if the last few weeks were any reliable indicator winter was going to be a real bitch this year.

Dalton stood in the middle of a small clearing among an innumerable host of trees, everything from red maples, sweet bay, black gum and sycamores. Their leaves were painted in a myriad of reds, oranges and yellows, as were their fallen comrades littering the lawn. The land was mostly untouched, with the exception of the blacktop highway that ran by the property on the other side of the tree line where his client should have arrived about eleven minutes ago.

He hadn't, though. Instead, Dalton paced the grass, kicking at fallen leaves, stray patches of clover and the occasional dandelion, trying to determine at what point he should give up waiting. He needed this client. Well, he wanted this client. It meant fulfilling a dream, a goal that he had put in place years ago. The opportunity to make a mark, to design something different, something unique among the classic architecture of the region.

He settled on at least another ten minutes before he gave Mr. Bostian a call. As long as the race car driver was on his way, or even planned to come, Dalton would wait.

A minute later, a brand new white Jaguar F-Type purred slowly through the opening in the tree line and onto the grass. It came to a stop next to Dalton's BMW and the engine shut off just before the door opened and Gavin Bostian stepped out on the uneven ground.

"Be careful there, it's not evenly graded yet," Dalton called out to his client.

His client stumbled slightly but managed to hold himself upright. Gavin grinned. His thick brown hair was spiked, nothing too aggressive, but just enough to compliment his youth.

For a driver, the twenty-eight year old was fit, Dalton thought, but he did not know many race car drivers. Sure, he lived less than twenty minutes from one of the most iconic speedways in the nation, but racing had never held his interest, especially after being trapped in the traffic jams it caused on I-485 and down Concord Mills Boulevard every race week.

"So what do you have here for me?" Gavin asked, extending his hand. Dalton accepted and gave it a firm shake.

"Well, this is only a small portion of the full lot," Dalton began, spreading his arms out to signify the area around them. "The full lot is exactly three point eighty-two acres bordering the lake. It's a wide lot, so that should give you plenty of room on either side for some privacy."

"So I assume the lake is just beyond the tree line there?" Gavin asked, pointing toward the other end of the opening.

"Yes, and if you want the house on the lake itself, it would be no problem to clear out an area of your choosing," Dalton explained.

"That's sort of what I thought you would prefer. I mean you're property would border the lake anyway, why not enjoy it?"

Gavin nodded, pleased, his hands clutched at his hips. Dalton brought the tablet up in front of him so that Gavin could see. In the view screen, the tablet's camera projected an image of the lot before it.

"So I took the liberty of drawing up some rough ideas. Of course, the look of the land may change, but this can give you an idea how things *might* look." Dalton swiped a finger across the screen from right-to-left and a mockup of a flat-roofed, white stone-walled house came into view overtop of the real landscape.

"Oh, whoa," Gavin stuttered at the gadget. "Now that's cool. The house design looks good, too."

Dalton grinned and explained how he felt that the flat roof style would enhance the utilitarian feel of the house while allowing Gavin to make use of solar-energy atop the structure without the visual blemish. Gavin nodded vaguely. Dalton felt he knew that expression, on to the next design.

Fifteen minutes and five mockups later, Dalton felt confident he was heading in the right direction. Gavin's reaction to the mockups had provided him valuable insight to what the man was looking for, and fortunately it was still down the same track the two had discussed over a month ago.

"I'd definitely want to push out onto the lake, but I like the property," Gavin assured Dalton. "Let me bring Kimberly by this weekend, let her take a look around. I'll give you a call on Monday and we can move from there, but I'm pretty sure she'll love it."

"That's great," Dalton was ecstatic, but he held in his pent up excitement. "Just don't take too long. You never know when someone else might come in and swoop it out from under you."

"Yes, sir," Gavin agreed and shook Dalton's hand again. "I'll give you a call. Have a happy Halloween."

Lenore tossed a second bag of party-sized Twix bars into the metal-framed buggy. So far the cart held two bags each of bite-sized Butterfingers, a variety pack of Reese's candies, peanut butter and regular Snickers and Smarties in addition to the Twix already in the cart. She might not enjoy Halloween, but she was not going to allow Mrs. Hightower, their neighbor situated at the end of their little peninsula about three hundred yards down the road, have the better selection. The last thing Lenore wanted to hear were kids whining about the *free* candy she gave them.

After the incident with the cat earlier that morning, Lenore had accomplished little in the form of real progress on her novel. A few edits here and there. A few elaborations. Nothing substantial, though. The climax was still nagging at her. It was not so much what should or could happen but how real the story should be. Life was full of surprises and rarely did a real-life story end with every seam and imperfection made right. How true to that fact she should stick eluded her.

Gliding down the aisle, Lenore dropped another bag of candy in the buggy, more Reese's. There was always room for more peanut butter. Rolling around the end of the aisle, past a display of flavored potato chips, Lenore moved into the frozen foods to pick up some of Aiden's favorite snacks; breakfast corndogs.

"Lenore?" a familiar high-pitched voice called out down the aisle. "It *is* you!"

Lenore raised the edges of her lips as a plump black lady approached her with arms outspread. It was her friend, and hair stylist, Tamieka Dula. Returning the gesture, Lenore gave Tamieka a generous squeeze, careful to mind her precisely-placed light brown hair.

"Tamieka," Lenore said. "Good to see you. How've you been?"

"I can't complain," the short, dark-skinned woman replied, with a

TO WATCH YOU BLEED

gentle staccato laugh. "Just doing some last minute shopping for dinner with Larissa tonight. She decided that she was over Halloween. Apparently it's only for little kids, so we're having dinner and a scary movie marathon instead. I'm going to make her watch the original Dracula."

"Oh, that sounds great! I wish I could convince my family to do the same," Lenore sighed. "Aiden's going to some party, Mara won't speak to me since she's grounded, and Dalton...who knows. I'd definitely prefer a movie night over handing out candy to a bunch of random kids in the dark. It frightens me."

"You?" Tamieka's eyes went wide, showing the bright whites and thin red veins surrounding the irises. "You, frightened? Surely not, I mean I remember reading that horror you wrote, what was it called..."

"*Beneath My Sin*," Lenore filled in the blank.

"Yeah, *Beneath My Sin*. That one was horrifying. Had me scared for nights."

Lenore chuckled quietly. It had been her most intense horror story, not her only, but definitely the most intense.

"But that doesn't mean I don't get scared. Sometimes I write about what scares me, to face it. Doesn't always help much in the end, though," she laughed.

"I guess so," Tamieka said, closing the glass freezer door and placing a box of some soon-to-be fried snack. "How's your *new* book coming? I cannot wait to find out what's going to happen to Kalem."

"It's coming along. I've hit a small rough patch, but I'm sure it'll work out fine. As for Kalem," Lenore grinned mischievously, "you'll just have to wait and find out."

"Such a tease," Tamieka threw her hands in the air dramatically.

"That's me. Have you read *Anonymous* yet?" Lenore asked.

"*Anonymous*? No, I don't think so," Tamieka answered. "Is that another of yours?"

Lenore took a pack of cheese sticks from the tall freezer and dropped it in her buggy. "Yeah, it's a bit more recent than *Beneath My Sins*, sort of techno-thriller slash horror. If you swing by tonight, I can get you a copy."

"Definitely," a wide grin crossed Tamieka's face. "Is four or five too late?"

"Not at all. I'll see you then. I've got to finish up my shopping," Lenore nodded with a generous grin.

"See you then," Tamieka gave her another hug and then made her way down the aisle.

Ten minutes later, Lenore was leaning back against the grey leather bucket seats of her Mercedes-Benz van with the wiper blades swiping intermittently across the windshield. The music played softly in the background, some random pop artist that she had never heard of, as she maneuvered the van left onto George W. Liles Parkway, matching speed with a late nineties-model Toyota Camry with a *COEXIST* bumper sticker.

She thought about her conversation with Tamieka at the grocery store, how her own voice had trailed off at the mention of Dalton. She huffed and pursed her lips. She doubted he would remember to be home on time tonight, he rarely did lately. Pressing the button emblazoned with a tiny green phone handset on her steering wheel, she initiated the car's onboard phone system through her phone's Bluetooth. Scrolling through the contact list, she selected *Dalton Summers* and initiated the call.

The familiar ring played on the car speakers as Lenore changed lanes, the Camry could not seem to manage a consistent speed. She tapped her fingertips atop of the steering wheel.

"Hello, Lenore," Dalton's voice came on the line, just as soothing as it had been almost twenty years ago when they were dating. The only change was a slight maturity, a gentle gruffness that had come with time.

"Hey," she answered, smiling though he couldn't see her wherever he might be. He sounded happier than he had in a while. "How'd everything go with your client?"

"It went great," Dalton was ecstatic, responding almost before she could finish her question. "Mr. Bostian really liked the lot I showed him. I think we'll end up cutting an opening out through the trees onto the lake, but that was expected. Who wouldn't want a lake view with the lake bordering your land?"

"That's true. So I guess you still have a lot to do before closing the deal though, right?"

"Oh yes. He still has to make a decision on the lot first, then we'll start working out the floorplan, then…" Dalton trailed off, realizing he was babbling. "Well, you know how all that goes. You've heard it time and time again from me."

Lenore could not help but grin, hearing Dalton excited. She sighed, "I've heard it before, but I don't have a problem with hearing it again. I'm glad it's working out."

She switched gears and spoke up again, "I know you're busy, so I wanted to remind you to be home tonight before the trick-or-treaters start up if you can, probably about six-thirty or so."

There was a brief, but noticeable pause on the other end of the line.

"I'll try, Lenore, but with Mr. Bostian coming around on the lot, I may have to stay late tonight," his voice had changed. It was still soft but Lenore could detect a wall, a sudden defense that had sprung up between the line. She frowned.

"Okay, but please try," Lenore said, trying to hide the disappointment in her voice. "You know how I don't like being alone with all the trick-or-treaters and the real crazies do come out in droves on

Halloween, too."

"Stop fretting, Lenore. It's Concord, we don't live in New York or Charlotte," Dalton failed at consoling her. "You've just watched one too many horror movies and way too many true crime documentaries. It's eating your nerves. It's childish really."

Lenore instinctively reeled her head back and looked at the LCD display on the center console, her brow scrunched and a frown drew across her lips.

"Childish? I tell you that I'm genuinely scared to be alone tonight, on Halloween of all nights, and you tell me I'm being child-ish? Really?"

"Lenore," Dalton was on the defense now. "Okay, it was the wrong word. Just don't fret, I'll try to be home as soon as possible."

Lenore refused to answer the poor attempt at an apology, if it even was an apology. He had sounded so dispassionate, uncaring. She looked ahead. Maples and sycamores lined the small two-lane road, red and orange leaves sprawling high over the pavement like a natural tunnel that blocked most of the sun on clearer days. She sighed.

"Lenore?" her husband's voice came across the line with only the slightest sliver of empathy in his tone.

"Okay." She would not give him the pleasure of a greater answer. She would work it out once she saw him tonight, but right now *okay* was all he was getting.

"I've got to go, Lenore," Dalton hurried. "Bye, see you tonight."

"Love…" The line went dead before she could finish her sentence, "you."

Eyes glued to the myriad reds and oranges of the leaves above her, a tear escaped the corner of her eye and traveled down her cheek. She looked up toward the sky. Rain clouds covered the pale blue that resided on the other side.

Her mind flashed back to happier times. Dalton stood in front of her booth at the arts festival in Georgia those many years ago. That silly grin on his face as he asked for a copy of her book, just a day after making the mistake of telling her he didn't like horror stories. The way his brilliant blue eyes mesmerized her just before he asked her on their first date.

Was that really so long ago? she thought.

The familiar ring of the release bell rang, the noise drilling into Aiden's classroom through the only entrance. While Mrs. Jackson tried to finish her sentence, the class erupted into the zipping of backpacks, shuffling of feet and scratching of chair feet against the floor. Aiden slid the oversized Algebra II textbook off his desk and into his pack. He leaned forward to catch the teacher's last words.

"Don't forget, pages thirty-two through thirty-four are due on Monday," the teacher yelled above the bell and the crescendo of noises building in the classroom as students packed up in a hurry. It was the weekend, and Halloween at that, no one wanted to be left at school for a second longer than required.

Stowing his last belonging, a green number two pencil, away in the front compartment of his pack, Aiden jumped to his feet and locked his eyes on his target. From his perspective, Aiden could not see Faith's emerald eyes and long black eyelashes, or the dimples in her cheeks when she smiled. He did not need to see them to imagine them. He had it all stored away in his mind, a perfect photocopy of her brilliance, but it was still nothing compared to the real thing.

He examined the gentle waves of her almost black hair. It cascaded back and forth halfway down her back before ending above the perfect shape of her hips and legs. She was beautiful, no longer the tiny little kindergartener that he used to spend most of his free time with as a kid.

He needed to get to her before she managed to get out into the hallway and lose him in the crowd. He had to ask her to Zed's Halloween party. It didn't matter to him that he had shrugged the idea off earlier when Mason had asked, he did want to, he just wasn't sure he could muster up the courage.

Aiden pushed his way up the aisle, dodging the occasional book bag flung around a shoulder or a classmate jumping up from their desk. Finally past the front row of yellow and orange metal-topped desks, he half-sprinted across the front of the room. He came to a stop by Faith. She turned and her eyes met his.

"Hey, Aiden," Faith started, her voice was small and silvery and her smile nearly took his breath. Flush red lips against tanned skin, her family's Hispanic heritage intermingled with a long line of European blends.

"Hey," he replied tautly and grinned stupidly. He tried to find the words that he had practiced the entire class period. Like some mental vacuum had rushed through, he found nothing.

Faith crinkled her brow, but the smile never left her face. "Are you all right?"

"Ah, yeah. I'm good," he stuttered. *No, my mind just went blank at the absolute worst moment ever*, he thought. "I…uh…I was going to ask if you were going to the party tonight, the one at Zed's."

"Yeah, I'm going," Faith confirmed. Her brow unwrinkled, her eyes opened a little wider and she looked at him, almost expectantly.

"That's great," Aiden filled in the gap. He laughed nervously. All the willpower he had mustered just seconds ago melted away into nothing. "I'm going to, too. I guess I'll see you there."

Hurriedly, Aiden turned and nearly jogged out the classroom door into the busy hallway before anything more could be said.

"Dammit," he muttered under his breath as he walked past a group of girls huddled by their lockers, earning a sideways glance. He half-grinned and cursed himself again inwardly for his cowardice.

How hard could it be, Aiden? I mean really. It's only a simple question. Will you go to the party with me? Dammit!

Up ahead, he caught a view of Mason's brown mess of hair and naturally smooth face. He started to turn and take another route, he wanted to avoid admitting his failure, but Mason had already noticed him.

"Aiden," Mason said over the rush of students, dodging around a pair of hand-holding seniors.

Aiden took in a deep breath and kept his trajectory steady as he met up with his friend. He grinned, hoping not to betray himself too quickly.

"So, what'd she say?" Mason half-begged.

Of course that would *be the first thing you ask, wouldn't it?*

"She's going," Aiden stalled, trying to take a neutral approach. It was the truth, but it was technically a non-answer, an avoidance.

"Well, I knew that, dumbass. But is she going *with you*?"

Aiden grinned cheesily, raising his right cheek high which caused his eye to squint slightly. He kept walking. Mason matched his pace, jumping in front of him, walking backwards with his hands outspread.

"Whoa there!" Mason stopped in his tracks, forcing Aiden to halt his escape. Mason cocked his head sideways and grinned ever so slightly. "You didn't ask her, did you?"

"Well," Aiden tried. "I about did, but I froze. I got nervous."

"You always get nervous when you try to talk to her, Aiden. *Always*," Mason stressed his point. "You've only got two more years here at Western and then it's off to college, and who knows where she'll be then. You need to get a move on it, man."

Aiden started walking again, head down slightly. Mason jumped in step and threw an arm playfully around Aiden's neck, shaking him a bit while he ruffled Aiden's perfectly-styled hair. "One of these days, man, you'll learn."

"Yeah, I know." Aiden shoved Mason, mostly to protect his hair, with a grin. "I'll talk to her eventually."

"*Tonight!*" Mason ordered.

Aiden shook his head slowly. Down the hall, a more fitful exchange reached his ears.

"Eff off, asshole!" The voice was calmer than Aiden would expect considering the words. Its calmness did not detract from its effect, though, as it echoed up the hallway. Aiden and Mason exchanged glances, eyebrows raised. A small crowd had gathered about twenty yards down the hall.

"Hey, get off him!" The same voice, the same deliberate tone.

Aiden stood on the toes of his shoes to get a look over the growing crowd. He watched as someone was shoved against the wall, a flash of bright red hair flaring out onto the tiled wall. Aiden pressed a hand through the wall of students and wedged through. *What's going on? Who's up there?*

"Come on, Aiden, let it go," Mason begged, throwing his hands down as his friend broke through the line. "Dammit!"

Past the crowd there was a chasm between the spectators and the entertainment. The entertainment was a group of four boys forming a semi-circle around two others. Aiden tried to assess the situation.

The first kid, the one doing the shoving, was Ben Corker, a junior. He was the jock type, second string quarterback for the school football team. He might have played three games since he joined the varsity team last year, but he thought he was "the stuff" as Mason put it. To his left, forming the farthest edge of the semi-circle, was another junior by the name of Liam and a boy that Aiden did not know but by face, broad and overly confident. The other boy was facing away from him.

Inside the ring were two more boys. Leaning against the wall, getting to his feet again, was Oliver Brooks, wavy shoulder-length red hair and all. He was a slim, almost scrawny kid, something his tight and brightly colored pant choice only made more obvious to the likes of Ben Corker. It was like an advertisement blinking the words *Beat Me Up*.

Next to Oliver, Chase Miller gave the boy a hand, pulling him up from his landing spot. Chase stood a full three inches above his counterpart at just a hair under six foot. His broad jawline and pale complexion stood in stark contrast to Oliver's tanned skin and V-shaped face. Dressed mostly in shades of grey and black, except for the white logo on his shirt, something Aiden did not recognize, Chase repeated his warning.

"Fuck. Off."

"Or what? You and your fag friend will beat *us* up?" Ben's annoyingly deep voice bellowed out.

"Just…" Chase started.

"What's going on here?" Aiden butted in, forcing his way past the boy on Ben's left, Nicholas Rivers, another football jock. "What's all the fuss?"

Ben jerked back in surprise, meeting Aiden's eyes.

"None of your damn business, Aiden," Ben retorted portentously before returning to his prey. "So you going to apologize, *freak*?"

Aiden took a step back, almost stepping into Nicholas. Ben stepped forward and pushed Chase, sending him back two steps. Chase came to a stop, locking his eyes again with Ben's. He seemed to be drilling through Ben's skull with those nut brown, almost black eyes, his chest heaving not from exhaustion, but from the pent up anger building behind his ribcage.

"Are you going to apologize for bumping your faggot shoulder into me or what?" Ben yelled at Oliver, only inches from his face.

"Stop calling him that, or I'll…I'll," Chase began to stutter, trying to find the words to get out of their situation.

"Just bug off, Ben," Aiden interrupted as he wedged his body between Oliver and Ben. "You're being pathetic. He accidently ran into you, get over it. It's not like he was trying to make sweet love to you in the middle of the hallway."

A small chorus of giggles rang from the mass of students surrounding them. Ben's eyes shot out to the crowd incredulously, searching for those who dared laugh at him. Abruptly the boy's demeanor changed. His authoritative manifestation disappeared into befuddlement, eyes darting about the crowd, searching for the eager eyes that had originally gathered. Instead he found them laughing at him. He took a step back and then spun around to face Aiden.

"Shut up, Aiden!" he yelled, "I didn't need you butting in."

"Just leave, Ben," Aiden held his ground. "It's not worth it. You're being petty."

Sensing the loss of support in the crowd, Liam and the others began to back up, distancing themselves from Ben. Likewise, Ben began to step back, his face angry again, but withheld. The crowd's giggles began to die.

Taking one last chance to keep up his persona, Ben jerked forward but stopped himself. Chase, Oliver and Aiden all jerked at the sudden motion. Ben grinned and then about-faced before catching up with his comrades down the hallway. Aiden rolled his eyes at the pettiness of his classmates as the crowd dispersed, leaving only Chase, Oliver, Aiden and Mason gathered by the wall. Mason kept his distance, lips pursed, ready to be done with this inconvenience.

"So," Aiden turned to Oliver. "You okay, Olly?"

"Yeah, I'm fine," Oliver replied, the irritation in his voice still rivaling his composure. "I didn't need your saving. I could have handled him."

A few feet behind them, Mason murmured something Aiden could not hear, and assumed he would rather not hear.

"Okay." Aiden smiled and then looked to Chase, "You good?"

"Yeah," Chase said, a hint of a grin crossing his lips, almost bordering on a thankful look. "Those guys are such pricks."

"That's jocks for you," Aiden joked. "Well, I gotta get out of here. See y'all Monday."

They nodded their goodbyes and parted ways. When Aiden's gaze met Mason's, the boy shook his head and let out an irritated sigh.

"What?" Aiden said once he was out of earshot of Olly and Chase.

"You! Always coming to the rescue of the *needy*," Mason said, throwing his hands up in the air exaggeratedly. "Like some modern Robin Hood, without the whole stealing from the rich part."

"Or the tights or cheeky accent," Aiden continued the train of thought with a light chuckle that Mason joined in on.

"Exactly," Mason grinned. "If you keep this up, though, tightless Robin or not, you'll be lucky to make it past your junior year, man."

"Ah, I'll make it." Aiden looked at Mason, eyes wide, and jeered at him, "Oh! You're worried about me."

Mason laughed, an exaggerated chuckle, and pushed Aiden away jokingly. "Shut up!"

Grinning still, Aiden shook his head and led the way out past the exit and to the parking lot.

"So, on a better topic," Mason started. "Are you seriously still going to the party tonight as Spiderman?"

"Yes!" Aiden shot back, faking a hurt expression.

"Okay," Mason threw his hands in the air defensively. "Okay! I just wasn't sure if you changed you mind and decided to go as some emo kid or something instead."

Aiden shook his head and answered his friend with one single raised digit on his right hand. The two burst out in laughter.

CHAPTER 5

Unable to restrain himself, Dalton smiled like a kid who had just opened a toy on Christmas day as he stepped out of the BMW. And that's exactly how he felt. Except instead of months, it had been years.

Out of habit, he checked his tie in the car window before traversing the pavement back into the office. He depressed the top button on his key fob and the car's amber light housings lit up. Then they dimmed back into obscurity accompanied by the sound of the locks engaging. Cars rushed to and fro behind him on Branchview Road. The office was nicely situated between Carolinas Medical Center Northeast, the Carolina Mall and I-85. Charlotte was less than a half hour drive southwest.

Dalton crossed the threshold into the office and the let the door shut behind him. Jenna's expectant face met him immediately at the receptionist's desk. Bright brown eyes begged to know how things had went. Dalton smiled.

"How'd it go?" she asked.

"Great. I think it went great," Dalton said, nodding his head. "I…"

"So, how did it go?" Daniel Cage entered the room from his office down the hall, a few seconds late in the conversation. His black hair was interrupted sporadically with signs of aging. Grey and white strands shined against the stark background. His gut hung just over his wide black belt and his forest green eyes were ready for good news. Dalton simply grinned.

"Like I was telling Jenna, it went great," Dalton explained, shooting his sky blues at Jenna and then back to his partner. "Gavin seems ready to move. He liked the property and I think he has a clear vision of where he wants to be. I cannot speak for him exactly, but I think he's going to go with the lot I showed him."

Daniel patted Dalton on the back in congratulations, though it was far from over. The decision on the lot was not in stone yet, or ink, technically. The design for the estate was only a cursory set of ideas and no firm direction on the overall style had been reached. Once they did close on a piece of property, Dalton and Gavin would certainly go through iteration after iteration of design concepts before ever coming to a concrete blueprint. And even that was far from the end.

"Congratulations, Dalton," Daniel said in his usual low pitch. "I know you've been waiting for this one for a while. Make sure you hit it out of the park."

"Or get past the finish line, in this case," Dalton corrected him. It only seemed right to use a racing analogy since his client was just that, an up-and-coming NASCAR driver.

Daniel pinched his lips and nodded before letting out a hoarse laugh. Dalton joined in. It was good to finally hit a goal, to be so close. He only hoped his client did not ditch and run further down the line.

"Well, once you settle the deal, we'll all have to go out and have a drink, on you of course," Daniel announced, earning a laugh from Jenna and a grin from Dalton. "Well, I've got to get back to Mrs. Sebastian. She wasn't happy that I asked her to wait in the first place."

Daniel nodded and turned to face Jenna. He tilted his head and eyed her. She raised an eyebrow curiously.

"Jenna," he started.

"Mr. Wayne?" she grinned. Dalton shook his head. One day he'd grow used to that.

"Are you busy tonight?" Dalton asked, ignoring the joke. "Care to join me for a drink after work?"

"Sure," she said without delay. She did not even bother to check her schedule. It wouldn't be the first time she had cleared her schedule for Dalton and she hoped it wouldn't be the last.

"Good," he replied. "Cabarrus Brewery fine?"

Jenna nodded.

"All right, I'll meet you there after work. I may be a few minutes behind," he smiled and then turned and walked into his office.

The hearty growl of an engine sifted quietly through the wall moments after the gentle two-note chime of the driveway notification echoed through the open living room. It seemed to drift over from the kitchen, past the tall vase of fluffy hydrangea blossoms and over the couch where Lenore laid sprawled out with her book of the moment, Dean Koontz.

Trapped in the mind of a disturbed nymphomaniac psychologist playing dangerous mental games with his patients, Lenore's attention left the beige pages and went to the kitchen. From the tone of the motor, she knew it was Aiden. Only his Camaro and Dalton's M3 had that deep throaty rumble. He would walk in through the garage in a matter of moments. Lenore put the book down on the end table after marking her spot with a green clip-on bookmark and stood to her feet. She crinkled her brow.

What is Aiden doing home? Wasn't he supposed to go to Mason's?

Around the corner, the door pivoted open with the slightest groan and Aiden stepped past the threshold. The door gently shut behind him as he slung his pack on the kitchen counter.

"Aiden, what are you doing home?" Lenore asked.

"I forgot my costume for the party," he explained, passing by her at a generous jog, taking the stairs two at a time up to his room.

Lenore lost sight of him at the top of the landing. She swiveled around and picked up a glass of water. It was no surprise that he had chosen to wear his Spiderman costume from last year. At least it had been no surprise to Lenore. The wall clinger was by far her only son's favorite comic hero, followed closely by Captain America. Lenore had advocated for a Cap costume, but had eventually given in to defeat.

Taking a sip from the clear tall glass, she wondered where Mara was, the one kid she had actually expected to see before late tonight. Her punishment mandated she come straight home from school, no side trips to friends' homes, no ventures to the store or any place else without calling and asking first. Lenore had received no such call from her eldest child. She groaned, feeling an additional two weeks were soon to be added to her daughter's punishment.

She took a quick glance at her watch, 3:26PM. Mara had another four minutes, but Lenore knew she'd give her at least until a quarter-till four. Mara needed to know her limits but Lenore hated being the bad guy all the time, especially so close to her little girl's graduation. Maybe four, she might could wait until four.

The thumping of Aiden's feet from the hall above echoed down the stairwell before Lenore saw his head crest the opening. She smiled. He was growing up. He had lost the pudgy cheeks of his youth and the adorable high-pitched vocal quality that had carried him through elementary and middle school. She watched him intently as he rushed down the stairs. He was moving fast, but she saw every detail like it was in slow motion.

The gentle sloping nose she still tapped on occasion and told him how cute it was. His tanned cheeks always turned so red when she said it in public. His chiseled chin and full pink lips. She adored the honey starbursts of his eyes. Without showing him, she cried a little inside, happy and wishing she could cradle him again all in the same moment.

"Hey! Do you know where Mara is by chance?" Lenore called after him.

Aiden stopped at the door to the garage, "I think she's on her way. I don't keep up with her."

"Have fun at the party," she said. "Love ya."

"Love you, too, Mom." The words echoed back to her from the garage as Mara stepped into sight from behind the same door frame.

"What was he doing here?" Mara asked, not attempting to hide the contempt in her voice.

Lenore huffed. *Wonderful. We're already starting off on the wrong foot.*

"He left his costume and had to come back to get it," she answered, checking the time. *3:29PM.* She pursed her lips and crossed her arms. "Cutting it a little close, aren't we?"

"You and Dad said three-thirty, so I'm home at three-thirty." Mara put on a fake grin and placed her right hand on her hip. "Reporting for solitary confinement."

Shaking her head from side to side, Lenore met her sarcasm, "Well, the warden won't be here for a few hours so you can roam the entire prison for a while."

"Funny," Mara mocked with a heavy breath and rolling eyes. "I think I'll stick to my room."

Lenore watched the gentle waves of her brown and blond locks bob up and down as she walked up the stairs and disappeared behind the landing. Lenore looked down to nowhere specific and leaned heavily against the wall. Her whole body sighed. Is this how their relationship was destined to remain the last year she would have her little girl at home before college? She felt a fracture forming in her heart. She wanted to reach out to Mara, be her friend, not a parent, but how could she be both?

*　*　*

The speakers thumped and the mirrors pulsed with each drop of the bass. The guitar hit hard for a long solo.

Instinctively, Aiden's head bobbed with the beat, just short of full-on head banging. He guided the Camaro down the country road that would eventually deposit him at Mason's place. Orange and red leaves were falling over the road way, swiftly finding themselves dispatched by the occasional car or swept into a cyclone and onto the roadside where the mass of the fallen debris had gathered in colorful heaps.

Occasionally the trees edging the road opened to a wide expanse of green fields or one of the many houses that dotted Enochville Road. Decorations varied from the Halloween apathetic, where only the colorful assortment of leaves on the lawn and roof indicated the season to the holiday enthusiast, or crazy person, who decorated to no end.

One house in particular had caught Aiden's attention, as it did every year at this time. Any other time of the year the house had a large open front lawn peppered with maples and other massive trees Aiden could not identify. A fancy circular stone-blocked gazebo that matched the façade of the house itself and well-manicured set of flowerbeds typically lined the front porch and the long driveway up to the house. Yet, the family apparently took Halloween very seriously. As he drove by, the full perimeter of the expansive lawn was cordoned off by shoddy distressed wood fencing and peppered with the occasional zombie, one in particular was impaled fully through the chest across a broken fence segment. As if that was not enough, the trees had cotton-based spider-webs splayed nearly halfway up their bare branches down to the lawn below, enveloping what appeared to be unsuspecting human victims. There was even a mammoth fake spider in simulated descent to toward its victims. Then there were the spindly life-size skeletons scaling the face of the house, threatening to break in at any moment.

It was cool, that much Aiden agreed with, but at the same time it creeped him out. The family decorated more for Halloween than they did for Christmas for crying out loud. As detailed and insane as the decorations were, Aiden had always decided against frequenting the house for trick-or-treating, or really any other time of the year to be honest.

Ahead, Mason's home came into view, the familiar Mustang sitting out front in the driveway. Aiden maneuvered the car against the curb in front of the house and cut the engine. He grabbed his costume and the pack of firecrackers, the real reason he had ventured back home before running off to Mason's. His mom would not have approved. School definitely would not have. So Aiden had decided to leave them at home and retrieve them afterward instead. In or out of school suspension for such a stupid school policy violation just did not seem worth it.

Before he could get half way to the front door, Mason swung it open. "What took you so long?"

"Quit your whining, it's too early for that," Aiden jeered back, earning a nearly silent snicker and accompanying grin from Mason.

Aiden followed Mason into the house, saying a quick hello to Mason's mom, a surprisingly young and attractive woman, as they ran to Mason's room. Mason shut the door behind them and Aiden dropped his costume on the bed.

"You brought them, right?" Mason asked.

"Yeah," Aiden assured him and then pulled the Spiderman suit back to reveal the unopened pack of firecrackers. Mason beamed at the sight. "Just remember, nothing stupid. We're going to follow the directions, stand back as far as it tells us and everything, none of the stupid shit you tried last year. I'd prefer not to have to call the fire department, especially since I'm the one who brought them."

"Oh yeah, no problem. We're just going to make a lot of noise," Mason assured him, picking Aiden's costume top off the bed. "You do realize this thing is going to be tight as shit, right?"

Aiden sighed. "Yeah, that didn't really cross my mind until last night, but it fits. I did try it on again."

"Oh, I cannot wait to see this," Mason jested with widen eyes.

CHAPTER 6

Dalton joined Jenna in the dirt parking lot that housed Cabarrus Brewery behind the old mill. The place had reminded Dalton of an old shed, maybe a barn. He felt like he should find a fleet of old half-rusted tractors within its shell.

He led Jenna up the steep staircase to the outer patio. The words *Cabarrus Brewery, Co.* hung overhead in large faded print above five closed bay doors where trucks used to dock before the building had been repurposed. It had a vintage vibe until you crested the stairs. Someone had forgotten the old, tattered and worn look when they put the patio boards down it seemed. Its wooden planks looked brand new, almost yellow, with maybe a half year of wear on them.

"So have you been here before?" Jenna asked, trying not to make a misstep up the stairs in her high heels.

"Once or twice," Dalton looked back to show her a grin, and then turned as his feet hit the patio. "You want to get a table? I'll get the beers."

She nodded as Dalton turned and walked in to get the drinks. Jenna scanned the crowd, looking for just enough space on one of the weathered wooden picnic-style benches while she hugged her light jacket to her chest. A few seconds later, she slid onto the edge of a bench with four others. Getting a table to yourself was near impossible on a Friday night, not to mention Halloween night. She smiled apprehensively at the occupants as they took notice of her.

Twirling a strand of red hair absently, Jenna was about to take out her phone when Dalton walked up on the opposite side of the table, drinks in hand. She smiled, biting her lower lip playfully.

"The beer has arrived," Dalton announced, placing the clear steins on the uneven surface, careful not to spill a drop of the dark amber liquid that sloshed inside.

"So, congrats," Jenna raised her glass. "Might as well start things out right. To more progress on your client."

With a nod, Dalton clinked his glass to hers. "Yes, progress please. I've waited so long for this. This one client, this opportunity. Hell, I've waited ever since I graduated from Charlotte."

She knew. Jenna may only have been with the firm for just under three years, but she had become intimately familiar with her two bosses. Especially Dalton. It had been his dream to design a home that could become his legacy, a mark on architectural history. Something that truly mattered, that stood out.

"Well, it seems that you're finally on track, Dalton," she grinned genuinely. "I'm happy for you."

Dalton took a long gulp from his glass. It was finally happening. His time may come after all despite what the dreary forecast seemed to have predicted. Through it all, it seemed that his savior was a man he would have never expected. He was not a painter, an author, director or hell, not even a musician. No, a race car driver. Dalton chuckled silently, his mind on his fortune and the way events came together. Rarely as one might expect them to.

"So how was the game last night?" he asked.

"It was great," Jenna replied. Her face lit up with excitement as last night came to mind. "I'm still not sure I know what was going on exactly. I'm not *really* into football, but it was exciting!"

"And we won," Dalton reminded her. It had been a home game for the Panthers. A good one that ended with the defeat of the Atlanta Falcons in the last two minutes with an interception and touch down after being down for an entire quarter. Dalton had missed the excitement of watching from the stadium with Jenna and one of her girl-friends, who was a die-hard Panthers fan. He had better things to do than fight off traffic in downtown Charlotte, or *uptown* as they were calling it these days. His online sports subscription had come in handy instead, lighting up a beautiful one hundred and twenty inches of glorious high-definition picture in his living room.

"That we did. All I know is that some big guy caught the ball in the last little bit and ran to the other side," she explained. "It was exciting, though. I'm surprised you didn't ask earlier."

"My mind was too stuck on Mr. Bostian this morning," he explained. He purposefully ignored the sad puppy dog whimper and frown. Dalton changed the subject. "Now, correct me if I'm wrong, but this coming Thursday you'll have been with us for a full three years, right?"

A sheepish grin stretched from cheek-to-cheek before she parted her red lips. "Yes. Three years since you and Daniel rescued me from the basement of Randall's Pest Extermination company."

Dalton laughed. Jenna had come to them only a few years out of college, stuck in a low-paying and less than desirable secretarial position at Randall's, a local exterminator. He still remembered when she had dropped off her résumé. She had been dressed in a tasteful beige pant suit which hugged the curves of her body just the slightest bit, just enough. Dalton and his partner at the firm would never admit how much her job offer had had to do with Jenna's curvature rather than her well-rounded experience and blooming attitude, which of course she had as well.

"Well why don't we celebrate your three years with Cage/Summers Architecture, too?" Dalton eyed her with a smile, and a bit too much longing in his eyes. "Another round?"

"Oh yeah!" Jenna nearly yelled, pulling back her arms and pronouncing her chest. "Let's celebrate!"

The room felt so lonely. Too quiet and empty even though it was filled with the same furniture and things as it had been for at least the last year. Lenore lounged back on a cushy mocha leather couch, eyes wandering from picture to picture. There was so much history in the portraits, so much love and happiness.

A large spring portrait from two years ago showed the family spread out on a thin white blanket among the grass, surrounded by magnolias. Another featured Aiden sitting up straight, with a flat top and his mouth shut tight; his first grade portrait and the day he lost his second tooth. He had been tormented by the thought of a gap in his smile for his school pictures. Lenore laughed lightly at the memory.

Next was one of Mara's school pictures, sixth grade if Lenore remembered correctly. Mara had been more agreeable back then. A simple pre-teen, unburdened with the needs of popularity and boys. And, best of all, she had yet to discover how her parents lived solely to hold her back from everything she wanted. Lenore huffed. Parenting had been so much easier when Mara and Aiden's thoughts never went beyond how much fun they could have at home with the family or with their little friends. Now there was no end to where their imaginations roamed. Being a parent and friend to two teenagers was anything but easy.

Right now was one of those less than amiable times. She felt so alone in the house. Mara was no more than twenty yards away, just a set of stairs and a locked door away, probably still bemoaning her ill-fated fortune of shelter. Lenore let herself laugh a little at that notion. What she would give to be under her parents' rules again, to live with the simplicity of a child's life. What she would give simply just to see her mother again. A tear escaped Lenore's eye unhindered. Five years seemed like ten and the sadness never seemed to dissipate. She had been a victim of Parkinson's.

Lenore wiped the tear from her cheek and placed the book she had been reading on the end table before making her way to the kitchen. The trick-or-treaters would begin to file through within the hour and she had yet to prepare the candy.

Dressed in a loose fitting white blouse and a simple pair of jeans, Lenore tore open the first bag of candy, Snickers. She eyed the small digital clock on the oven. Eight till seven and Dalton was nowhere in sight. Lenore cursed herself for thinking the man would come home when asked. She opened the second and third bags and poured their entire contents into a large orange plastic bowl shaped like a smiling jack-o-lantern.

Lenore heaved the heavy bowl off the counter and shuffled over to the front door. She dropped the bowl on a waist high mahogany table by the frosted glass entry door. Satisfied with the placement, she walked past the plain white columns dividing the open foyer from the kitchen, dining area and living room back into the kitchen and rummaged through the junk drawer for the lighter. She hooked her index finger through the spindly handles of two old-timey looking lanterns and walked back to the foyer and then outside.

The air had grown cooler. It nipped at her nose as she placed each lantern on a separate table on either side of the door. She hated the cold, and constantly had to remind herself that it only lasted a few months before North Carolina's warm spell started up again. It was cold, though, autumn, a cold autumn and it did not show any signs of warming. Lenore shivered as she lit the oil wicks and stepped back into the house, hurriedly shutting the door behind her.

It would only be a matter of minutes, maybe less, before the first group of annoying little trick-or-treaters would knock on the front door. She imagined their greedy little plastic or paper bags held high, expecting nothing less than some sugary treat.

Trick-or-treat my foot. More like trick-or…well, just trick actually. When else did little kids get away with walking up to a total stranger's doorsteps demanding candy or some stupid ass trick? It was definitely just a trick.

Lenore looked up toward the staircase leading to the second floor where Mara was fortified in her room sulking. Maybe, just maybe, she could convince Mara to come down and help her with the kids. Mara had always been good with kids despite her more recently attained lack of restraint.

She made her way up the stairs and down the upper hall, walking past more photographs, her legacy. A picture of Aiden in basketball shorts and a jersey poised to make a shot, which Lenore was pretty sure he missed. One with a four year old Mara, grinning from ear to ear, mustard smeared down the whole right side of her mouth. Lenore's heart brightened at the sight.

Ahead she came to Mara's door. It was shut, just as expected. She stopped and went to turn the knob but then froze, thinking better of it. Instead she rapped gently on the door with her knuckles.

"Mara?" she called through the heavy wooden frame. She waited, nothing. She frowned. "Mara? Come on, Mara, talk to me."

"What do you want?" Mara finally responded, the irritation more than evident in her almost distressed answer.

"Uh…" Lenore stuttered, hurt more than she would ever admit to Mara. "I just thought you might want to come help me with the trick-or-treaters, dear."

"Uh. No."

Lenore frowned behind the cover of the door. "Come on, Mara. You used to like passing out the candy."

She waited. Nothing. Lenore leaned her cheek against the door and closed her eyes. She sighed and pursed her lips.

Lenore swallowed the sadness in her throat. She took a deep breath and raised her head, staring at the solid door as if she could see right through it. She imagined Mara lying on her bed, angry, with headphones stuck in her ears. She turned and walked back downstairs. Mara was just angry, a teenager deprived of a night out and unable to understand the reason why. It would pass and she only hoped the sadness would, too.

"Man, you've *really* got to get a new costume," Mason leered behind Aiden.

"Are you staring at my ass?" Aiden asked, his left brow raised and forehead crinkled with a contradictory friendly grin. "I mean I can't blame you, but—"

Mason cocked his head sideways, the unruly brown and sandy tufts displaced further down his brow. He tossed the strands back up and his eyes met Aiden's, an attempt at displeasure in his eyes.

"No," Mason retorted. "It's just *really, really* tight. I mean…"

He put his hands out, waving in a broad up-and-down motion to signify the entire outfit. He had trouble finding the word, trying not to sound wrong.

"It's just *really* tight."

"Yeah, I know," Aiden said, trying to hide the embarrassment. He had not expected the costume to be this formfitting, and he was not excited about it. "But this is *the* last time I'm dressing up, and it still *technically* fits."

Up the stone path from where they stood sat an imposing stone-faced home, Zed's. Vines and other greenery twisted over the face of the home's two oversized levels. Windows dotted both levels in perfect symmetry. The driveway overflowed with a plethora of cars. They ranged from growling muscle cars to the giant Ford crew-cab with a ten-inch lift kit and accompanying American flag waving beyond the truck bed.

Aiden brushed a hand through his milk chocolate brown hair, pushing it back, as he pulled up the Spidey mask and secured a piece of Velcro at the nape of his neck. The two stepped up to the entrance landing and took a quick glance at their reflections in the large glass door.

To his right stood a short and spindly version of Mike Myers, complete with a blood-filled plastic knife and off-white latex mask. Then Aiden's eyes traveled to his own figure in the glass. He sighed at the sight of every overly-emphasized curve under his Spidey suit.

Only another few hours.

Mara stared up into the white speckled ceiling. It was dark. The lights were off and the faint glow of the moon was largely held at bay by heavy white curtains. The tiny glowing dots on her ceiling had faded noticeably over the past hour, her indoor illusion of the night sky slowly fading into the clutches of pitch black night.

Music flooded through her ears, a constant rhythmic beat of R&B and indie label hip-hop. Halsey's *New Americana* had been playing when Lenore had knocked at the door. Mara heard her just above the chords echoing in her ears but held back any extra response other than a quick *No*. She huffed at the ceiling. Clad behind the iron bars of her parents' imprisonment was not how she dreamt spending her last Halloween as a senior, but nonetheless here she was.

She raised her iPod and checked the time. *7:18PM.*

Where the hell are you, Nathan? she nettled.

The sooner he arrived, the sooner her prison sentence could finally be commuted for at least a few hours, of course without Mom or Dad's knowledge. That was the genius of a prison break after all, though hers did not require actually leaving the house.

Come on!

Mara sat up in her bed and threw her feet over the edge before tapping a dull light to life on her nightstand. The tiny shimmer of the glowing specks on the ceiling suddenly became insignificant as the grey, almost blue walls came to life with photographs and a stenciled white silhouetted scene of flowers rising from the floor nearly to eye level. Her light nightgown hung loose around her small waist where it stopped inches above her knees in laced frills. She tugged the lime green band at the back of her head loose and let her gentle curls unfurl and drop around shoulders.

Cinching the gown's straps tighter, Mara walked over to her vanity and took a seat on the cushy tall-backed wooden chair. She lifted a large-bristled comb from the multiple options on the table and combed her hair, inspecting the color and texture of her sun-kissed skin and double-checking her makeup.

Clack!

Her head snapped to the left, eyes glued to where the noise had come from. The window closest to her. She loosened up.

Nathan?

Mara rose from her seat and started to walk toward the window. The familiar shadow of a waving tree limb swayed ghost-like behind her curtains. She parted the curtain, letting the gentle moonlight shine into the room, lighting up her face. Beyond was the same bare red maple tree limb that had haunted her bedroom since they had moved in. Beyond it sat the lake shimmering in sparkles of white and black just beyond the family's tiny dock bordered by more trees.

She peeked through the glass, angling her head to get a better look. Suddenly something hideous jumped in front of the glass, slapping into the surface with a loud clinking. It was *Predator*.

Mara stumbled back, barely holding in a screech that would have seemed a beacon for help to her mother downstairs. She took a step toward the glass, an indignant frown slashed across her lips. She heaved the window open as the mask lifted to reveal a wide jaw and toothy grin followed by a set of chestnut brown starbursts gazing back at her in obvious amusement.

"Nathan!" She whispered yet yelled at Nathan at the same time. She reached out and helped him cross the window's threshold, "What do you not understand about *sneaking* into my bedroom? About causing me to scream doesn't qualify as sneaking, idiot."

"But you didn't," Nathan retorted, his boyish demeanor only dinted in the most minor bit by her complaining.

"That's not the point. If my mom realizes you're up here, they'll never let me see you again," she whispered.

"Sure they will," he said. "They can't keep you locked away forever."

Mara couldn't help but grin at him. She leaned forward onto his chest and nuzzled her cheek against his as he bent down slightly to her level. At five foot ten, he was short for his role on the high school football team, first string running back, but that didn't make it any easier for Mara. She let her arms wrap around him as his hands reached down, latched on to her buttocks and lifted her the remaining few inches to put them eye-to-eye.

"That's better," Nathan grinned.

She smiled, looking straight into his eyes, enjoying the feeling of his palms tight on her butt, her breasts against his hard chest and his balmy breath on her cheek. Finally, his lips met hers. Mara closed her eyes as his tongue worked its way between her open lips, and she gasped lightly. Instinctively she slid her hand down his back and then under his t-shirt. Slowly her palm explored the soft contours of his waist before she found her hand sliding back up the slopes of his back.

"Much better," his eyes held a longing, a deep need as he opened them just long enough to take a quick look before kissing her again. Still carrying her, Nathan walked a few steps back and gently laid Mara down on the bed.

CHAPTER 7

The nippy wind took one last bite at Lenore's ankles as she closed the door. The candy bowl was dwindling. About a third of the chocolatey treats had made their way into the bags of a handful of trick-or-treaters. It was a benefit of living on the end of a side road rather than off the main road, and having a long driveway. Fewer cars made the turn off the main road and fewer parents cared to make the additional trek down the path to further fill their kids' candy bags.

The usual suspects had already come by. The Flandry kids, an eight-year-old blond-haired and blue-eyed boy with a growing tummy and his always skinny eleven-year-old blond sister. She lacked the blue eyes, though, instead she took after her mother, brown. Then Noah James, a spindly little kid of six or seven, sandy brown hair and grey-blue eyes. His mom, Beth James, had struggled to keep Noah from sprinting off up the path and to the front door. Lenore had smiled at the boy's exuberance. They were the only people Lenore had recognized.

The last group had consisted of four kids. Judging by height, Lenore assumed they were each around ten except for the fourth kid, who was likely an older brother serving as the obligatory chaperon. The stale "Tell the lady thank you" had said as much at least.

Lenore dipped her hand in the candy bowl and pulled back a miniature peanut butter Snickers, ripped open the wrapper and popped the peanut buttery goodness in her mouth. *Where are you, Dal-*

ton?

She knew better than to expect him home on time, but an hour late was even beyond her tolerance. Huffing, she finished chewing up the candy, licked away the remaining chocolate from her lips and fingers and reached for her cellphone in her pants pocket. She was not worried, no, she was agitated bordering on choleric.

She tapped the recent calls log, chose Dalton's name from the list and put the thin phone to her ear. Just as it had twenty minutes ago, the phone played the familiar ring on the other end, beckoning Dalton to answer but earned no answer, again. *Maybe he doesn't have signal. No. Not likely.*

No, the more likely scenario was that Dalton had gotten too involved in his work. He had probably left late and did not want to explain it over the phone. He always did prefer to confront Lenore's temper head on. It used to work, but lately, the tactic just got under Lenore's skin.

She called again. Voicemail. Lenore ended the call. "Come on, Dalton!"

Lenore thought of her brother, Daniel. He was probably at home helping Lori hand out candy down in Pensacola right now. She could see him smiling happily at the little kids as they ran back down the concrete sidewalk to their parents, his arm wrapped around Lori's waist, hugging her to him. She looked down, placing the cellphone back in the pocket of her blue jeans.

She stepped back up to the entrance door and spied out the peephole between the two pieces of frosted glass. The coast was clear. Lenore turned and made off for the stairway. In her heart she knew it was a futile thing, useless and better left untried, but her mind told her it couldn't be that bad. Conquering the stairs, she stepped before Mara's bedroom door and knocked. A faint yelp sounded from behind the door and Lenore tensed slightly.

"Mara? You okay?" she asked, her sea green eyes squinted ever so slightly.

"I'm fine, you scared me!" Mara's yell came muffled through the solid wooden door.

"Could you please come help me, Mara?" Lenore asked, almost pleaded, though she tried to keep the supplication to a minimum. She wanted to reason with her daughter. Tell her how lonely it was downstairs, how they could talk, maybe watch a movie. Anything.

"No," her voice came quieter this time, but still a yell, though she sounded exhausted. "I'm in solitary, remember?"

Lenore let her forehead rest against the door, her healthy brown locks crested her shoulder and flopped down against the door and hung below her. She knew she could unlock the door and tell her to come downstairs and help. She had the authority and in that moment of rejection, she felt like exercising it. She let a few seconds pass to allow herself to think more clearly.

"Please, Mara," she asked once more. "I could really use the company."

"Solitary," was all she got back.

A forced smile replaced the frown on Lenore's lightly painted lips. She shook her head and sighed as she turned in defeat, tucking tail and moving out and down the stairs back to her own solitary. Her punishment for attempting to be a good parent, she esteemed.

She took the phone from her pocket again and dialed Dalton. The phone to her ear, Lenore peeked outside through the peephole again. To her dismay, a small Kia SUV turned into the driveway as the chimes sounded in the living room. The phone continued to ring.

"Answer, Dalton," she willed him. Nothing. The sound of the pre-recorded voicemail message played in her ear as one, no, two kids jumped from the SUV and were led up to the front door by their mother.

The clatter of a hundred loud voices echoed out of the main brewery onto the patio where Dalton and Jenna sat. Lips pursed, irritated, Dalton swiped at his phone, rejecting another phone call from Lenore.

"Was that Lenore again?" Jenna inquired. Her eyes had grown harder over the past half hour with each call from Dalton's wife. Her pale arms were beginning to show signs of the cold, tiny little chill bumps crawling up her normally smooth skin.

"Yeah," Dalton confirmed sourly as he pocketed the phone. "I'll be home when I get home."

"You did tell her six thirty or seven, though, didn't you?" Jenna asked, not intending to play devil's advocate, but finding herself in those shoes nonetheless.

He didn't answer. Instead, Dalton stared back at her with a brow raised and took another swig from his second pint. He let the glass hit the table a little harder than he had intended which earned him a slight twitch from Jenna.

"Don't you think you should at least answer?" Jenna kept trying. "Maybe she's worried."

"She's not worried. She's just needy, selfish." Dalton was surprised at how quickly the words had come out. He had not downed enough beer for his mind to be on autopilot yet, but it felt good to vocalize the sentiment finally.

"Too used to being in the lime light," he continued. "She can deal with the little douches on her own tonight. I'm staying right here, with you. What am I supposed to tell her anyway? Oh hey, Lenore, I'm just out at the brewery with Jenna."

Jenna's gaze remained steady on Dalton though she shifted on the wooden bench. The crowd around them had grown denser as the sky grew darker, revealing the eerie orange lighting that hung over the bay door entrances to the brewery's interior.

She was surprised to see so many adults in full Halloween get up. Already she had noted at least three scantily clad cats, one devil complete with tail and pitchfork, a giant condom and keg couple, too many Jasons to count and one Thor.

"No," Jenna paused. "I don't know, but it just seems you should at least answer. Hell, if I think you should answer, that should tell you something."

"Jenna," Dalton started. "I wasn't going to mention this yet, but I've already had divorce papers drafted up. I've got them in my briefcase."

He nodded toward his car in the parking lot below them. Jenna's eyes wandered across the crowd, past the newly arriving set of costumes, and to the stairs leading down to their cars. Was it true? Was the next step to them being together sitting only thirty yards away? She couldn't help but let her eyes brighten. Dalton noticed.

"It's going to take some time, but it won't be long now," he explained. "I just have to sign the dotted line and start the process."

"What are you wa…." She stopped herself. A sudden rush of resentment flushed through her cheeks. She pursed her lips and looked at Dalton sternly. "You're still married, though. She at least deserves an answer to her call."

"Seriously? You're on her side?" Dalton asked incredulously.

"I'm not on anyone's side, Dalton, it's just common courtesy. I mean it isn't like she's stalking you," Jenna tried.

"I can't believe what I'm hearing," Dalton said, his voice louder than it was a few seconds ago."

In the rumbling of the crowd and music, his voice did not carry any further than did their loud mouthed neighbors, but Jenna's eyes darted around them instinctively, hoping no one was witnessing their conversation. She felt something she had not expected, pity for Dalton's wife. Would Dalton so easily throw her aside? No. It was different with them. He loved her, they understood each other. But, even still, Dalton was not willing to discuss it right now.

"I think I'm going to head on home for the evening," Jenna said, getting to her feet and pulling her jacket tighter to her chest. "It's getting cold anyway."

"Whatever," Dalton mumbled, refusing to make eye contact as he took another gulp from his glass.

Her eyes darted to him, but she held her tongue. She diverted her eyes, trying to hide the hurt she felt.

"Night, Dalton."

Shutting the door behind her, Lenore stepped past the stoic white pillars of the foyer and down a small step to the low-lit living room. She let her right hand caress the thick mocha leather of the oversized recliner where Dalton usually sat before she crossed between it and the sofa and fell back into the couch's cozy depths.

A scene from the Rob Zombie *Halloween* remake was playing on the television, part of a Spike TV horror marathon. Lenore had watched absently between visits to the front door to greet the masked kiddies and bestow chocolate goodies on them. On the screen an attractive young lady roamed the dark recesses of her house, knife in hand. It was a testament to the fact that Zombie could make something horrific without all the crazy.

Lenore picked up the remote and leveled up the volume just high enough that the sound was immersive yet not too loud to prevent her from hearing the door chime. She curled her feet up on the couch and laid her head on one of the wide black and white plaid cushions.

A scream rang out from the speakers mounted around the room as Myers, face ensconced in his gray mask, suddenly appeared in a door way. He wore an oil-stained mechanic's jumpsuit, his hair carelessly combed back, haphazardly flowing out from behind the dirtied mask. Lenore kept her eyes on the tube as the action began. The running. Mike Myers actually moved faster than a walk in this version, much to Lenore's approval. The screaming. The eventual carnage that would ensue.

Thirty minutes later, the credits began to roll. Lenore rolled back on the couch and let out a breath, an approval of the cinematic remake. At the bottom of the screen the title of the next movie appeared. *Sinister.* Lenore shrugged and reduced the volume as the credits quickened while the next movie's opening credits began.

The gentle chimes of the driveway sensor rang quietly in the background, signaling a new arrival. Lenore rose from the sofa with a belabored sigh. She walked to the kitchen to refill her glass before the new trick-or-treaters arrived. She passed by the open foyer where the gentle flame of a small oil lantern sent dancing rays of orange light onto the entrance door and filtered outside through the frosted glass. As her bare foot crossed the threshold into the kitchen, the ditty of the doorbell rang affably throughout the space.

"Dammit," Lenore muttered. "Those little buggers are quick."

She altered her course after depositing her glass on the nearest countertop and stepped back up onto the foyer landing. She could already see several shadows behind the frosted glass. Lenore opened the door and put on her best grin.

"Trick-or-treat," came the usual chant as the door opened. But, instead of the shrill voice of an elementary school boy or girl, the voice was an octave lower than any of the night's earlier patrons. Not an adult, but the owner had at least hit puberty.

Three masked figures. Considering both the previous vocal tone from whichever had spoken and the flat contours of their chests under graphic tees and simple blue jeans, it was a pack of boys, tiny plastic bags in hand. Each stood at least five-seven to five-eight except for the one to her left wearing the eerie crimson skull mask that wrapped around the full extent of his head. He stood even with Lenore at about five-six, not a piece of skin exposed except for his spindly wrists and hands. Even the boy's eyes were a mystery behind the mask's grated mesh eye sockets. The boy on the right donned a familiar Freddie Kruger mask. Brown eyes cried out behind the tortured but gleeful façade covered in sinuous umber and carmine fibers of simulated burnt flesh.

The last boy, standing front and center, wore the simplest guise. It was a homely achromatic disguise. A white hard-plastic mask with six openings. The first hole was a slit along the plastic but life-like lips which revealed the boy's full pink lips. Another two openings created passageways for air in the nostrils of the mask and yet another two revealed two almost-black eyes. They glimmered in the small lantern light behind her. The last hole was a simulated bullet hole just below the boy's temple. It cascaded out into innumerable cracks and fragmentation marks like the skull had been a piece of glass.

"Happy Halloween," Lenore said, surprised to see teenagers at her door. She put her finger up, "Ah, yes. Candy, right?"

Silence. The three just stood there, waiting. Lenore tilted her head awkwardly and turned back toward the candy bowl. The rustle of feet sounded behind her. She turned to find the group standing within the doorframe.

"All right now, I'll bring the candy to you," she uttered, showing more authority.

No one moved. They stood in place, staring back through their masks. The black abyss of the middle kid's orbs bored into her.

"Come on now. I said you need to wait outside," she tried again.

The kid with the bullet hole mask, Bullet, stepped a foot's breadth closer. His friends immediately followed him, Freddie and Skull-face.

"I said out!" Lenore raised her voice, mustering equal parts thunder and command to disguise the trepidation building in her lungs. "Out!"

When no one moved, Lenore took a step toward them, hoping to scare them. They were probably just a group of pranksters who couldn't let go of their little prank. She would end that quickly, she thought. Lenore came to a cold stop when Bullet's hand came out of his treat bag. Her eyes widened at the sight glinting metal, a long sharp blade. She stepped back involuntarily.

At first she wanted to kick herself for falling for such a trick on Halloween, but when the flame light gleamed off the ten inches of curved silver steel, her mind went into stunned fright. She stood, frozen.

"No," the lips behind the bullet-holed mask moved. Another knife appeared in Freddie's hand, smaller, but still a large kitchen knife likely swiped from the family knife block. Her mind imagined dark ominous lips snarling behind the mask as her heart pounded, paralysis holding tight to her legs.

Mara! her mind screamed.

Breaking from her stupor, Lenore defected a step back before swinging her body around and sprinting off. She had to warn Mara, but she did not dare lead them to her. Lenore's feet pounded off the foyer landing and down into the kitchen as the three formerly stoic figures burst forward. Maybe she could get her own weapon. Three against one were bad odds in any fight, even a knife in her hand couldn't change that, but it couldn't hurt either.

"Come here, baby!" one jeered but Lenore couldn't tell which, she didn't care which.

She bound around the tile-covered counter and sprinted for the utensil drawer where the most readily available knives were stored. Before she could reach out and pull the drawer open, a hand gripped her shoulder and wrenched her around. It yanked her body close, chest to chest. Those black eyes were only inches from her frightened green counterparts.

Lenore's breathing came in short rhythmic gasps. Her body tensed at the feeling of the boy's hardened chest pressed firmly against her breasts and stomach. Fear jetted through her veins alongside the adrenaline. She struggled to loosen his grip around her back. His hand was planted firmly in place. She stopped her struggling as the knife came back into view, hovering dangerously close to her neck just above her clavicle. She felt the cold edge of metal meeting skin, a singe of excited terror coursing through every vein in her body. She shivered.

"Now, now, Lenore," the lips behind the bullet-holed mask spoke her name in a young but raspy tone, moving inches from her face. Lenore's eyes widened at the sound of her name. "Just calm down and everything will be just fine."

He waited. Lenore's breathing steadied only the slightest bit. She exhaled in abrupt stutters. The boy's grip loosened and Freddie took hold of her around the waist, pulling her to him, her back to his chest.

"Well, not everything will be fine, but eh," Bullet jeered, an almost sociopathic air about his voice. "So, where's the whore?"

"Yeah, where's the little whore at, Lenore?" Freddie jeered before she had a second to compute the original question. The voice behind the mask was immature, maybe a hint of gang-like quality or the attempt at a deeper tone by a medium-octave voice. She didn't care.

Whore? What? Lenore's mind was ablaze. Should she run? Should she stay put and chance her luck as the submissive captive? Should she escape the blade and warn Mara?

"Mara, the whore," Skull-face spoke up for the first time, a more shrill sound than she had expected to come from behind such an ominous mask.

Mara?

"She's not here," Lenore lied without even thinking. "She's out."

"No she's not," Freddie said between quiet chuckles.

Bullet tilted his head, digging his black eyes into hers. Even in this situation, this horror, Lenore could not help but admire the deepness of the boy's eyes, a quality that betrayed him as both kind and heartless, a contradiction that she could not reconcile.

"Don't lie to me, Lenore," Bullet said in a softer tone that gave the slightest credence to the softness in his eyes. "We know she's here, so where is she?"

His voice remained calm as he spoke the last few words slowly and deliberately. As if she had woken from a trance, Lenore suddenly realized that they were using her name and used the recognition to bypass the question.

"How do you know my name?" she asked between stuttered breaths that were finally beginning to regulate.

A hard grin formed between the lips on Bullet's mask. Skull-face seemed to bob with some pent-up excitement that was waiting to burst within him. Freddie just nodded, his amber eyes calm behind his mask.

"We know a lot about you, Lenore, and about Mara, Dalton, Aiden. All of you. But we're just here for a little fun," Bullet explained candidly, like it was any other conversation. Then his voice slowed to a decidedly more deliberate pace, the raspy quality heightening, "Now, let me try this again. Where is Mara?"

"She's not here," Lenore tried again, letting her voice drop into more despair. "I'm telling you, I'm by myself, everyone's gone for the night."

"Maybe so, but they'll be back eventually," Freddie quipped, the hot stench of his breath coating her neck and right ear from behind.

"Don't be a fool, Mara's here," Bullet chided Freddie before looking back at Lenore. "So where is she?"

The three masked figures turned on her, their human and inhuman eyes drilling into her. She shifted her gaze quickly between them, unsure what to say, what to do. Bullet took another step toward her. He angled his head to the right and then back to the left, taking in a deep breath as if examining her soul behind his screwed up mask. Lenore closed her eyes, but did not say a word, trembling in Freddie's grasp.

"Either you show us where she is, or we'll break down every door in this house to find her. If we have to break down doors, Lenore, you're not going to like how we bring her downstairs," Bullet reasoned. He huffed lightly, pursing his lips in an ominous grin just within sight through the slit on the mask. He let the massive blade float around playfully under Lenore's chin. "No, you really won't enjoy watching that. Take us to her and things will work out a *little* more in your favor."

Opening her eyes, Lenore looked down to the floor shamefully. How could she stop them? They would find her either way, and if Bullet was true to his word, Lenore could only imagine what they would do to her. She cringed at the thought. The sight of metal came into view as the blade tapped under her chin and lifted her view, pressing dangerously against her skin. She trembled.

"So what's it going to be, Lenore?" Bullet asked calmly.

"Upstairs," she said after a few seconds. Suddenly, revulsion for her own soul welled up inside her. Had she made the right decision or simply damned them both to an earlier grave?

"There we go. See, that wasn't that hard," Bullet jeered. "Lead the way now."

Lenore frowned and reluctantly turned to lead the way. The tip of the blade left her chin. She walked to the stairs and grasped the wooden railing along the wall to support her shaking body. She did not dare look behind her. She knew what was there. Three dangerous kids, bent on something horrible. What their goal was, she didn't know, she didn't want to know. No, she just wanted them out of her house.

Cresting the top stair, she led the trio down the hall. For a brief second she entertained the notion of taking them to the wrong room, leading them off to some empty room and making a run for it. The knife prodded her gingerly in the back. She decided against the ruse, it could only make matters worse.

Just a few feet down the hallway, Lenore stopped at Mara's bedroom door, her prison as she had referred to it the past two weeks. Lenore shivered and turned cautiously to face her captors. She nodded at the door and immediately looked down.

"Call her out," Bullet whispered. He motioned with the curved blade like it was just another appendage, not a sharp-edged weapon. Lenore began to shake her head in refusal. "Do it."

A tear escaped her eye, she swallowed and looked up toward the ceiling before knocking on the door. "Mara."

"Go away," Mara yelled back angrily.

"Oh my," Freddie giggled, looking back to Skull-face who joined in quietly. Bullet just stared at Lenore, steel-eyed, waiting.

"Try again," he said.

"Mara," she started and looked back at Bullet. "Get out! Out the window! Ru…"

Bullet shoved his body against her, pinning her painfully against the door frame and his body. He shoved the knife precariously under her throat. He seemed to growl as he barked out a command, "Get her! Now!"

Freddie and Skull-face immediately went to work banging at the door with their feet. Freddie took a swipe at the heavy solid wood door with his knife, burying it a mere eighth of an inch. It was useless.

"Come out, Mara," Bullet bellowed out, "or I'm going to slit your mom's throat right here, right now!"

A stirring echoed from inside the room. Feet pattered on the floor but no one said a word on the other side. They waited.

"I'm going to give you to the count of five to open the door and walk out. Don't try anything stupid," Bullet commanded. "Five... Four..."

Lenore's body shook with fear as the blade laid against her neck. The cold metal stung as it moved ever so little, nicking her skin. *Mara. Just run.*

"Three... Two..." he continued the countdown.

Suddenly, a latch clicked from the other side and the door slowly moved inward. Eyes peeked around the small opening, Mara's eyes, and opened wide in fright as she saw the knife around Lenore's neck. For a second she rethought her actions and began to shut the door. Freddie wedged his foot in the gap.

"No, no," Freddie said. "You're coming out to play now."

Freddie shoved his body against the door, using his weight to knock her off balance. The door swung wide and Mara stumbled back but stayed on her feet.

"Looks like someone was ready for bed," Freddie quipped, noting the tan of her soft sculpted stomach, pink panties and a matching bra that left less to the imagination than a skimpy bikini showing behind the open gown. His eyes moved up and down her with a grin that no one could see behind the mask. Mara reeled the gown shut and cinched the cloth belt around her waist.

"Aw, come on," Freddie whined. "Whatever, you're coming downstairs regardless."

He moved forward, Skull-face following a few footsteps behind him. As he advanced, Mara stepped back, her eyes were those of a child as she cried, "Get away!"

As Freddie passed the threshold, another body jumped from behind the door, wrangling its arms around him. He was pulled to the ground with a hard thump. Before he could react, a fist rammed into his side and he gasped. Mara moved forward to help but suddenly saw her mother standing in the doorway, a blade held tight to her neck and Bullet shaking his head slowly. She stopped. Then Skull-face rushed in, a glint of light shining off his blade as it curved through empty space and found purchase in her boyfriend's calf.

As quickly as the struggle had begun, a stunned scream echoed behind Freddie as Nathan lost his grip. His arms coiled back and he fell to the ground. Freddie reeled around and brought his knife up into the air. Mara screamed, "No!"

"Stop," Bullet's raspy voice penetrated the chaos.

Freddie stopped his blade's plummet a mere inch over Nathan's chest. He let the small but sharp blade hover in place for a few moments as he stared into the boy's eyes intensely. Nathan curled up in pain and fright and turned away. Skull-face wrenched the knife out of Nathan's calf, earning a grunt and moan of pain. Nathan screamed in pain, gingerly touching his wounded calf.

"Well that was stupid, Mara," Bullet said without emotion or empathy. "Are you trying to get your boyfriend killed?"

Mara stood in place, shaking, wanting to run to Nathan and to her mother, but afraid to move in either direction. Freddie got to his feet and kicked Nathan in the side for good measure before stepping up to Mara. She took another step back. Freddie huffed angrily.

"Stop that shit, or my buddy back there is going to slit your mom's throat right in front of you," Freddie commanded angrily. Bullet tightened his grip around Lenore and let the blade move just enough to bring blood from her neck. Mara's eyes lit up.

"Okay! Okay!" she cried, tears running down her cheeks.

Freddie moved in and wrapped an arm around her stomach, bringing his blade up against her neck. Mara lifted her neck, trying to keep it from touching her. She shivered as Freddie's body writhed slowly against her back. He moaned pleasurably.

"This is more like it," Freddie said before his palm found purchase on her left breast and squeezed tight. "Yeah!"

Mara jerked, the need to get away clouding her memory of the edge of the knife against her neck. Freddie's arm wrapped staunchly around her waist, letting the knife move out to keep from slicing through her fragile neck.

"I'll slice your pretty little neck if you don't calm down, I swear it," Freddie said more calmly than she had expected. Slowly she stopped struggling and let his grip tighten around her.

"Please stop, please just stop," Lenore pleaded between sobs.

"We will. In time," Bullet assured her.

Still on the ground, Nathan's eyes burned with rage at Freddie. He tried to get up but his wounded calf sent him tumbling back to the floor.

"What do you want?" Nathan asked angrily.

"Well, that has nothing to do with you," Bullet said from the door. Nathan craned his neck back to see the white-masked figure. "So…" Bullet sighed. "This might work, though."

"What do you mean?" Nathan's voice had changed. It had lost its anger in a scared confusion.

"Doesn't matter," Bullet said. "Let's get them downstairs."

Immediately Freddie complied, shoving Mara forward past Nathan and out the bedroom door into the hallway. Skull-face kicked Nathan in the side gently.

"Get up," he ordered through the red mask. It almost seemed as if the boy had painted the crimson skull on his mask with blood.

Struggling, Nathan propped himself up on his hands, cringing as his calf moved, planting his hand on the vanity table. He took in a deep breath and pulled himself up with the table, careful not to put any weight on his right leg where blood seeped through his jeans. Finally, he managed to stand.

"Let's go," Skull-face said.

Nathan stepped forward with his bad leg and immediately pain blossomed up and down his leg. His nerves went haywire up and down his body, and his leg suddenly when numb. He dropped to the ground with a thump and groaned.

"Dammit," Skull-face huffed. "Here." He reached down and took hold of Nathan's arm, hefting him up. Nathan struggled to get to his feet even with the boy's assistance, his small arms proving to hold little real strength. As he got to his feet, he thought about fighting the boy, trying to wrench the knife from his grasp. As if reading his thoughts, Skull-face brought the knife to Nathan's bare throat. It was the type of blade Bullet had. Long and crooked. Every sliver of light in the room seemed to reflect off its cold blade. Nathan put his arm over Skull-face's back for support and let himself be escorted from the room, useless.

Downstairs again, Skull-face deposited Nathan on the recliner by the couch where Lenore and Mara crouched fearfully and teary-eyed.

"Looks like your boyfriend is going to stain your chair a little," Skull-face said.

No one answered. Skull-face shifted his head, "It was a joke."

The other two just looked at him aimlessly through their masks without a word. "Whatever," he pouted.

Bullet returned his attention to Lenore before moving on to Mara. He let his gaze settle on her sky blue eyes for a full half-minute before Lenore caught a slight grin form behind his mask. He nodded his head for a moment without saying a word. Then he turned to face Nathan and frowned.

"I was not expecting a guest in our little game tonight," Bullet complained as he eyed Nathan. He turned and grinned at Skull-face and Freddie, "It seems, though, that fate smiles back at us."

Nathan's brow furrowed, confused. Mara broke her gaze from the masked figures to look at Nathan, begging to find understanding in his eyes. There was none there, only more unknown, more fear. She looked to Lenore who attempted to fake a grin to comfort her daughter but retreated back to a tear-stained frown.

"Now we're only missing one person," Bullet continued. "Where is Dalton?"

"He's not here," Lenore said, hoping the crazed boy behind the mask would hear the truth in her words.

"Oh, I know he's not here," Bullet said. "I think we can fix that, though. You're going to call him, make him come home. I think he'll want to."

"I've tried all night," Lenore told him. It hurt now more than it had minutes ago. Before it had only been an irritation that her husband would not answer her calls, that he was somewhere else, ignoring her. However, now it tore at her heart. Had he been here, maybe he could have stopped them. Maybe he could have done something. But that was over and gone, it was too late for maybes.

"Well try again, bitch," Bullet growled.

CHAPTER 8

Alone among a throng of unfamiliar faces, Dalton's eyes burned into the rough wooden table top. His beer had yet to leave his hand. He occasionally raised the glass to his lips to console hidden wounds.

He had been cruel, he admitted that much. His thoughts too often mirrored only his needs and wants. But was he expected to always reside in the shadow of his wife? Her success, her name. There was nothing quite as demeaning as trying to make your mark and then finding yourself constantly referred to as Lenore Summers' husband. He was the architect, dammit, she was his wife.

Taking another gulp of the amber liquid, he thought of Jenna getting up and leaving. She had not stomped off like a ten-year-old who had just been told she could not have the Transformers toy in the middle of the supermarket. No, she had simply told him goodnight and left, still dignified, leaving Dalton as the sullen loser. He wished she had stomped off instead. He wanted something to pin on her rather than admit his own temper and psyche.

Things were about to change, though. He finally had the client that could provide him the upward momentum he wanted, to being someone finally. Not just her husband, or well, her ex-husband. With Gavin Bostian in his portfolio, Dal-

ton could finally become Dalton the Architect, his own man to
the world rather than on the wrong end of a relationship.

He lifted the glass to his lips. A miniscule drizzle sloshed
at the bottom. He sighed and lifted his legs over the bench to
order a third ale. On his way to the bar, his phone began to
vibrate in his pocket. *Shit, would you just stop already?*

Approaching the bar, he allowed the call to go to
voicemail. He could only imagine how many messages she
had already left, at least five. Each one probably said the same
thing, complaining that he was not home yet. *Sure, it would be
an argument tonight, but how was that any different from any other
night,* his less than intact mental process reasoned.

Dalton placed his glass on the bar, "Another ale, please."
The bartender nodded, taking the glass and going to work behind the counter. His phone vibrated again. A pulse of aggravation ran up his spine. He shoved his fingers into his pocket
and dug the phone out.

Lenore was spelled out on the large LED display just below
her portrait. Soft brown hair, green eyes and rosy cheeks. Dalton pursed his lips and hovered his index finger over the call
reject option. It continued to vibrate in his hands. He imagined
the number of missed calls was dangerously near tipping into
the double digits.

What could he say? There was no scenario in his mind that
answering the call would start or end with a jovial little talk.
No, but maybe Jenna was right. Maybe he did at least owe her
the respect of answering her call. With a sigh, he swiped to
answer the call.

"Yes, Lenore," he huffed into the phone, immediately
wishing he could start the call over again without sounding
like a complete dick.

A heavy silence followed. No sob or angered condemnation, just silence. Dalton waited for a moment. Maybe she was trying to find the words to really let him have it. Maybe she expected him to grovel, explain, something.

"Lenore," Dalton tried again, "I'm sorry, I should have answered earlier."

Still no answer came. On the other end, Dalton detected a faint noise. Breathing. It was faint, but just enough to hear over the line. He squinted and moved away from the bar and over to the staircase leading off the patio where the noise echoed less prominently. He leaned toward the phone as if it might help amplify the sound on the other end.

"Lenore?" he asked.

"How sweet. An apology," a raspy voice masked in a dark undertone sounded in his ear. There was an odd youthful quality to it. "You really ought to come home, though, Dalton."

The small hairs on the back of Dalton's neck stood up instantly as his eyes widened and his heart beat quickened.

"Who is this?" Dalton asked. He tried and failed to keep his voice calm and deliberate. His cheeks went white. The cold fall wind whipped hard against his jacket like a whirlwind.

"That's not important, Dalton. The important thing is that you come home before anyone gets hurt," the voice explained. "You don't want any of your family hurt, do you? Lenore. Mara. Nathan."

Dalton felt the blood that had drained from his face begin to rise again, the warmth of his anger beginning to boil alongside the fear that ravaged him. *Had the voice said Nathan?*

"Oh, I forgot. Nathan's not family, is he? No, that's right," the voice laughed. "He's not supposed to be here, is he? That's right, he was upstairs screwing your daughter. I'm sure you're not pleased with that."

The voice paused to let Dalton take in the thought. Dalton's mind worked to take in the information over the adrenaline. Suddenly, what Nathan and Mara might have had planned seemed ineffectual under the weight of the unknown voice on the phone. Yes, he wanted to unleash a beating on the boy. How many times did he have to deal with the kid before he would respect his decision? It didn't matter right now, though. His mind shot back to the raspy voice. In steps, his anger re-centered on the unknown person behind the call.

"Let me help you out with that," the raspy voice said and went silent for a moment. Suddenly, screams echoed through the line. *Mara! Lenore!*

"What are you doing?" Dalton yelled into the phone, ignoring the odd looks his yells received on the patio. "What are you doing?"

On the other end of the line, Dalton heard Mara's voice raging above the others, "No! Don't do it! Nathan!" Her screams turned into agonized squalls and then suddenly attenuated to sobbing. The other voices quieted.

"What did you do?" Dalton asked again, his voice beginning to shake.

"I fixed the problem," the voice came back on the line. "Well, I almost fixed the problem. You might have to clean up a little bit once he finally bleeds out, but the bright side is you won't have to worry about him screwing your daughter anymore."

Dalton dropped to the ground, letting his legs flail onto the stair steps below him. He gripped the railing with his free hand. He felt as if the breath had been sucked right out from his lungs by some cruel vacuum in outer space. His mind went blank, aimless.

"Why?" was all he could muster.

"Well, I mean if you're having second thoughts about the boy, you might should hurry home. He…" the voice paused as though he was calculating some figure, "Well, he might have twenty minutes left."

"Don't touch my family," Dalton's words trembled despite all the anger he placed behind them.

"Well, then come home, Dalton," the voice said. "Oh, and no cops and no help. That would just sully all the fun."

For a few moments, there was silence and Dalton. He was about to hang up and make a dash for his car when the raspy voice spoke up again. This time the voice seemed almost gleeful but with a hint of something darker, something deep and ominous.

"Hurry home, Dalton. Before I kill them all."

"Why?" Lenore pleaded, her voice barely audible behind the tears. "Why?"

"Why not?" Freddie asked, kicking Nathan lightly in the side while he lay flat on his back on the rough tan tile floor. The boy was grasping his neck, trying and failing to hold back the blood rolling from the open wound. It was beginning to paint the tile a red hue. His breathing came in spasms, more from fear than the injury. His face had already went pale, his thick arms focused only on the life pouring from his neck.

"Stop whining, asshole," Freddie chided the once strong and confident boy on the floor.

"Stop it," Mara screamed at him. "Stop it!"

She jumped from her seat, arms up and ready to unleash on Freddie. Her fists met Freddie's chest, clashing against soft flesh under the cold façade. Freddie jerked with the first blow, not expecting the attack, but quickly rebound, pressing her backward and onto the couch.

"Don't touch her," Lenore yelled, reaching out, beginning to move to her daughter's aide as Skull-face reminded her of the blade at her neck, letting the metal sink dangerously into her neck, just enough to frighten her but not enough to cut.

"Sit down!" Bullet railed angrily. He stared at them through the sockets of his white mask for what seemed like minutes. The sobs continued, but no one moved. "Oh my god, just be still."

"Why?" Lenore asked. Her mind needed answers. Why had they hurt Nathan? Why had they doomed him to bleed out on the floor? Why had they broken in? Why did they not just take what they wanted and leave?

"Why?" Bullet repeated the question. "If you're asking about poor Nathan here, well, one, he deserved it. Two, it should light a fire under your husband's ass, right?"

He paused, waiting for a response. None came from Lenore. He huffed and then continued, "Or why did we come at all? It's Halloween, Lenore. We're just having a little All Hallows' Eve fun. Right?"

Behind the mouth slit in his mask, the grin on his lips expanded and eyes became narrow horizontal slits which dug into her. She trembled.

"You know all about the fun we're going to have, Lenore," Bullet said.

She looked at him quizzically through tear-stained eyes. How did she know? She frowned even more.

"You'll understand soon enough," Bullet explained cryptically.

Lenore's eyes followed the boy as he turned and walked the few steps to Nathan's side where he knelt beside the bleeding boy. He reached down and tried to pry Nathan's hands away from his neck. The boy fought him, feebly. Bullet reared back and punched Nathan across his right cheek. Nathan groaned. Bullet tried again and managed to pull back Nathan's palms. He examined the laceration he had inflicted minutes before.

"Hm," Bullet muttered. "It's starting to clot up. Can't have that now, can we?"

Deliberately, Bullet reached down with his left hand and placed his thumb and index fingers on each side of the bloodied cut and pressed down and out. The tiny bit of scabbing tore open with a nasty wet noise and blood poured out more quickly again. Nathan screamed in agony as he began to kick and jerk.

"Hold him down!" Bullet yelled at his comrades. Without hesitation, the two boys pinned Nathan's body to the ground, Freddie latched down on Nathan's legs and Skull-face's hands found purchase on his hips.

With his free hand, Bullet brought his crooked blade around and let it touch down again on the fresh wound. He carefully and slowly drew back the blade, slicing a layer deeper into the tender skin. Nathan's body jolted and jerked as the blade glided through his pink skin and blood started to flow more freely.

Something in the horrible scene before her kept Lenore from turning her eyes. Her stomach churned, begging her to look away. Mara screamed, pleading with them to stop.

"Stop!" Mara yelled. "Please stop!"

As Bullet lifted his blade, the trio let go of their grip on Nathan. His hands latched to his neck again where the blood flowed freely, the wound deeper. He didn't scream this time. He just stared up at the sky, his eyes wide and steadfast on some unknown point on the ceiling. His breaths came in quick stuttered beats.

"Are there any weapons in the house?" Bullet asked, looking at Lenore whose eyes were glued to Nathan. "Hey, I'm talking to you, bitch! Are there any weapons in the house?"

She snapped out of it, shaking her head to try to clear her thoughts. It didn't help, but she was at least able to compute what Bullet had asked. She wished she had a different answer, maybe it would have given her a chance.

"No," she answered.

"Are you sure?" he asked again. "I don't want any surprises."

"There are knives in the kitchen, but no weapons," she assumed he meant guns or tools meant specifically for killing, but her set of culinary knives could be just as dangerous.

Bullet eyed her for a moment, boring those black orbs into her soul. Freddie crouched over Nathan's head, knife ready. Skull-face stood beside Bullet, his unknown eyes probably staring back at her as well.

"Good," Bullet finally said. "Because if I find anything, we might be inclined to make use of them."

He let his eyes break away from Lenore. He looked to Skull-face and barked a passive order. "Search the house for weapons. Make sure she's not lying to us. And close and lock all the windows."

* * *

Laughter and the barrage of forty, fifty, maybe eighty voices buffeted Dalton as he attempted to think, to divide up the alarms that rang in his mind. The gentle glows of tiki torches dotted the patio, lighting up the area under a cloudy night sky.

Could any of this be real? Was it some elaborate trick his mind was playing on him? Had he totally lost it? He pushed aside the notion. He may have problems in his life, who didn't, but he was not crazy. He just knew he wasn't.

Were Lenore and Mara safe? Aiden? Aiden was at the party, and then he was going to Mason's house, right? Right. He should be fine. But the girls? Had they hurt them? Touched them? The thought sent a boiling pulse of anger through Dalton's body. He took a deep breath. And what about Nathan? What had he been at the house for? Did it really matter now? No. Had the person behind the phone killed him? Please no.

No cops, alone. That had been the only rule given by the voice. Dalton raised to his feet abruptly and sudden dizziness shook him. *Dammit.* He grasped the railing and took the stairs slowly at first, then accelerated until he hit the gravel and then sprinted for his Beemer. His finger fumbled for the tiny lock button on the door handle and eventually hit it, earning a *Beep, Beep* and two accompanying amber flashes from the turn signals.

He slung the door open and slid into the front seat. He tried to even his breathing as he depressed the *START* button and the engine roared to life. He tapped the steering wheel-mounted shifting paddles and shifted the manual transmission into reverse. It would take him at least fifteen minutes to get home in normal traffic at the speed limit. Nathan might not have that long, though.

Dalton rammed the accelerator and dropped the clutch. Gravel dinged the undercarriage and the car yanked backwards as the tires gained traction among the rocks. The BMW swooped around and came to a jolting stop as Dalton hit the brake.

He shifted into first gear and took off, gravel flying as his tail end fished out for a brief second before catching and sending him flying forward. His back pressed against rich scarlet leather bucket seats. Dalton was glad when the road transitioned from gravel to asphalt and the tail end of the Beemer stopped shimmying back and forth on the solid surface. At the parking lot exit, Dalton did a precursory glance in both directions before shooting out onto the four lane. He careened across the first two lanes and found a home in the third lane, earning a loud screech from his tires and a few others along with a flurry of angry horns.

Dalton's foot and mind fought on how to control the accelerator. He had to avoid being stopped by the authorities on his way home but he had to get home quick. Reluctantly, he gave into reason. He let off the accelerator a little. He decided that ten to fifteen over was going to have to be enough until he hit the more rural roads where he could drop the accelerator to the floor.

The BMW maneuvered around a slow moving Toyota sedan. Dalton pushed the accelerator, fighting to keep the needle below sixty. He wanted to engage the emergency flashers and lay down on the accelerator, to cut the time home in half and, and what? *What am I going to do?*

What could he do? Maybe he could snatch a pair of hedge clippers from the storage room? But if he entered the driveway, he knew the driveway chime would sound off in the liv-

ing room and kitchen. They would know he was coming before he could get closer than two hundred yards from the
house. Maybe he could park out on the main road and sneak
onto his own property and get one of the shovels before sneaking around back and through the back door.

Minutes later, after nearly running two other cars off the
road, he cut off the main highway and onto a small state road
only a few miles from his home. Dalton floored the accelerator
and leaned into the curves, letting the low sitting BMW dig its
haunches in and pull him around. Suddenly, the car speakers
rang. An incoming call. His eyes shot to the center console
where Lenore's photo and name appeared on the LED display.
He put his eyes back on the road and gulped before pressing
Answer.

"What do you want?" Dalton challenged the voice. He
grimaced, unsure it was the best tactic.

A second of silence echoed over the speakers before the
raspy voice came through, "Just a warning. If I so much as
think you're trying some brave heroic shit or the cops are coming, I'll slit both their throats. Right in front of you."

Dalton was stunned silent, his arms stiffening as he
mounted another curve. A tire left the blacktop and the BMW
bounced on the rough shoulder, bringing Dalton back to himself.

"Did you hear me, Dalton, or do I need to go ahead and
kill them now? It'd be a shame if you weren't here yet, to witness it." The voice became more authoritative before it sof-
tened in a false sense of empathy.

"I hear you," Dalton blurted as quickly as he could manage.

"Park in the garage. Come in with your hands visible,

pockets empty," then the connection ended.

Eyes glued to the steady path of the bluish-white beams on the pavement in front of him, Dalton kept the car moving. His options had suddenly vanished into thin air. If he tried anything that might give him an upper hand, however slight it may be, it would immediately be met with Mara and Lenore's death, if the man behind the phone was true to his threat. Dalton did not feel like testing him.

The two-lane road became curvier as he closed in on his street and made the turn onto Rankin Road. The maples and sycamores that lined the road suddenly appeared ominous, a quarter of their branches barren and ghastly, the others reflecting shades of red and orange back down to him. A heft of the dead leaves blew up over his hood and then fell haphazardly to the ground.

The decorations on their closest neighbor's house were now disturbing as he passed the large Victorian home. Eerie oversized spider-webs, glowing jack-o-lanterns and a set of skeletons along the front porch, and the lonely headstones jutting unevenly from the ground. Dalton swallowed.

Finally, his home came into view around a green patch of holly bushes, the long driveway wound around a series of cherry trees leading up to the house. He steered the BMW past the entrance gate, knowing that his presence had just been announced inside the house. Following the path between the cherry trees, he brought the car up the driveway and around a late nineties model Camry he was unfamiliar with, probably *his* car.

He tore his eyes from the Camry and tried to peer into the house through the large glass front door. It was frosted, a useless effort he knew, but he still felt he should try. Pressing the garage door button above the rearview mirror, he drove on as the garage door opened and then swallowed his car whole.

Dalton brought the car to a stop and cut the engine. He sat still, eyes glued to the door. Behind it was the kitchen and then behind that he assumed he would find Mara and Lenore, and Nathan, trapped in his own home with who knew who. His hands shook. His mind went to the hedge clippers just feet away from him in the storage closet on the opposite end of the garage. He wanted a weapon, he needed a weapon. But, he knew better. Instead, he emptied his pockets into the center console. A set of black and blue pens he always carried, his wallet and lastly his phone, his one chance at reaching someone. He stared down at the device and huffed.

He stepped out of the car and shut the door. *What am I going to do?* His whole body shook as he approached the kitchen door. Standing with his hand outstretched, hovering over the doorknob, he inhaled deeply and closed his eyes.

Then he turned the knob.

CHAPTER 9

Raucous screams shrieked from the neighboring room. Aiden jerked a step back and peered around the corner, trying to seeing past the writhing bodies and flashing lights. Finally, the screams died down to riotous laughter and he found the source.

A tall boy. A senior if Aiden was right. The boy had his body pressed tight to a younger girl dressed in a skin-tight black dress that was lucky to reach below her ass and a set of cat ears atop her head. He was nibbling playfully on her neck before he pulled back revealing a set of large fake vampire teeth to go along with his overly dramatic Count Dracula cape. The two had apparently been playing out a scene from the movies and it had garnered more attention than just Aiden's. Half the room was in one state or another looking on at the spectacle.

"I guess some girls are into that," Mason said.

"Guess so," Aiden shook his head playfully, holding his cloth Spidey mask in his left hand. He returned his attention back to their small group. They stood over in the corner of the house's living area by a mammoth black display case that held all manner of art. Aiden could not begin to fathom the point behind a single piece of it.

"So have you all seen that new Eli Roth movie?" Gage asked. He was a stocky guy, tall, football material if he would ever try out. The flashing orange and white lights muted his icy blue eyes and tea brown hair.

"Yeah, that's some messed up shit, man," Brian reacted before anyone else could speak up in his usual manner. His brown eyes matched his ear-length close-cropped hair. Brian's slender build extended up to his face, but it did not hold him back from being a star-athlete on the school baseball team. He held the third highest record in school history for homeruns in a season. He always said he was going to beat even that before he graduated.

Mason grinned before chiming in with his own thoughts, "Oh yeah, and the main woman in it. Talk about hot."

The group's collective gaze settled on Aiden, expecting his input. He sighed, "I've not watched it. You guys know my stomach cannot handle all the gore."

"A little blood too much for you, Aiden?" Gage jested.

"You call that a little blood?" Aiden asked. "Didn't they say it made his last movie look like child's play or something?"

Mason patted him on the back, "Yeah, and they meant every word of it."

Aiden intentionally shivered at the thought. His stomach just could not take it. The guts, the flying pieces of meat, the hands ripping at tender flesh, blood pouring from open wounds. It made his insides roll at the simple thought.

"Well, it was great," Brian chimed back in.

The conversation continued along the same avenue for the next five minutes, recounting every gory detail and psychotic mental element. Aiden let his ears drown out their voices with the thumping beat that enveloped the room and the unintelligible voices from neighboring conversations or high-pitched giggles. The occasional nod was enough.

As Gage switched gears to another recent movie, Aiden let his eyes scan the crowd behind him. So many familiar but unfamiliar faces. People he had went to middle school with and now attended high school with for years but had never spoken to. Others that he was well aware of. Jacob from biology class stood in the corner with a question-able beverage in a red solo cup talking to his girlfriend, Sarah, who was dressed in a naughty nurse outfit. At least they were talk-ing, *if* people could communicate through mouth to mouth. He won-dered when the two took the time to breathe.

Next to them were two faces he had never seen before. Maybe they went to Northwest Cabarrus, maybe not. A few feet more and Aiden found a group of girls sitting along a vast set of black leather couches in the center of the room. All Aiden knew for sure was that they were juniors, gorgeous juniors. Lots of long blond and brown hair, slim curvy bodies and short skirts. Behind them was the unoffi-cial dance floor. He counted at least four couples doing one dance or another, or some excuse for a dance. Most of the dances were more an excuse to twist and rub body against body without calling it foreplay.

A gap opened in the "dance floor" and his eyes locked onto Faith Moreno. She stood across the room, cup in hand, talking to one of her friends. He smiled, then smiled even more when he noticed her cos-tume. She was dressed in the iconic Wonder Woman outfit. He could not help but move his eyes over her. Strong tan legs, small waist above an ample posterior. She held her chest high, exaggerating her already appealing form which the low-fitting costume held back. Thick flat crimson painted lips, broad jaw. And emerald green eyes that Aiden could not get enough of yet he could never manage to maintain eye contact with at the same time. Her long brown, nearly black, hair hung in gentle waves below her shoulders.

Step aside, Gal Gadot and Linda Carter. You've got nothing on Faith, Aiden thought.

"Aiden. Aiden!" Gage's voice managed to pierce the cacophony of noises that competed for Aiden's attention.

Aiden turned in surprise, "Yeah. Sorry, I got distracted."

"Yeah, why don't you go *talk* to her rather than standing

here awkwardly staring at her," Gage suggested with a raised brow.

"I'm with Gage," Mason piped in. "It's about time you finally did it."

"You better hurry," Brian jumped in on the peer pressure. "Otherwise I'd be happy to let Wonder Woman over there lasso me in."

"Slow down there, Brian," Aiden put his hand up. "If that lasso's getting anyone, it's me."

"Then you might want to go on over there then," Mason urged. "We'll be all right without you for a little bit. I promise."

Aiden grinned at Mason and shook his head. Mason had tried in one way or another to get Aiden to talk to Faith for the past two years. And failed. If Aiden was honest, he was glad his friend was persistent, but at times he just wished he would shut up. Now was not one of those times. It may be just the incentive he needed to finally speak to her, to *really* talk to her.

"Okay," Aiden said.

The surprised expressions on his friends' faces, mouths hanging open as wide as their eyes, said all he needed to know. Aiden shook his head. Before he could second guess himself, Aiden about-faced and started off across the large space. He angled between everything from a Mike Myers look-a-like to a massively bloated Minion. He involuntarily jumped a step when an ample-breasted witch decided to slide a palm over his butt. He glanced behind him at the grinning witch, gave her a nervous grin and swallowed before turning and resuming his calm walk.

Finally out of the most crowded area, he made his final approach. *What do I say? Hello, Faith. Hey, Faith. No. Faith, I'm surprised to see you here. No, that's stupid, she told you she'd be here at school today.*

"So how's the Amazon these days?" Aiden blurted out. His voice was as awkward as the choice of phrase was cheesy. He kicked himself. *Anything would have been better than that. Anything.*

She turned and locked eyes with him. Her emerald green eyes were easily the most beautiful green he could fathom. She may not have the height of the Amazonian, but she honored the grandeur and dignified presence of any Amazonian, past or present.

"It's good," Faith replied with a large smile. "How's Queens?"

Suddenly, he no longer felt stupid. She was perfect, just as she had always been. Aiden laughed.

"I've just been hanging around." He put a hand to his mouth and coughed. "Ah, now that was cheesy."

Faith laughed, not at him actually, but rather with him. Aiden captured the sight of her smile like a photograph, an image he would keep on record.

"Yeah, it was," she said between laughs. "But that never stopped you before, now did it?"

"No, don't think so."

For a moment the two stared awkwardly at each other. A multitude of shared childhood memories sprung into Aiden's mind. The silly antics of elementary school kids. Building elaborate blanket forts in Faith's playroom. His old red bike imagined as a car in hot pursuit of her imaginary vehicle.

"So," Faith ventured. "What do you think of the upcoming DC movie?"

Saved from his utter despair at having actually wandered over to see her without the words to say, Aiden nodded his head vigorously. For minutes they talked about the newest installment in DC's comic to movie series, *The Flash*. Aiden failed to realize how easy his words flowed, how he was actually talking to her again, and he didn't absolutely suck at it. It was an act he thought he could not manage just ten minutes ago.

After exhausting the upcoming movie's many rumors, Faith looked down nervously. Her mouth twitched subtly. When she looked back up, she was no longer smiling brilliantly as she had been just seconds ago. A serious demeanor had taken over.

"Why did you stop talking to me?" she asked. Her smooth voice held an almost hurt tone.

"What do you mean?" Aiden asked, confused. *No. Don't ask that question. Please don't.*

"No, I mean why did you stop talking to me after eighth grade?" she clarified, boring her eyes into his, searching for an answer.

Aiden looked away skittishly. He had hoped the question would not surface, that they could just glaze over it. So much for hope. The truth was simple, but he could not speak it, not to her.

"I don't know. I just did," Aiden said without meeting her eyes. "Things just got awkward for some reason."

"Awkward?" she dug.

"Yeah, awkward," he said. "I don't know why, they just did."

Fighting the urge to tuck tail and run, Aiden punched himself inside and lied to her. Well, maybe not a lie. An omission. No, he knew it was a lie, the real reason was integral to the whole, not some outlier. They had been best friends since before he could remember. They grew up together, pre-school, elementary school and middle school. Only high school had been different, separate. It had been at the end of their eighth grade year when he distanced himself, and it really was simple. He thought of her as more than just a friend, a friendship that could be more maybe. But, there was always a but, he had felt too foolish to say anything. Instead, he built up a wall that ended in the empty chasm that stood between them now. He felt like a coward standing in front of her now.

"Well, that's just nonsense," Faith grinned again, tossing a deep brown lock back over her shoulder. "I'm glad you finally decided to talk to me again. Even if I do happen to be dressed like Wonder Woman."

The door cracked open to reveal the kitchen much as it had been when Dalton had made his exit for work earlier that morning. The sink was empty, as were most of the cabinet tops with the exception of a lone glass that came into view at the far end of the room and the toaster oven. There was no sign of anyone.

Dalton let out the breath he was holding. His eyes scanned as he stepped up on to the threshold and entered the kitchen. He stole a look back into the garage where his BMW sat, engine beginning to cool. For a brief second his mind urged him to retreat, to bolt back to the car and down the road. To go anywhere but right into certain trouble. But Mara was here somewhere, scared and distressed. Her blue eyes and big smile flashed through his mind. *Mara.* And Lenore, she needed him, too.

What am I going to do? What can I do?

His mind rushed with question after unanswerable question. No scenario was certain, and every action he devised was sure to end less than desirably, even disastrously. He wanted to call the cops, retreat back into the garage and wait. Dalton's thoughts went to the knives stashed in the utensil drawer, his eyes followed and he stepped toward the drawer.

If I so much as think you're trying some brave heroic shit, I'll slit both their throats. Right in front of you. The words ran through Dalton's mind like a neon light. He stopped, losing his gaze to the tile floor. He took a breath and stepped forward. His heart beat hard against his ribcage, its rhythm thrumming in his ears.

"We've been waiting for you, Dalton," a raspy but youthful voice called from around the corner. Dalton froze. It was the voice on the phone. "Come on in, I'm just dying to begin."

Willing himself to move his feet, Dalton trudged forward. He glued his eyes to the dividing wall that would soon reveal the living area, and whoever dwelled behind it. Five feet felt like five miles, like a tight-wire strung taught between the roofs of two skyscrapers.

He exhaled carefully as he breached the corner and Lenore came into view. Tears stained her face, fear stamped across her eyes. Dalton's heart sank an inch, then he saw Mara in the same disheveled state and his heart dropped. He had not been there for them. The need to protect prompted him to step out into the open. Immediately he found the masked intruders standing just feet from his wife. He took in every detail.

The figure closest to Mara was the thickest of the three, but for his height, his build was average at best. The jeans and band t-shirt indicated either a male or extremely flat-chested female, of at least fifteen or fourteen years. Dark gloves concealed their hands. The creepy Freddie Krueger mask was overly theatrical but did its job, only revealing the smallest bit of the boy's eyes.

Standing in front of Lenore, the next figure was largely in contrast to the former. Visibly shorter, a male, boy, Dalton thought. His black skinny jeans betrayed his thin frame and made him an unusual candidate for the large curved blade in his right hand. The red skull mask only further made the boy behind the mask an enigma, casting a demonic glare to his spindly presence.

A step behind the other two stood the last intruder. Dressed in black jeans, a simple black t-shirt and a white mask with a bullet hole in the forehead, he was adorned in the simplest disguise. Yet, the sight of his large black eyes staring back at Dalton in contrast to the white mask jarred Dalton. Then he spoke.

"Welcome, Dalton," he said, affirming Dalton's assumption. His voice was the one on the phone, that raspy devil that rung in his head like some tormenting demon.

"It sure did take him long enough," Skull-face rattled.

Dalton checked another point off in his mind. Teenagers. The immaturity in their voices betrayed them. Maybe he could use that to his advantage, he thought. Maybe they were just on a momentary high, drugged out, or just out for a few kicks. The sight of Nathan lying barely conscious on the floor complicated his theory, though. Still, drugs were a possible culprit.

The faint rising and falling of Nathan's chest assured Dalton he was still alive despite the bloody gash across his neck. Dalton cringed, diverting his eyes to Mara and then Lenore.

"Are you okay?" he pleaded more than asked.

Neither spoke. Lenore nodded sporadically while Mara whimpered, her eyes digging into Dalton's heart and then shooting back to Nathan on the floor. Dalton held back the tears that their looks caused to well up inside of him. His heart broke as quickly as it burst into a fury of flames. It burned hot, a hatred he had never felt before, all aimed at the three kids that threatened his family. His eyes shot to the middle boy, the one who seemed to be at the lead. Dalton stepped forward aggressively.

"Slowly now," Bullet ordered. Before Dalton had time to think, the boy placed his feet squarely in front of Lenore and lowered the tip of his long silver blade precariously under her chin. "You wouldn't want me to *accidently* slit her throat now, would you?"

Dalton froze, his feet steeled in place. He reached out as if by some mere will of the mind he could stop whatever ill intent the boy had ravaging through his mind. Lenore's eyes widened and her chin lifted in a futile attempt to put space between skin and blade. Her breathing quickened, as did Dalton's.

"Come on now." The words came from Skull-face. It took Dalton a moment to connect the octave-too-high voice with the red mask. "Sit."

Following the spindly digits on the boy's hands, Dalton stepped carefully forward. He came around the recliner where he was expected to take up residence. The boy did not move as Dalton stepped inches from his body. He was confident in his status as captor and Dalton's as captive. Dalton slowly took a seat and sank into the cushy leather recliner. He kept his eyes on those of the skull mask, wondering what face lie beneath it. Something deformed and hideous came to mind, something that matched the boy's outward character.

He let his eyes meet Lenore's and then Mara's, trying to console them. He knew that simply being here could do little to assuage their fears, but he would still try his best. Dalton's eyes fixed on Lenore again. *Had she been calling all night, confined here by these…these freaks?* He grinned sadly at her, trying to apologize. *No apology could ever make up for that. Never.* Just under the frown he saw her force a tiny smile. It was barely perceptible to the naked eye, but enough. He knew he didn't deserve even that.

A meow echoed quietly around the corner as the cat plodded down the stairs and pranced into the living room. There was no hint of despair or fear in its tiny voice, just a cat who had found more hands to attend to it.

"They've got a cat?" Freddie groaned.

"Is that a problem?" Bullet asked, his raspy voice gaining an almost sarcastic flair.

"I hate cats," Freddie replied.

"It's a fucking cat, who gives a shit?" Skull-face jeered, keeping his eyes firmly on Dalton.

The conversation felt surreal to Dalton. These boys stood before him and his family in masks with knives at the ready, they had slit Nathan's throat, and they were worried about a cat. Dalton wrinkled his brow and parted his lips slightly in confusion.

"Just kick it outside, man," Bullet ordered with a shrug. "We don't need the distraction."

Skull-face nodded and lowered his knife before scooping up the family feline in his spare hand. The other two steadied their weapons on Mara and Lenore as Dalton fidgeted in his seat, hoping for a moment of opportunity. It was becoming evident they were not going to make it easy.

The front door opened and Skull-face tossed the cat out onto the porch and slammed the door quickly shut. On the floor just feet from Dalton, Nathan coughed suddenly. His whole body quaked. Dalton turned just in time to see a spout of blood bloom over his lips. The kid moaned, slowly coming out of shock. Skull-face turned to see what was happening and bolted back over in front of Dalton.

"No, no, no," Mara begged, "Nathan."

Dalton forced himself to look up and into those dark eyes behind the white mask. "You cannot just leave him there to die. He needs a doctor."

Bullet stared back, his eyes squinted in what Dalton thought seemed like confusion. For a moment he did not speak, he just studied Dalton. It felt like he was calculating Dalton in his mind, trying to understand him. Finally, Bullet moved. He stepped over Nathan's body and squatted down by his head. He looked down at Nathan thoughtfully and then back up to Dalton.

"You care about this boy?" Bullet asked, a hint of the confusion Dalton sensed in his eyes emanating from his voice. Before he spoke again, Bullet brought his blade down to Nathan's open wound but stopped just short of contact. "I thought you'd want him dead."

On the floor, Nathan jerked weakly and tried to speak, but Bullet's hand quickly covered his mouth. He brought his knee down heavily on Nathan's chest and kept the boy on the ground. The knife hung in place over Nathan's neck. Nathan stopped jerking. The fear of the blade slicing deeper down into his neck was like a numbing agent.

"What? No," Dalton stuttered. How could he want the boy dead? Sure, the kid was a thorn in his side, but he was just a boy, a kid. Of course he made stupid decisions and yes, he deserved a good scare, but death? No. "Just think about what you're doing. Put the knife down."

"You seriously want him around?" Bullet asked. He tilted his head.

Skull-face and Freddie shuffled in place, chuckling lightly at the thought like it was funny somehow. Dalton did not see the humor in it. He only saw horror.

"Don't hurt him," Dalton pled.

"You do realize what he was doing to your daughter behind your back, right?" Bullet continued. "In your own house."

Dalton didn't answer, he didn't want to know the answer. He didn't need to know. Nothing warranted the horrid intention behind those black eyes.

Bullet looked at Dalton intently. He emphasized his words. "He was *screwing* your daughter, in your own house."

"You know. Ah! Ah!" Skull-face shrieked playfully, thrusting his hips back and forth.

Dalton clenched his eyes shut and tried to block out the boy's noises. He breathed in deeply. *It doesn't matter right now, Dalton. It doesn't matter right now.*

"Let him live," Dalton pled more quietly, letting his fear and anger for the masked trio outweigh the hurt and anger he felt toward Nathan.

"No," Bullet said coldly before turning to Nathan, "Karma's a bitch." Without delay, Bullet pressed the blade down into the boy's flesh and sawed back and forth. Blood squirted from the gaping gash where Nathan's neck bent unnaturally back the further the blade sliced. He gasped desperately for air. He tried to block the opening with his hands but Skull-face held them back.

Dalton went to move but Skull-face's blade greeted him. It hovered a foot away, daring him to move. He sat back down, afraid and horrified.

Finally, Bullet pulled the blade back and hovered over the bleeding boy. Crimson flowed freely from the gap in Nathan's neck and out his mouth. His body shook violently, stuttered noises escaping his jaws between gurgled breaths. Mara screamed in agony and jumped from her seat only to be hurled back into place by the strong arms of Freddie. He placed his blade on her throat to remind her to stay still.

"Why? Why?" Dalton implored the white mask. "Why?"

Bullet let his face turn and fixed his stare on Dalton. Behind the mask, a menacing grin caused Dalton's insides to curl even more than the sawing of his blade. Dalton broke eye contact to look to Nathan. He did not want to see it happen, he did not want to witness it, but something in him made him need to see it.

At first Nathan's body began to move less, jerk less. The gasps and blood-filled gurgles became less frequent. Then as his air passage filled with the very crimson liquid that gave him life, his body ceased to move, his chest failed to rise and his eyes went glassy.

"No. No. No. No," Mara said over and over again.

Dalton could not remove his eyes from the cold lifeless orbs of the boy that used to be Nathan. Now he was nothing more than a corpse, a reminder of what had been and what would never be.

"You really should thank me, Dalton," Bullet spoke up finally.

Jarring him from his stupor, Dalton let every ounce of anger he could muster fill his face as he met the monster's gaze.

"What do you want?"

"What do I want?" Bullet asked, as if it was the question he had been waiting for all along. "What do we want? We just want to have a little All Hallows' Eve fun, you know, trick or treat. Like I was telling your wife here. We want both, though. I mean look at this place, there is bound to be money here somewhere, right?"

TO WATCH YOU BLEED

Bullet's lips formed into a huge grin, his eyes narrowing as his cheeks rose behind the mask. The look seemed almost gleeful. Not demonic or mad, but excited.

"You can have whatever the hell you want!" Dalton yelled, "Just leave my family alone!"

"Oh, I plan on having whatever the hell I want," Bullet's grin became mad. "But not before we have a little fun."

Fun.

The simple word amplified in Dalton's head. It was such an unusual word to be used immediately after slicing someone's throat wide open. His imagination conjured up images of flashing billboards and neon tube lights like those outside a rundown hotel on some back alley street in Los Angeles strobing the promise of *fun*. His eyes, on the other hand, saw anything but the brilliant flashes of light.

On the floor Nathan was dead, his own blood soaking his collar from the gaping wound across his neck. Mara was shaking, likely in shock, tears pouring down her face. She rocked back and forth, repeatedly muttering the same despairing word over and over again. *No, no, no, no.* Closest to him, Lenore sat on the couch next to Mara with her arms encompassing her shoulders. Her eyes were averted from the mess on the floor. They pled to Dalton with a frightened gaze.

Stop them. Please.

Her green eyes bore into his soul, not in spite or anger, but in need. Dalton didn't know what to do. He was defenseless. He had no weapon, no advantage, no foreseeable plan to overcome these boys.

"Let's move the body out of the way," Bullet nodded to Freddie. "Wouldn't want it to get in the way."

Freddie turned to face the plain white mask, then his face moved down to the body on the floor, blood pooled beneath it, and then back up to Bullet. He didn't move.

"Uh..." Freddie mumbled as Bullet crouched down and found purchase under Nathan's armpits, his wrists smearing the red liquid across the tile.

"What are you waiting for?" Bullet asked incredulously. The boy didn't move. Dalton could imagine scared eyes behind that nasty mask. "Come on, don't be a pussy on me! Pick him up."

The boy snapped out of his stupor, shook his head slightly and then bent down and wrapped his hands under Nathan's limp ankles. The boys hefted the body up by the head and feet and drug it a short distance away before depositing the shell next to the artificial fireplace. They let the body drop with an ungraceful thud. The head smacked hard against the black ledge of the fireplace. Dalton winced. He knew there was no more pain there, no more consciousness to register the hard drop to the tile floor, but it still nagged him.

"So where to begin?" Bullet wondered aloud, eyes flicking between his three captives and Freddy, a grimace on his lips between the small slit in the mask. Dalton squinted angrily when Bullet's eyes met his own through the cut outs in the mask. The edges of Bullet's lips rose in satisfaction. He lifted his right hand and let his index finger jut out slowly, swaying portentously between Mara and Lenore with eyes still fixed on Dalton, toying with him.

"No, if you're going to do something, do it to me!" Dalton yelled out, almost jumping to his feet, fighting the urge to get up and pounce.

"That's not how this works," Bullet explained. "See, I'm making the calls, and right now it's just not your turn, Dalton. How selfish of you."

"Selfish bastard," Skull-face muttered, a mix of disgust and glee in his voice.

"Let's see now," Bullet continued. He diverted his attention from Dalton and let his eyes go back and forth with the motion of his finger. Back and forth between Mara and Lenore. "Ah."

His finger stopped and his eyelids transformed his pupils into slits. "Mara," Bullet exhaled, his raspy voice a mix of calm and derision.

"She's mine, right?" Freddie's voice lifted, taking a step forward. Bullet grunted, then nodded his head as he stepped around the couch. Dalton watched intently as the masked figure took up a position directly behind Mara.

"I've been waiting on this for a long time," Freddie said. He stepped up in front of Mara and pocketed his knife.

"What are you doing?" Dalton asked.

"What I want," Freddie replied dryly.

"Don't worry, Dalton, we're not going to kill her." Bullet paused, caressing her neck dangerously with the sharp end of the blade and smiled. "Well, not yet at least."

Dalton's eyes went wide. *Not yet?* The two syllables repeated in his head. Dalton begged, "Please, don't hurt her."

Carefully, Freddie lifted the front of his mask, rolling the latex up just above his mouth, revealing dark black skin and thin, chalky black lips. He leaned forward, tried to kiss Mara, but she butted her head forward, smacking hard against his forehead. Freddie reeled backward, cradling his forehead.

"Bitch!" he yelled at her, rearing back his gloved hand and smacking her across the cheek. Mara yelped in pain.

Dalton's instinct and emotions overrode his restraint. He sprung to his feet and bound toward Freddie, hands ready to deliver a pounding blow. Seconds slowed to minutes. Dalton watched as Freddie turned to see him, a slow motion picture, a target.

Suddenly something caught his ankle and time sprung forward as Dalton's chin met the tile floor with an explosion of pain up his jaw. Shrill screams pierced through his head from the couch. His vision blurred for a split second before the sight of Freddie's black tennis shoes came into view.

"What do you think you're doing?" one of them asked, Skull-face Dalton thought.

"Do you *want* me to kill her?" It was Bullet, there was no doubt in Dalton's mind. That raspy voice would be stuck in his head for all eternity.

Dalton put a hand underneath his chest and pushed himself off the floor. Blood trickled from his chin onto the tile. He faintly realized his blood was mingling on the floor with Nathan's. It pooled into tiny puddles along the grey borders. He wiped his mouth as he went to get to his feet. Something small and hard slammed between his shoulder blades, sending him back down to the ground. He barely kept his face from smashing onto the plain stained tile again, bracing himself with the palms of his hands.

"Let 'em up," Bullet ordered.

With Bullet behind the couch and Freddie standing in front of him, that only left Skull-face behind him. Dalton imagined the small-framed kid smiling gleefully behind his mask, though he couldn't put a face to the image in his mind.

"Now sit down, and don't move unless you want her on the floor next to Nathan," Bullet explained, bringing his blade around and placing it under Mara's neck. In pain, Dalton propped himself up and got to his feet. Bullet looked at Dalton and maneuvered his face down next to Mara. His mouth almost touched her ear, "Now you're going to cooperate like a good little girl, aren't you?"

Mara nodded vigorously, keeping her chin high, trying to avoid the sharp edge of the blade. Dalton took his seat nervously, his eyes never leaving Mara. Bullet nodded once to Freddie and the boy stepped forward again, leaning down and putting his thin lips on Mara's.

Gripping the arms of the recliner tightly, Dalton shook angrily as

Freddie's lips parted and continued to kiss his daughter.

"Stop, please stop," Lenore pleaded.

Ignoring her, Freddie continued. Gradually his hand moved from its perch on the leather cushion where Mara was seated. It slid closer until it reached her bare leg. Freddie swatted away the thin fabric covering Mara's leg and locked his palm on firmly. He squeezed her smooth flesh, sliding his hand up and down in a rush of lust.

He moved back for a fraction of a second to look into Mara's scared blue eyes. They pleaded with him to stop, begged his heart to find some semblance of empathy, to see the monster he was. Her eyes were met with a wicked grin, with a pleasure-filled sigh. Freddie moved back in and devoured her lips. His hand jumped from her leg to her stomach and then moved up, grasping at her breasts under the gown.

Mara whimpered and a tear slivered down her cheek. Dalton shook as the sound broke his heart and he burnt with rage. He went to move, but Skull-face stepped closer with his knife held ready. His attention diverted momentarily from Mara, Dalton noticed that Bullet was staring at him. He had his head cocked to the side, propped up against Mara's ear. His knife was still held precariously below her neck. Even when Dalton met his gaze, the boy did not look away, instead he shook his head calmly and shimmied the blade in warning.

"Stop!" Lenore began to yell. "Stop! Dalton, make them stop!"

Eyes locked with Bullet, Dalton's heart tore. Lenore's screams, begging him to do something, to do anything, felt like his heart was being ripped from his chest. What could he do? What option did he have that did not end with Mara's body laying lifeless beside Nathan's? Maybe if he moved, maybe they wouldn't kill her. Maybe. But they had already proven their willingness to end a life. He couldn't take the chance. It hurt, and it pained him beyond his understanding, but if he remained still maybe she would come out of this alive, bruised but living.

Lenore continued to scream but dared not take any physical action against their captors.

"Would you shut your mouth?" Skull-face yelled. She continued to scream.

"Close your mouth, bitch, or I might slip," Bullet warned.

In mid-scream, the noise ceased to exit Lenore's lips. A new fear, one that brimmed with the realization that there was nothing she could do, etched her high cheekbones and soiled her eyes. Before Dalton could comfort her with a meaningless but well-intended smile, Mara yelped again.

Dalton looked to find Freddie yanking the glove from his hand, revealing five black digits. His lips still working lustfully, Freddie placed his naked hand on Mara's bare leg. He caressed her soft skin, moving further north, twisting down around her inner thigh. Dalton wanted to look away, to imagine this was all a bad nightmare, but he was afraid that if he looked away something worse might happen.

"Now you can't turn me down like before," Freddy said, but no one dared to respond.

Inch by tormenting inch, Freddie's hand disappeared between Mara's thick legs, shielded from view by the contours of her thighs and useless gown. Suddenly Mara gasped. Dalton gritted his teeth. She whimpered between restrained and fitful groans.

Mere feet from Dalton, Skull-face chortled in a darker tone than had previously exited his lips. Dalton's face burned hot, his body shaking with anger-filled need. His eyes shot to Bullet who was still staring at him. As if reading his mind, he shook his head again in warning. A tear escaped Dalton's eye as he watched his daughter convulse. She whimpered, begging him to do something, anything.

Within that brief moment, a world of shame and horror overtook Dalton. His heart felt leaden. Each beat of that sinuous mass in his chest felt like some foreign beast pummeling his fist, unhindered by any defense, in rapid succession into Dalton's ribcage. The rage running through his veins was equaled only by the ignominy that flooded over him, the uselessness he felt. If he moved, if he made any action in defense of his family, to stop this maniacal and savage scene before him, the only outcome he could imagine ended with him slouched over a body in tears.

"Do you like that?" Freddie teased, looking Mara dead in the eyes. A grin formed on his lips barely in view under the curled mask. Mara turned her face and closed her eyes. Her body shook again as Freddie thrust and withdrew his arm.

"Stop. Please stop," Dalton begged in little more than a whisper. "Please, I'll give you whatever you want."

Bullet's gaze had remained steady on Dalton, unmoving. Only his grin had changed, vanishing into a nearly flat line. "You already are."

"No," Dalton cried. "We've got money, valuables. You can take any of it. All of it! Take the cars, anything. Just get the hell out of my house."

The blade at Mara's neck drifted away and out of sight as Bullet rose from his crouch. He raised the knife over Mara and extended the handle toward Freddie. Freddie's hand reappeared and took the knife. He let the sharp end touch Mara's thigh, letting it lie there precariously.

Bullet reached behind his back and pulled out a compact pistol. Its black frame was menacing and the unguarded trigger sent a new chill down Dalton's spine.

"No, no, no," Lenore begged as her eyes locked on the weapon.

He waved the firearm around carelessly, his finger fidgeting on the trigger like it was a toy. He aimed the gun at Lenore, "Yes, yes, yes."

Lenore kept repeating the same word, over and over again. "No, no, no, no." Dalton looked at her for a brief second before returning his eyes to Bullet. She was breaking, or broken.

"No, let's talk about this," Dalton begged. The radiance of her sea green eyes was muddled by tears and the hundreds of thin red veins that haphazardly streaked across the whites of her eyes. Her lips frowned, streaks of water-torn makeup lined her cheeks. The weapon came to a stop directly behind Mara.

"Ah. No. The last thing I want to do right now is talk about it, Dalton." Bullet dug the tip of the barrel into the back of Mara's head, pushing her forward. Mara jumped involuntarily at the realization of what was against her skull. The cold singe of the blade at her thigh became only a minor nuisance in light of the horrid device now fixed in place behind her. Freddie pushed the blade down just enough to remind her of its presence but without drawing blood. She tensed, stuck between two uneasy endings, and froze.

Dalton began to rise, but before his body could break contact with the recliner, Freddie yanked the knife back. Mara yelped in pain as sanguine lines formed hastily across her thigh. Crimson ribbons streaked in indiscriminate patterns along her tan skin and onto the couch.

"Sit!" Bullet bellowed, his raspy voice thundering in an authority he had yet to present. "I told you not to move, Dalton."

"Why?" Dalton begged. Lenore sobbed uncontrollably.

"Just sit still and keep your mouth shut," Bullet ordered. He signed and looked to Skull-face, "Get the first aid kit and patch her up."

The boy nodded and stepped away from Dalton after he placed his blade far out of reach. He then extracted a white box from one of the "candy" bags they had brought with them and placed it on the edge of the couch.

Dalton looked on in bewilderment as the thin boy opened the box and removed a series of bandages and swabs and began to bandage his daughter.

What the hell are we dealing with?

CHAPTER 10

It had been over three years since Aiden remembered talking to the angel in front of him in more than a quick passing "Hey" or "Bye" in the school hallway. The small talk, catching up, had been easier than expected. The stuttering and blanks that typically overcame him in her presence had vanished after the first few awkward seconds.

"So I hear you have a little sister now," Aiden half-asked, half-stated. He hated feeling this detached from her.

"Uh huh, Gloria," Faith said. "She'll be two in December. She's super cute, a little testy though."

Aiden giggled in the deepest tone he could muster. Orange and white light flashed brilliantly around Faith. It highlighted the curves of her waist under the red and blue costume and glinted off the plastic golden tiara. Her emerald eyes sparkled in the light, like some mesmerizing hypnosis. Aiden wished he would never have to look away.

"I don't have any younger siblings, so I wouldn't know," Aiden continued. "But I do still have Mara and that's a trip sometimes."

Laughing, Faith grinned, looking down for a brief moment. Aiden kept smiling. About ten yards on the opposite side of a group of teens to his right, Aiden caught sight of Mason. He had a crooked grin plastered on his face and quickly raised his fist with his thumb erect. The boy was proud of himself, and presumably of Aiden. Aiden shook his head but could not wipe the grin from his own lips.

He returned the thumbs up sign just as Faith looked back up.

"What's that about?" Faith asked, her left brow raised but still smiling.

"Just Mason," Aiden half-laughed. "If he hadn't pushed me, I likely would never have come over here."

He paused for a second. He grimaced a bit and then continued, "I wanted to talk to you. I really did. I've wanted to talk to you for the past two years, but I couldn't ever get up the courage to approach you again. Mason's been trying to get me to talk to you for a while."

Faith stole a look over her shoulder and found Mason. She grinned and gave him another thumbs up. Mason's grin intensified. *Yeah, he's never going to let me live that down. Ever.*

"Well, *maybe* I'll have to thank him one day," she said.

His grin grew larger than he thought possible. Aiden was overwhelmed with excitement. He had always thought she wouldn't want to talk to him, that she would eventually walk off in disinterest. Instead, here she was, still talking, laughing, reminiscing.

"You want anything to drink before they run out?" he asked. It was getting late. The crowd had already thinned significantly despite the constant throb of the bass thumping through the house. Warm bodies, enveloped in all manners of costumes, still roamed the living area, kitchen, dining room, hallways and Aiden was sure the bedrooms, though fewer costumes remained secured there.

"Sure," Faith said.

"What do want?" Aiden asked.

"Surprise me," Faith responded with grin.

"Dr. Pepper then," Aiden shrugged. "Yep. It's Dr. Pepper then."

She giggled and shook her head. "I said surprise me, not bring me exactly what I expect you would drink."

Aiden grinned. She remembered such a small detail about him. Something about that thrilled him.

"So no Dr. Pepper then?" he asked. "Surely you're not going to say no to Dr. Pepper."

"Bring me a Dr. Pepper," Faith replied in fake defeat. Her grin was magnificent as she gave in.

Giving her one last grin, Aiden took her cup and made his way through the dwindling crowd to the drink bar. He picked up the proper two liter and poured his own cup first. As he began to fill Faith's plastic red cup, he felt an arm wrap around his shoulder. *Mason.*

"It seems to be going good over there," Mason's voice barely made it over the music in obvious approval.

"It's going well," Aiden agreed, grinning at his friend.

"So now. When are you going to admit I was right?" Mason jeered, shaking Aiden jokingly.

He nearly missed the cup a few times until Mason let him loose. Aiden capped the bottle and placed it back in its spot on the table and picked up the cups.

"Never, Mason," he rebelled. "Isn't going to happen."

Mason laughed, "Sure. Well, I'll let you get back to your girl then I guess."

Aiden gave him a simple nod and grin and the two parted ways. Ahead a small group of girls had formed around Faith. He recognized a few, her usual group, but he didn't really know any of them, except for Erica. She had went to the same middle school while Aiden and Faith had been friends, and had always been one of Faith's closest confidants.

Dressed in a form-fitting black suit that reminded Aiden of the Black Widow, Erica was the first to see him coming. She was a pretty black girl, almost one with the suit she wore, with long black braids running down well below her back.

"Here he comes," Erica grinned at him. Faith turned to see him, smiling still. "We'll see you later tonight, Faith."

The group began to disperse as Aiden approached. He returned a nod from Erica as she turned and left. He was surprised to receive another soft slap on the butt by one of the other girls. He jumped forward slightly and turned the other cheek.

"Nice ass, Spidey," a short blue-eyed girl said with a crooked grin.

"Never mind her," Faith apologized. "She's harmless."

Aiden raised an eyebrow and sighed with a gentle smile. He passed Faith her cup, "Maybe I should have worn something else."

Faith simply giggled and grinned at him. He was not sure how exactly to take that but chose not to dwell on it long. Twenty minutes later, the crowd had withered to only a handful of costumed guests.

Mason walked up as Faith was talking about one of their blanket forts. The elaborate creations of their childhood in her family's basement that had doubled as a toy-filled playroom.

"We were pretty creative," Faith reminded him. "Remember all the tunnels and rooms we'd build with nothing more than blankets, comforters, chairs, tables and whatever else we could get our hands on?"

Aiden laughed. It seemed so childish now, but it had been so much fun. For a moment he wished he was back then, in the simplicity of it all, oblivious to the deeper feelings that would come in the years to follow. "Yeah, those were crazy."

"Crazy?" Mason asked. "What was crazy?"

"Nothing, Mason," Aiden shook his head. "I'll explain later."

"Okay. Well, I hate to break this up but it's time for us to be hitting the road. Parents expect us back by ten," Mason explained. "Stupid curfew."

"Okay," Aiden said, looking at Faith. Neither of them said a word. They just stood awkwardly, like simply stepping away from each other would be too odd to actually commence in the action.

"Well then," Mason said slowly, emphasizing how odd the situation was. "Why don't you just kiss her and say goodbye."

Aiden glared at Mason. Yes, that's exactly what he wanted to do, but his body didn't want to move and his mind was too horrified to override it. Suddenly he relaxed and shook his head.

"Why don't you go start the car, Mason?" he suggested.

Mason grinned mischievously and left them alone with the other guests. At least they were not standing inches from them, expecting a scene. Aiden looked down and then back up at her with a grin.

"Do you have a ride?" Aiden asked. "I'm sure Mason wouldn't mind dropping you off."

"No, I'm good," she replied. "I'm riding with Erica."

Carefully, Aiden took a step closer to Faith. He stood a mere half foot from her body. He smiled, unsure how to proceed though he knew exactly what he wanted. Faith smiled back and crinkled her brow, her emerald eyes expectant. Aiden shook his head and laughed quietly at himself before taking a deep breath.

The awkwardness in his bones finally banished, he leaned forward and kissed her gently. His body chilled at the feeling of her lips against his own. Strawberry, simple and delicious. Then he stepped back, such sweet parting, and looked her in the eyes. They gleamed intensely and her smile looked as though it could never be erased. He was sure it matched his own expression.

"Goodnight," he said.

"Night," she replied happily.

"Stop, please stop," Dalton begged pathetically.

Bullet's knife slid gently in wide slaloms across Lenore's bare leg where the raspy voiced-boy had ripped her right pant leg open with the same blade. A thin line of red left a trail along her leg. Lenore held her lips tight, refusing to give him the pleasure of a scream. Instead she whimpered as the sharp edge etched a tiny line through her skin. Her whole body shook in shock.

"I'm begging you, please stop," Dalton continued, quieter and with less force. "Take anything you want, anything! What do you want from us?"

Those black holes, excuses for eyes, behind the plain white mask dug into Dalton. The boy didn't even watch were the knife went as he traced aimlessly along Lenore's thigh, then knee. He kept angling his head as if in contemplation of Dalton, taking in every emotion and torment from the father's eyes, every tear and sob, every last drop of pain and grief.

"Stop!" Dalton yelled this time. His entire body shook with the words, his voice booming in the large living space. Bullet sank back an inch, his blade stopping halfway down Lenore's calf. Freddie and Skull-face were jarred to attention, heads tilted. It was a more menacing scene than Dalton could have expected. Three foreign figures, all cowering behind eerie masks, staring at him, wondering at him almost. He suddenly felt more uncomfortable than he had a moment ago, but he refused to let it show. He had to do something. But what?

Signaling for Skull-face to watch Lenore, Bullet rose from his crouch. His eyes never left Dalton as he stood to his full height. At first he simply stood there, looking at Dalton with a masked expression that Dalton could only imagine. A senile freak. A raving lunatic.

"What do you want?" Dalton yelled furiously.

The masked boy stepped forward quicker than expected and perched himself directly in front of Dalton. He looked down at Dalton, the hard plastic of his mask almost making contact with Dalton's nose. The knife jutted out precariously only inches from Dalton's neck. Those dark eyes bored into him. Then he yelled, the raspy quality of his voice giving way to something more childish, almost a squeal. "Shut up!"

"What do you want? You can have any…"

A fist hammered into his nose. His head reeled back, his vision blurred, and pain seared up his nostrils, eyes sockets and forehead. Dalton jerked back. He tried to shake the pain out of his head, tried to restore the clarity to his vision. His vision clarified. He raised his hand to his nose where most of the throb came from. He felt something wet and warm on his index finger. Blood.

"Oh that felt good," Bullet exclaimed. It was an almost joyful melody. Dalton ducked as his vision caught sight of another fist heading straight for him. He closed his eyes. Nothing. He opened his eyes again and found Bullet bouncing like some boxer, pumping his fist in and out barely out of reach of Dalton's face.

"Yeah, that felt real good." Bullet stretched his shoulders and wrenched his neck from side to side like he was preparing to step into the ring. "How'd you like that, Dalton?"

"Please, just go," Dalton begged.

"If you'd just shut the fuck up maybe we *would*," Bullet argued. He stopped the theatrics and sighed. He let his gaze shift around to Lenore and Mara and then back onto Dalton. "Well, once we get what we want, we'll leave. But not until then."

"What do you want then?" Dalton begged for an answer. His mind needed something solid, something concrete, some demand he could meet.

"Like I said, we just want to have a little fun, then we'll get to the real business and leave," Bullet explained vaguely.

"Yeah, we have to have some fun first," Skull-face chimed in from behind Bullet.

"Just a little Halloween fun," Freddie added.

Searching those dark eyes for something more, some unspoken detail, Dalton tried to piece together what they had said. *Fun, then we'll get to the real business. What was the real business?*

"You're just going to continue to hurt my family, like some twist-ed game, aren't you?" Dalton asked, needing some validation, an an-swer.

In the periphery of Dalton's vision, Freddie and Skull-face began to nod slowly and deliberately. There was no attempt at shadow or disguise, no covering their intent. Bullet did not move. He bore his eyes deeper into Dalton's, his head tilted as he stepped closer, but still out of reach. His eyes narrowed to slits behind the holes in the mask and his lips pinched into a dreadful smile.

"Hurt me, not them. Hurt me," Dalton begged, his voice shaking.

"I am, Dalton. I am hurting you." The words came out calm and clear. He paused once more for a mere second before continuing, "By hurting them. Can't you see that?"

An icy chill laced through his body like an electrical current. His eyes widened in realization. He let his mouth fall open but he could not form the words to speak. Had he heard right? Yes. He knew he had. Finally, he let out a breath he had not realized he was holding. His eyes darted in quick jumps to Lenore and then Mara, and then back again and again. The realization that he somehow was the center of this cruel game sank in, deep into his marrow. He was the center and his family were the pawns. His eyes communicated such deep sorrow to his wife and Mara, then he looked down.

"But why?" he asked one more time, expecting to be punched again for the question.

"Because I can," Bullet explained.

The words felt like a knife through his heart. The still beating or-gan felt like it was thumping around the thick blade, causing cut after cut with each expansion and release. What type of monster was stand-ing before him? Could he be real? Was any of this real? Human? If he was, if this was anything more than a dark nightmare, the boy that stood before him had a soul as black as hell itself.

"I believe it's my turn next," Skull-face broke the silence. He looked at Lenore. "It's your turn, honey."

CHAPTER 11

The bright light emanating from the television screen cast a faint glow over the plaid sofa at the opposite end of the room. Its red and green stripes looked to be shades of gray in the flashing light.

Tamieka Dula sat on the couch immersed in the television's light next to her daughter, Larissa. The rays projected from the grayscale image reflected in Larissa's glasses, tiny imitations of the story playing out on the old tube. The glare almost hid her bright brown eyes bordered by dark brown skin. She sat bundled in a large plush mocha blanket, feet tucked securely under her and wrapped in more blanket.

On the tube, Bela Lugosi walked with unnerving grace in shades of black and white through a large ornate room. His gaze was steady and cunning as he approached an unsuspecting female who, unknown to her, was the next on his list of blood donors.

"Here we go, here we go," Tamieka said, patting Larissa on the shoulder excitedly. Larissa just looked at her with a blank expression then went back to watching the screen.

Smoothly, Dracula took the damsel in his arms and stared into her eyes, hypnotizing her with his gaze. Finally, his eyes flared in hunger and his mouth opened wide, exposing hidden fangs, and he bit down onto her neck. The woman didn't struggle, she just laid back like nothing was happening. Another of Dracula's victims.

"That was intense," Tamieka exclaimed.

"Intense?" Larissa asked. She looked at her mother, confused. "Were you watching the same thing I was?"

"Yeah, that was good," Tamieka asserted.

"That was old, and corny," Larissa retorted. "You all actually thought that was scary back in the day?"

Tamieka rolled her eyes and feigned shock, "Back in the day? Yes, that was scary." She let a grin spread across her cheeks again.

"Interesting maybe, I wouldn't call it scary. If you want scary watch one of the Dracula movies in color," Larissa explained.

"Ah, all you young'uns just like the nasty junk. Gore and sex," Tamieka said.

"Well, at least it's genuinely scary," Larissa teased.

"I can't argue with that," her mom agreed.

Larissa laughed, confident that her mom would eventually come to her senses. Tamieka stood up and began to make her way to the kitchen. "You want anything to drink?"

"Nah, I'm good," came her daughter's reply back in the living room.

Tamieka nodded and made her way into the kitchen. She worked the fridge, retrieving a jug of good ol' southern sweet tea and poured herself a glass. Family time had become so much more important for the two of them over the past year. Shaun, Tamieka's husband of fourteen years, had died in a fatal car accident just thirteen months ago. Thirteen months and two days. Moving on had felt near impossible then. It still did at times, but she made herself get out of bed each morning and smile for her daughter. She missed him.

Out of all the heartache, one good thing had come. It had brought Tamieka closer to her daughter. She had even asked to stay home this Halloween instead of going out with her friends or out trick-or-treating like she had two years ago, before the accident. She had confidently explained that at thirteen she was too old to go door-to-door like a little "kid" begging for candy. Tamieka did not argue. She was grateful for the time with Larissa. Losing Shaun had taught her to hold on to every moment, and she wanted to be there for Larissa for every one of them.

Abruptly, a thought popped into Tamieka's mind. Lenore's book. She had told Lenore she would be by tonight to pick up one of her books. *Which one?* She shrugged off the question, sure Lenore would remember.

I can pick it up tomorrow. Uh. But I told her I'd be there tonight.

"Larissa," Tamieka called into the living room from the hallway as she made her way back to the sofa. "I might have to go out for a little bit. I forgot that I was supposed to go by the Summers' house earlier."

"What are you going over there for?" Larissa inquired.

"She's getting me a copy of one of her books," Tamieka shrugged, "I can't remember which one, but one of them. I could go by tomorrow probably."

"I'll be fine, go get your book," Larissa smiled. "I know how much you like a new story."

Tamieka grinned. The girl knew her well, even if the understanding didn't run as well back the other direction. A teenage girl, although she had been one, was no easy book to read. Tamieka figured there was no use arguing, she did want to pick up the book after all.

"All right," Tamieka said. She stepped back into the hallway and snatched the car keys off the hall table. "Get your shoes on, we'll go on and be back in half an hour or so."

"Come on, Mom, let me stay here and watch movies. I'll be fine," she tried, holding herself tall and confident on the sofa.

"I don't know, Larissa," Tamieka said. "I don't like the idea of leaving you all alone. Halloween night can be crazy."

"Go, Mom, I'll be fine."

With a gentle grin, Tamieka gave in, "Okay. Keep the doors

locked and don't open them for anyone but me. And I mean anyone, but me."

"Okay, Mom!" Larissa pleaded with her to just stop.

"Love you, I'll be right back." She turned and walked out the front door.

"Love you, Mom."

The cool night air rushed over and under Aiden's red and black gloved hand as he let it wave up and down outside the car window. The brisk breeze was refreshing as it seeped through the thin breathable fabric of his costume. It cooled his blushed skin. With his Spidey mask off, his pale pink lips arched upward in what was possibly a permanent grin. The dark and light browns of his hair ruffled in flurries as the wind sloshed them furiously. The light brown of his inner iris seemed to overtake the usually dominate outer honey brown circle. It gave his eyes a brighter look.

"Hey, man, are you still on Earth over there?" Mason inquired, momentarily taking his eyes off the curvy road.

Snapping back to reality Aiden grinned even more. He smiled at Mason and then looked back out the window at the passing night forest. "Yeah, I'm here."

"Really? Cause you definitely look like your somewhere else," Mason jeered. "So was it good?"

"Yeah," Aiden started, trying to find the words. "Yeah, it was great. I actually talked to her."

Mason visibly slumped in the bucket seat of his Mustang. He shook his head at his oblivious friend.

"I mean I *actually* talked to her. Yeah, I was horrified at first, but after I started, I was fine. Yeah, it was good."

"Uh, yeah, that's nice and all but," Mason continued with a renewed grin," but you kissed her, right?"

Aiden's gaze pulled back into the car and over to Mason with a sideways grin. He laughed at himself, realizing his mistake.

"Of course," he answered. "Of course it was good. It was great, really great."

"You kiss her upside down?" Mason continued to joke.

"No," Aiden laughed. "You're crazy, man. I may be Spiderman for the night, but I'm not that good."

"Well don't tell Faith that," Mason advised him. "She might think she's getting the whole package. Wouldn't want to disappoint her too quickly now."

He punched Mason playfully and looked back out the window. The thrill of her lips on his still sang through his mind like the sweetest guitar rift with a hint of strawberry. He swore he felt a tingle on his lips again. He played the moment over and over again in his mind, wishing he could feel it again, really feel it again. He knew he would. Somehow he just knew it. All the time he had wasted in useless fear seemed to disappear for the moment.

"So, you ready to admit I was right?" Mason chimed in, left hand on the wheel, the other on the shifter in the middle of the car's console. He shifted down a gear as he accelerated around a curve.

Aiden looked at him with a raised brow. He grinned mischievously. "Never. But I will happily beat your ass in Call of Duty again tonight."

"Hey, now," Mason retorted, "I beat you a few times this week."

"Yeah, try like six times…out of what, at least twenty rounds," Aiden grinned proudly.

"Whatever…" he shrugged. Then Mason's eyes widened and a crooked grin painted across his lips. "Oh my goodness, Aiden! Did you realize we didn't even take the firecrackers in? I knew I forgot something."

Aiden shook his head. Firecrackers were the last thing on his mind. "It never crossed my mind."

CHAPTER 12

Dalton's hands shook. The reality of all that was happening had finally sank in. It now coursed through his veins and set his body on a small steady rhythm.

"Do you have any buckets around here?" Skull-face asked.

"*What?*" Dalton asked. He raised his brow, confused. He had heard the question, but it seemed so odd. The cadence of the words were so nonchalant, almost respectful. It was almost as if the voice had not sprung from behind a dark skull-covered mask. That it somehow belonged to someone decent, someone who didn't hold the slicing edge of a knife to his neck.

Freddie and Bullet looked on quietly. There was no reading Freddie, all his facial features hidden behind the grotesquely detailed Freddie Krueger mask. Just feet in front of Freddie, Bullet stood silent and expressionless. The small slit in his mask that revealed his lips showed a flat line and the eye sockets revealed even less.

"Buckets. Do you have any buckets?" Skull-face asked again. This time his tone held the slightest tinge of irritation, or maybe it was sarcasm.

"Uh..." Dalton thought aloud. He stopped shaking. What did a bucket have to do with his wife? Were they done? Did they need something to haul out their loot? Dalton's mind lifted just enough to come crashing down as another thought broke into his stream of reason. Knives. Buckets. *They don't plan to carry us out in buckets, do they?*

Dalton's heart began to race quicker. His mind strained to fight for control over his emotions and fears. He was losing the battle. He squeezed his eyes shut and forced himself to focus on the question, to take each thing as it came. It was useless, pointless, to attempt to predetermine what the trio of masked freaks planned. It was an exercise in futility that took vital attention away from the here and now, from what mattered, the only thing that ever really mattered. In that split second, his fear dissipated just enough for the weight of who he had become to crash down into his metal lap. *The only thing that ever really mattered.*

In a fraction of second, his mind raced through a lifetime of memories. Mara's feet leaving the concrete driveway as she finally managed to pedal her tiny pink bicycle on her own. Aiden smiling widely at just two years old while Dalton spun him in circles by his arms. Every single time he'd kissed his children on the head while they slept. Lenore in a simple white dress, walking slowly toward him with her father. Lenore.

"It's not that hard of question, man," Freddie's voice arched over the others, interrupting the flood of memories and the joy and grief they brought. There was that gang-like sound in the boy's voice again, just a hint.

Opening his eyes, Dalton finally spoke, "No. I don't have any buckets. We have some boxes out in the garage, but no buckets."

"Hm..." Skull-face pursed his lips for a moment. "Pots. I assume you have some large pots, right?"

"Yes, of course," Dalton answered quickly, not wanting Lenore to have to speak to the monster. He was not one to cook but he witnessed the large pot of water or tea on the stove more than a few times so it was an easy answer. "In the kitchen."

"Good," Skull-face said. "That should do I guess."

After a nod to Bullet, Skull-face walked lightly out of the living room and into the kitchen out of Dalton's sight. The other two monsters spread out before the sofa and recliner. Freddie swooshed his knife in a slow arch between Mara and Lenore, daring them to move while Bullet kept the muzzle of his pistol aimed dangerously at Mara's temple. Neither bothered to show him any attention with their destructive instruments, but preferred to torment him instead with their targets.

Their intent was clear, keep Dalton seated. He cursed them silently, wishing there was some way he could get them far enough away from his wife and daughter, from his life, to make a move, any move. If they were too close, though, Dalton's attempt at rescue could turn into the very instrument of murder. He couldn't bear that burden. He couldn't. Instead he sat, eyes fixed invariably on the leader, on that cold white mask.

Clangs and pings echoed into the living room. The noises came from the kitchen, surely originating from Skull-face's search of the cabinets. Apparently he had found *something*.

"Found them!" the boy's youthful voice yelled from the opposite room. Dalton crinkled his brow, wondering still why the pots were needed. He hoped his mind was simply running rampant.

In the silence that followed, Dalton's ear caught the subtle flush of water pouring from a faucet. He kept his eyes peeled on Bullet, the edge of his pistol and Freddie's knife visible in his peripheral vision. They waited as the sound of running water continued, followed by a quiet clang of metal on metal.

Suddenly, the sounds from the adjoining room changed. The water ceased to fall and the sound of footsteps replaced the clanging. From the corner of his vision, Dalton saw the skinny boy walking carefully around the recliner with a pot filled to the brim with water. He looked at the silver pot quizzically.

"You'll figure it out in just a minute, just be patient," Skull-face assured him, like it was some game that all teenagers played. "I hope you don't mind a little water on the floor, though."

The boy's mixed words confused Dalton. It was as if he tried to be polite and cruel all in the same instance. Dalton wanted to question him, to ask what he was doing, but he held his tongue.

Skull-face turned and returned to the kitchen. Seconds later, he returned with another pot, a slightly smaller one of the same set, also filled to the brim with water. Again he returned to the kitchen and came back with another pot, again smaller. In the end, Skull-face lined up three pots along the earthenshaded tile floor. Two of the pots were from a silver set Dalton had bought Lenore four years ago at Christmas and a smaller pot from an older set made of cast iron of the decorative variety. Each was filled to the brim with water.

The boy's gaunt figure seemed to bob with excitement as he stood by his pots of water. Dalton imagined a thin face with wide crazed eyes, crooked nose and thin lips smiling insanely at the preparations he had made. Still unsure what purpose the water served, Dalton looked back to Bullet who stepped back to let Freddie move in front of him.

Without a word of warning, Freddie took hold of Lenore's

arm and yanked her forward. Horrified, but unsure why, Lenore jerked away. Freddie lost his grip and she fell back to the couch.

"Get up," Freddie commanded angrily. It was like Lenore had disobeyed an obvious command, as if she had willfully knew and rebelled.

Lenore's eyes widened. She scanned the pots, wondering what purpose they served. At first she didn't let her body move, but as Freddie insisted with another pull, she scooted forward and let herself be led to a standing position. Dalton could see her body shaking, the fear in her eyes, the small string of blood that etched from thigh to mid-calf in a drunken fashion. Her eyes turned to Dalton, pleading with him to do something. Dalton met her pleading eyes. He refused to look away in her moment of need, but he was unsure what he could do. Inside his heart sank another notch, a notch he thought did not exist.

"On the floor," Skull-face commanded, his youthful voice gaining an edge of authority. "Lay down. On your back, now."

The confusion in her eyes grew. She stood, questioning the command by her inaction, her mind trying to understand what they had in store for her.

"On the floor, bitch!" All of Skull-face's odd politeness vanished as he bellowed the command angrily.

Obeying out of fright, Lenore got to her knees and laid back on the cold tile floor. Her body tensed at the awkward feeling of the hard tile against her back. Above her, Freddie moved down and straddled her legs before placing his full weight onto her knees. The weight of the otherwise light boy was more than her knees were accustomed to holding up. Pain blossomed up her thighs as her knees bent backward, pressed flat to the floor. Nothing popped or broke, but she gasped as the pain jumped up both legs.

"Shut up, this is nothing," Freddie griped.

"Here," Bullet said to Freddie, passing him the gun-metal grey pistol. "Keep it on her," he commanded, nodding back to Mara, keeping all of his bases covered. Keeping Dalton at bay. Bullet's eyes caught Dalton's and a small grin formed behind the smile opening in the mask. Dalton's lips writhed in anger, and hate.

Bullet dropped to his knees just above Lenore's head and reached out for a small white kitchen rag, one of the thin square variety that Lenore kept on hand. He rolled the rag like a large joint before wrenching Lenore's mouth open violently and shoving it into her mouth, a hand holding on to each end of the roll by each cheek. Lenore gasped as the back of her head was pressed against the tile and the rag pressed against her lips. Dalton cried inside as Bullet pushed down harder, pulling the edges of her lips back further than they were meant to go.

"You ready?" Skull-face asked.

"Stop! You're hurting her! " Dalton blurted out.

The three boy's stopped what they were doing and looked up at Dalton. The eyes he could see stared back at him, laughing at him.

"Uh. Yeah," one of them said. Dalton couldn't tell which, but it had not been Bullet, his mouth had not moved.

"Please. Stop!" he begged

"Have at her." Bullet nodded to Skull-face. He grinned at Dalton.

"No..." Dalton whispered.

"I've been waiting for this," Skull-face commented as he

retrieved the smallest of the pots, the cast iron one. He stooped to his knees by Lenore's face. When he spoke again, his voice was young and gleeful again, "Open wide."

Immediately Dalton realized what was happening. He kicked himself mentally for being so blind. Slowly, Skull-face tipped the pot and let the water pour into and over Lenore's mouth. She fought, twisted and shook, but Bullet and Freddie held her down. Suddenly she began to gasp and choke on the water, unable to prevent the life-giving liquid from pouring down the back of her throat in time to breathe. The water continued to pour. Lenore's body jerked, trying to loose itself from its human bonds as she choked. Horrible gurgling noises escaped behind the constant stream of water.

"Stop!" Mara screamed. Dalton's attention shot to his daughter. She had finally come out of shock and her eyes conveyed terror at what she was watching. Dalton grimaced harder and then looked back to Lenore.

The water continued to pour. Lenore's body jerked and convulsed as it lodged in her throat and windpipe, cutting of her ability to breathe. Finally, the last drop of water fell from the pot and Bullet let her up just enough to expel the water from her lungs. She coughed and choked again and again. Water dribbled off her lips.

"Now to the next bucket," Skull-face informed her.

"Stop, please stop!" Dalton begged them. He met Lenore's eyes. "I'm so sorry."

None of the three blessed him with an answer or even a reaction. The thinnest of the boys twisted at his waist and retrieved the next smallest pot and turned again to dangle it where the first had been just moments ago. Dalton kept his vision of the boy's crazed countenance in mind as he focused all of his hate on the monster behind the skull-marked mask.

Again water flowed from the pot, falling through open space and splashing against Lenore's lips and on the rag holding her mouth open, then down her exposed throat. She choked again and again, gasping for air when the singular deluge lessened for less than a second and then choked again. Her body jerked and jumped, almost threatening to knock Freddie from his painful perch atop her knees.

Again the water ceased and Skull-face went for the last and largest pot, his excitement peaked. During the transition, Lenore begged for air as she choked on the water in her windpipe, retching and gagging on the liquid. Water spewed from her mouth and around the cloth Bullet still held harshly between her jaws.

"Here comes the big one," Skull-face warned her, but the excitement in his voice betrayed the warning. Lenore's eyes did not widen, instead they rolled in their sockets, bloodshot and scared. Her white blouse was soaked, the black lines of her bra showing suggestively under the thin wet fabric. Her soft brown hair was sodden with the burdensome water that pooled around her upper body.

She whimpered, begging them to stop between coughs. "Please... St... Stop."

"Please just stop," Dalton begged.

"Please," Mara joined him in a chorus of stuttered unheard pleas.

Unheeded, water began to pour from the silver pot. Dalton watched as the first droplet raced down, pulled by gravity to its destination. Gentle lamplight reflected off the droplet as two, four, ten, twenty, then countless more clear droplets came together in an amorphous free fall before colliding across Lenore's lips, then sloshed along her tongue and caught in the back of her throat. He watched her gag and retch as the usually innocuous liquid cut off her life-breath.

What had been a slow trickle amassed into a torrent of rapids peeling over the cleft of Lenore's soft lips, slaloming down her cheek and ears, over her chin and splashing on her chest. Abruptly her body wrenched up as she began to panic for breath again. She jerked side-to-side uselessly. The pot in Skull-face's hands followed her as she managed to move just a few inches under Bullet's tight grip. Water seared over the torn flesh at the edges of her mouth where the rag had rubbed back and forth. Unlike the other pots, the water just kept pouring. Dalton went to get up, but Freddie was quick to remind him of the pistol pointing at Mara. He took his seat again.

"Please stop," Dalton begged.

"If you insist, Dalton," Bullet rasped and nodded at Skull-face. The boy tipped the pot over and let the remaining content dump over Lenore's face haphazardly. The water ceased, the pot emptied of its contents. He grinned wickedly behind his mask, letting the rag go slack in his hands and slip from Lenore's mouth. She coughed spasmodically. Her body jerked and water spewed from her throat. Instinctively Lenore tried to escape. Before she could get far, Bullet regained a hand of control on her collar bone. He slammed her back down to the wet floor. "Did I say to get up?"

She didn't answer. Instead she continued to heave, expelling the water from her lungs. It spilled over her lips and eyes and neck. Finally, she could breathe. The air came in heavy gulps but she wasn't choking anymore. Her eyes darted from corner to corner, from person to person, scared. Finally, Bullet got to his feet. Freddie unmounted Lenore's legs and stepped to the side.

"Get up," he barked.

Dalton looked at his wife who still laid on the ground shaking. She was in shock. He wanted to go to her, reach out and lift her up gingerly. Pull her to him and envelope her in his arms and hold her gently. He wanted to shield her, to be there for her, to *love* her. He looked to the ground shamefully just before Skull-face yelled out.

"Get up, bitch!"

"She's in shock, asshole!" Dalton yelled, almost jumping to his feet defiantly. Words were dangerous, but not as dangerous as a misinterpreted action in his situation, so he remained still for a moment. When no one moved, he began to step forward.

"What did you say?" Skull-face roared as deeply as his shrill voice could manage. It was a delayed reaction. He had not expected the defiance.

"I said she's in shock, as..." Dalton began to repeat himself as he stepped forward.

"Stop!" came Bullet's raspy tone. He was neither angry nor amused, simply resolute. He reached down and cupped Lenore's underarm in his palm and wrenched her upwards before Dalton could take another step, "Get up."

On her feet with Bullet's rough assistance, her eyes met Dalton's. He tried on a sad grin, trying to convey any strength he could muster to her. Abusively, Bullet shoved her to the left and onto the couch. She stumbled onto the soft leather and managed to position herself into a sitting position next to Mara, who reached out and wrapped her arms around her mother, trying to comfort her.

"How sweet," Bullet said.

* * *

Silence ruled the expanse of the open living room for what felt like half an hour. It had been a mere three minutes. Positions had been resumed, or assumed.

Freddie stood behind Mara, hovering over the sofa with the sharp end of his knife against the nape of her neck, his free hand laying on Mara's neck just over her collar bone. His dark ungloved fingers lingered on her sensitive skin, earning quiet whimpers. Skull-face was planted directly in front of Lenore, a new bounce in his step and his curved blade hovered before her. Dalton let his eyes burn with hate anytime the boy's masked eyes wandered his way.

Just feet in front of Dalton stood Bullet. His knife, a near replica of the one in Skull-face's hands, was angled at Dalton. It seemed the pistol was a less desired tool, pinned behind Bullet's shirt between pant and skin. His eyes bore into Dalton's head but Dalton refused to give him the pleasure of his attention. Instead he kept his eyes on Lenore and then Mara, and back again.

"Why do you care so much about her?" Bullet's voice questioned with surprising authenticity in his bewilderment.

"Why?" Dalton repeated the singular word disdainfully. "She's my *wife*."

His answer was met with a laugh. Not a comical sound, not the laugh of a crazed lunatic. No. It was the laugh of a calculated decision, of knowing, slow and belabored as it escaped between closed lips.

"Well that's obvious," Skull-face jeered, looking momentarily at Dalton who glared at him and then to Freddie who cackled along. They were like a pack of two wild hyenas. Ravenous and crazed.

"Yeah, I sort of get that," Bullet nodded. "But that's not what I mean. You know exactly what I mean."

Bullet's black eyes dug into Dalton as if working to unearth some hidden jewel, or black stone. Dalton stared back, meeting his gaze with all the hatred he could muster, but unable to hold back the confusion that crossed his face.

"What about that other woman?" Bullet asked pointedly.

"What other woman?" Dalton asked.

"You know who I'm talking about, Dalton. Stop playing dumb," Bullet insisted. "That woman you work with."

Jenna. Her face sparked in his mind. *How do they know about Jenna? Who are these people?*

For a long moment, Dalton stared back at his masked foe, not wanting to meet his wife's eyes, not ready to meet the accusation that was sure to be there, not ready for the truth. He gulped, trying to find the words to say. During the hour that had passed, or had it been an hour, or more, his mind had worried only about Lenore and Mara. The need for her had resurfaced, a need to see her safe had surged to the forefront. He shook his head, finally letting his blue eyes meet Lenore's questioning gaze.

He frowned and moved his eyes to the floor before fixing them again on those two black abysses behind Bullet's mask. "Why are you doing this?"

"Is it her hair? That nice figure?" Bullet prodded. "Or is it just because she's younger?"

"Stop," Dalton bellowed angrily.

Bullet toggled his attention from Dalton to Lenore and then back again, a smile eking out from the thin slit in the mask. He nodded toward Lenore, "She doesn't know, does she?"

Lowering his head, Dalton attempted to gather himself. The fear in his bowel notched up. His stomach churned. His heart twisted in agony not for his own shame, but because he knew how much he had just compounded Lenore's suffering. He dared raise his head and steal a glance toward her. In her damp sea green eyes, she conveyed a typhoon of emotions. The lancing pain and mental anguish wrought from physical torment, fear in the twitching of her unsteady gaze and the visceral torrent of emotions heightened by the revelation of his disloyalty.

The thought of the divorce papers in his briefcase made him feel dirty. What had he been thinking? He locked his eyes with Lenore's, trying to convey his shame.

"Jenna?" A flicker of realization shot through Lenore's eyes. "You were..."

"So her name's Jenna?" Bullet half-asked, half-stated. "So you were screwing Jenna then?"

"I never..." Dalton stopped himself. It would not have been a lie exiting his lips, but it was a useless statement, a useless plea. Now was not the time to prove his innocence of a mad man's claim. Instead, he apologized. "I'm sorry, Lenore. I'm so sorry."

"See, he didn't deny it, Lenore," Bullet jeered, nearly prancing. Dalton loathed the pleasure the teen seemed to derive from this torment. "He screwed Jenna, over and over again."

Dropping his eyes, Dalton muttered a quiet "What?" as a revelation washed over him. It was a simple revelation, nothing profound or unusual, just frightening. These boys knew him, they had chosen his family for this night.

"What was that, Dalton?" the raspy voice came again.

"Why?" Dalton whispered, still not looking at the intruders, still talking to himself more than the boy in front of him.

"I couldn't make that out, Dalton. What were you saying?" Bullet asked again.

"Why?" Dalton raised his head and glared at Bullet and asked. "Why us?"

"Why you?" Bullet asked, cocking his head, looking back at Dalton sideways.

"This isn't random," Dalton stated with confidence. "You chose us. You didn't just randomly come to my home tonight. You planned this. Why?"

Behind the alpha male, Skull-face fidgeted nervously, the long curved blade of his knife swaying a little lower. Freddie tightened his grip on his weapon and pulled it dangerously close to Mara's neck.

The tips of Bullet's thick lips raised. He swayed confidently, resting his free hand on his hip. "We know a good deal about you, Dalton. But, why? Well, it's just not time for that yet."

"No, what do you want? Why are you here?" Dalton demanded.

Bullet looked to Freddie and the knife around Mara's neck threatened to dig deeper. Her taut skin began to contort around the blade. Dalton reached out, "No, no!"

"To watch you bleed," the voice came dark and raspy from behind the white mask. The blade lifted as Bullet flicked his fingers dismissively at Freddie.

"What?" Dalton asked, hiding the fear that had suddenly chilled through his spine. He had heard the cruel words, but he could not believe them.

"You asked what I wanted," Bullet reminded him. The raspy nature of his voice thickened as he repeated himself. "I want to watch you all bleed. I want to watch *you* bleed."

The pallid expression that overwhelmed Lenore's visage was a mirror of how Dalton felt. The chill of those heavy words had immobilized Dalton's limbs. He could feel his legs and feet beneath him, his arms and phalanges at his side, but he felt powerless to move them. His eyes were locked with the alpha predator's black holes in an almost hypnotic trance.

Gradually the wicked grin behind the white mask raised at the corners and the head bobbed with a whispered but guttural chortle. His head twitched to the right but never broke their stare. The others, the sheep, remained at their post, knives bared and ready.

"Why?" Dalton finally spoke. He immediately wished he could take the word back.

"How many fucking times are you going to ask that?" Bullet bellowed louder than he yet had. "Did I not just tell you?"

"Yes, yes. I'm sorry," Dalton apologized in flurry of words and nods as he drew back into the recliner. Why did this man, this boy, want him to *bleed*? Deep inside he knew what that meant, though he refused to countenance the word, or the idea. He had to remain strong for Mara and Lenore and that would be impossible if he broached the inevitable conclusion of the boy's words. He shook the thought away.

"Let's take a little break," Bullet stated, stepping a few feet backward.

"Yeah, wouldn't want them *too* roughed up *too* soon," Skull-face giggled darkly as he let the blade drift away from Lenore. He let it sway back and forth between her, Mara and Dalton, then back again. The black kid in the Freddie mask, as evidenced by the ungloving of his hand, relaxed the weight of his blade on Mara's neck. He stood straight, behind Mara. A reminder of the threat of his presence.

"Nah, wouldn't wa—," Freddie began to repeat his counterpart as a gentle chime echoed in the open space. "What the hell is that?"

Dalton's body tensed. It was the driveway bell. The short tone that let them know when someone ventured onto the concrete path leading to their estate.

"It means someone is coming up the driveway," Dalton explained. But who? *Please don't be Aiden.*

"Did you call the cops?" Skull-face jumped toward Dalton with the blade sweeping a hair too close to his face.

"I said no cops, Dalton!" Bullet yelled. He hooked Dalton by the collar and hauled him to his feet, nose-to-nose. His dark black irises became the only thing Dalton could see. "Tell me you didn't break my rules."

"I didn't," Dalton almost pled, trying to reason with the boy. "I promise. If I had they would have been here a long time ago. I don't know who it is. I swear."

He refused to admit what he feared aloud, that it might be Aiden driving into a trap. *If it's you, Aiden, please just turn around*, he willed his son, wishing he could warn him of what waited for him.

Bullet cocked his head sideways before releasing his grip on Dalton's shirt and belting out commands. He refused to say the name of his counterparts to get their attention. Instead, he pointed with his long index finger. First to Freddie and then to Skull-face. Dalton dropped back to his seat and fell backward into the soft leather.

"You, keep the women down and quiet. You, make sure *he* doesn't move or speak," Bullet barked. He looked in Dalton's direction, his eyes narrowing as he met Dalton's gaze. A warning, daring him to break his rules.

The sound of old brakes screeched as a car came to a stop outside. Bullet half-jogged to the front door and eased the window curtain back just enough to peek outside. He reeled back. His eyes dotted back and forth aimlessly over the living area where the rest of the group stood or sat where he had left them.

"Who is it?" Skull-face whispered.

"How the *fuck* would I know?" Bullet replied quietly.

There was something new in the boy's gestures. He fidgeted with the handle of the knife between his fingers. His eyes remained low and sporadic. He was unsure what to do. Dalton tried to draw strength from the boy's insecurity, from the fact that he was not in complete control.

Dalton heard the sound of muffled footsteps mounting the porch just as Bullet did. Bullet moved away from the door. He backed up by the bar in the kitchen, knife up and ready again. Seconds later, a faint silhouette materialized along the frosted glass of the entrance door. Then came the knocking on the door frame.

No one said a word. While Dalton stared worriedly at the silhouette behind the glass, Bullet, Skull-face and Freddie stood rigid and tense. Silence overtook the open space with the exception of Lenore's still ragged breathing.

Again, the person outside knocked on the door post. The silhouette moved like a dark spirit waiting outside in contemplation of whether to break the threshold. It waited. Then it spoke.

"Lenore," a familiar voice echoed into the house. No one answered. Bullet's head shifted back and forth like he was trying to make a decision. A few seconds later, the voice came again. "Lenore? It's me, Tamieka. I'm here to pick up that book."

Again no one responded, no one moved. A full half minute passed and no one moved, it felt like no one even breathed. Then Tamieka shifted to the left outside the door.

"I'm probably too late," she said more quietly, talking to herself. Her silhouette faded out of view in the frosted glass. She was leaving.

Bullet visibly relaxed. He loosened his grip on the knife and stepped closer to the door. He looked back to Dalton and shook his head.

"That was close," Bullet barely even whispered.

Unsure whether to be glad or disappointed, Dalton let his eyes drop. *What could she have done? Nothing.*

"Give her a little bit to leave, and we can get back to business," Bullet continued, his voice barely audible across the expanse. He began to walk back down into the living area.

"Help!" a voice squealed loudly. Dalton's attention darted toward his daughter. It had come from Mara. He shook his head vigorously.

"Shut the hell up!" Skull-face warned her as Freddie's knife dug into her skin, summoning a thin trace of red from her neck. She closed her lips, fear and pain overwhelming the need to get away.

Bullet froze in place about five paces from Dalton, another eight to the entrance door in the opposite direction. Skull-face waved his knife in front of Mara's face angrily and then brought his index finger up against her lips. "Shhh."

CHAPTER 13

She jammed to a stop at the bottom stair, cocked her head to the side and listened. Tamieka had heard something. A scream. She swore it was a scream from inside the house.

Between her and the dented golden Camry she had driven the past ten years, the frigid October air was dark. The expansive mani-cured lawn nearly disappeared into the blackness of night as did the weaving driveway about sixty yards out behind a setting of trees. Be-hind her, bordered by white stone columns in varying shades of slate, brown and red rock, the entrance door sat ominously in place. A set of black wrought iron chairs were to either side, accompanied by matching tables. The dual fans that normally circulated the air on hot summer nights sat dormant overhead. An old lantern was perched on a small wrought iron table just by the door, a gentle flame flickering to and fro inside with no apparent rhythm. Amorphous shadows flashed over the house and porch.

Tamieka turned and faced the house. Her ears were piqued, lis-tening. She stepped cautiously back up the stairs and planted her feet on the edge of the porch. There was nothing, no noise. Just quiet ex-cept for the usual chirping of crickets out amongst the grass and bor-dering forest.

Despite the quiet, Tamieka couldn't shake the feeling that some-thing was off, that something was not right. She pulled her jacket clos-er to her chest and inched closer to the entrance door. Her eyes darted across the porch and then back to singular glass door.

"Lenore?" She raised her voice just above a subtle whisper. Her mind told her to be silent, don't speak, just walk away. At the same time it told her to investigate, find the source of that noise, the scream. With caution she let the need to know take her feet closer. "Are you there, Lenore?"

She stepped a foot closer, waited. More of the same. Crickets, the shuffle of her own feet on the roughly-textured concrete. She pursed her lips and shifted to try a peek through the windows. Stepping lightly the last few feet, Tamieka reached the window by the entrance door to the right and searched for a breach in the concealing curtains on the other side of the glass.

There was light on inside the house, that much was clear the moment the house had come into view from the driveway. That was about all she could tell even squinting inches away from the glass. The thick curtains were impossible to see through. Softly she moved past the door to the window on the opposite side. More of the same.

She sighed, biting her lip gently. Her mind told her to leave again, to get off the porch and get the hell out of there. Her heart was worried, though. And winning.

A subtle commotion inside suddenly grabbed Tamieka's attention. She stood upright, stiff. Her eyes darted to the entrance. Fighting the cold chill in her spine, she spoke again.

"Lenore?" she called. Silence occupied the space again. Tamieka looked down, trying to make a decision. Stay or leave? Stay or leave? She shook her head and opened her mouth again. "Lenore, if you're okay, please say something."

She paused, waited. More silence. A full minute passed. "Lenore? Mara?"

* * *

His index finger held erect to the opening in his white mask, Bullet faced the women, expecting Dalton to know better than to speak up. The sharp edge of Freddie's blade still rested precariously against Mara's neck and Skull-face kept the point of his curved blade within striking distance of Lenore.

Dalton sat submissively. But inside he raged, his mind a flurry of anger. He watched as the unexpected rocked their captor's plans. Even in that moment, though, he found himself helpless, anesthetized to any reliable course of action.

Just leave, Tamieka! Dalton begged.

"Man, we can't have the police coming out here," Skull-face complained in hushed syllables. His confidence had dwindled, a fear of his own taking root.

"I know." Bullet jumped back but kept his voice to a subtle whisper.

The woman's shadow flickered on the frosted entrance door. Bullet redirected his attention to that shadow. Dalton watched him, the intensity of thought behind the holes in his mask, the black and white orbs working overtime. Abruptly the boy looked back to Lenore and then back to the door and grunted.

"Guys," Bullet began in a whisper. "I'm going to answer the door."

"What?" Freddie almost forgot to whisper, bringing his tone down quickly. "Are you crazy?"

"Huh?" Skull-face cocked his head sideways. Dalton wished he could see the expression behind the red skull plastered on his mask. He wished he could see the fear.

"I'm going to tell her I'm Aiden, that Mom's busy," he said, feigning air quotes at the word *mom*. "Tell her to come back tomorrow."

"Are you sure?" Freddie asked. "I don't know, it seems like a bad idea to me."

"She's one woman," Bullet responded. "I can deal with one woman, more than a shit load of cops."

Both Skull-face and Freddie nodded as if their approval was somehow needed. Dalton knew better. This boy would do whatever he wanted, no one was getting in the way of that.

"All right, here we go," Bullet whispered before raising his voice to a slight yell and stepping off toward the foyer landing. "I'm coming."

The form on the other side of the door remained still, only the shadow moved ghostly along the window. Dalton scooted in his seat to watch the boy go to the door. He bounded up the single step to the foyer platform and reached the door in a few long steps. He hid the long curved blade behind his back in his right hand.

"Who is it?" he called, leaning up against the door frame, looking back at his audience. He was playing a part now. Dalton thought he could see one of the boy's signature grin escaping from the thin mouth slit.

"Tamieka Dula. Who am I speaking to?" she asked, an edge of doubt seeping through door frame.

"Aiden, Lenore's son," Bullet lied.

After a long pause, probably sizing up the response she received, Tamieka spoke, "Are you going to let me in?"

"No, I don't know who you are," Bullet said.

"Tamieka Dula," she repeated. "I'm your mom's hairdresser. She told me to come by tonight to pick up one of her books."

Bullet craned his neck around and looked at Lenore with a smile and a fake congratulatory nod.

"Can you come back tomorrow?" Bullet started, trying to build an excuse to keep the woman away. "Le—, Mom's in bed already. Rough night."

He shook his head. Dalton grimaced at the misstep. Bullet waited for the woman's reply on the other side of the glass.

"I thought I heard someone say help," Tamieka said after a pause. Her voice came through the wall with a careful, wary air. "Is everything okay in there?"

"Everything is fine," Bullet said.

"I'd really feel better about it if you'd just let me in so I can be sure," Tamieka tried.

Bullet bit his lip, contemplating whether or not to open the door. He looked back to his confidants. Both were shaking their heads adamantly in obvious opposition, screaming at him to not let the woman in. He looked back to the silhouette and sighed. With his free hand, he reached for the doorknob. He stepped behind the door itself and brought the knife out from hiding behind his back.

No! Dalton screamed inside, but he could not form the simple words on his lips before it happened.

The door wrenched open with blinding speed and Bullet swung forward. He brought the curved blade around, pulled by his body's momentum. The silvery metal disappeared with a disconcerting squishing sound as it gored its victim. Tamieka gasped. Her eyes blinked spasmodically, her breath becoming short gasps.

"No!" Lenore screamed, daring to move before Skull-face's blade reminded her of her place. Mara remained still, shock convulsing through her body.

Bullet wrenched the knife side-to-side, mutilating whatever organs were in the blade's path. Tamieka screamed and groaned as new pain surged through her body. Blood began to spurt between her lips and dribble down her chin.

"Stop!" Dalton yelled. Begged. Pleaded.

His eyes met Tamieka's as she began to slip away. He wanted to say something, anything to absolve himself of the viscous act, but there was nothing he could say, nothing of value.

Bullet yanked the knife back and took a step backward. The woman dropped to her knees. Her body jerked with each labored breath, blood pouring down her grey Duke t-shirt behind a thin cloth jacket. The look on her face transformed from fear and pain to a blank stare. Dalton watched, mouth hung wide, as Tamieka abdicated her place on this Earth with a loud thud on the tile floor.

Why? Dalton wanted to ask so badly, but he had learned the question was unwise.

"Well, that's unfortunate," Bullet commented apathetically, a hint of contradiction in his tone. His attention drifted sluggishly back to his captives. He grinned and crouched down by the corpse. He reached down with two thin fingers and slid them through the growing puddle of crimson around Tamieka's body.

He stood erect again and made his way back down by Skull-face. Looking at Lenore, he snickered. It almost sounded like the boy was excited.

"How does it feel to know you brought her to such an unfortunate end?" Bullet chided her.

Tears streaming down Lenore's face, her eyes were glued to Tamieka's inanimate body. She refused to look at the mask as she began to cry again. Her body shook with each sob.

Bullet passed his knife to Skull-face and bore his eyes into Lenore. His eyes narrowed and then he wrapped his clean palm around her chin.

"Look at me!" he demanded. Lenore's eyes met Bullet's. A terror brimmed up behind them. Satisfied, he took his right hand and smeared a swath of Tamieka's blood down her cheek. "Good job."

He released her and stepped around Skull-face, nearly straddling the arm of the couch as he leaned over Mara. Just as he had done to Lenore, he wrenched Mara's face toward him with a firm grip under her chin. His hand gripped just an inch above the knife Freddie held to her neck.

"You know, really it's your fault she died, though," Bullet began.

"No, stop!" Dalton begged him, trying to spare his daughter. "It's my fault."

"No, really, Dalton, it *is* her fault," Bullet said matter-of-factly before fixing his eyes back on Mara. "It's *all* your fault. If you hadn't screamed, she might have left. But no, you had to be a little bitch and call for help. You practically begged me to cut her open. To gut her."

He let go of her chin and stepped away, turning to face away from them for a moment. "Not that I mind, though."

CHAPTER 14

"Jo—," Bullet started before abruptly silencing himself. Freddie's attention shot to Bullet. His hand still held the blade steadily at Mara's neck. He cocked his head as if to say, *Be careful, man!*

Joe, or Joseph, Dalton thought. The horror on his face made it easy to conceal his thoughts. The boy had slipped up. He had said Freddie's name, or at least part of it. That much was evident from the immediate reaction from the boy with the Freddie Krueger mask on.

"Get the body and move it over by Nathan," Bullet finished, nodding in the new corpse's general direction. A large pool of blood surrounded the body. It veined along the symmetrical lines of the foyer tile and dripped off the landing's edge, splashing onto more tile.

Freddie, or *Joe,* let his knife break contact with Mara's skin and slid the short blade between his belt and the waist of his pants. He huffed, and then walked to the body and took hold of Tamieka's feet. He hauled her backwards, dragging the body away from the door. Blood marred the path in a wide swath of crimson. The lifeless skull cracked against the tile floor as it dropped from the foyer landing to the main floor. Dalton looked away and grimaced. Freddie did not stop, he continued to pull the body across the living room until it laid precariously beside Nathan's lifeless body. Satisfied, he left the bodies to themselves and took up his place behind Mara again. He produced the blade again and pressed it against the red mark along Mara's neck.

"Where were we?" Bullet's voice had regained the authority and calm that had dominated the room since its arrival a few hours ago. "Ah, yes. Your incessant question. Why? Why *us*?"

Dalton moved uneasily in the recliner. He longed for an answer. Why them? What had drove these psychos, these kids, to his doorstep? Why were they so bent on hurting his family in front of *him*?

"I've been...we've been watching you and your family for a least a year now. Studied your habits, your schedule." Bullet paused for a moment, looking at Lenore and then back to Dalton. "Your love interests. It's how we knew about Jenna. How we know that Lenore is an author who stays at home most of the day, and when she does go out it's either alone or with Mara or Aiden. He's at a party tonight, right?"

Dalton did not answer, neither did Lenore. If his heart could drop anymore, it would have. Instead he stared back at the boy, trying to find some recollection of those black eyes in his memory. If they had really scouted out his family for so long, surely he had seen the boy at some point. Nothing. The boy's eyes were unusual, dark abysses like the pits of hell the boy would one day surely occupy. Dalton thought for sure he would remember them. But he could not recall. There was nothing of use in the recesses of his memory, at least nothing that came to mind.

"But why? Why did you choose us? What have we done to...to deserve *this*?" Dalton begged quietly, refusing to answer Bullet's question.

Bullet grinned. It confounded Dalton. It was an almost kind grin, like he was happy to answer the question. Then he pursed his lips and huffed, "Let's just say we didn't randomly select your family."

There was a pause. A long silence. "You did."

Mara and Lenore shot their heads toward Dalton. He curled back in the recliner, eyes wide, brow crinkled in confusion. *What? How?*

"What do you mean, I did?" Dalton asked, suddenly more aggressive, but still aware of the fear in his bowels.

The boy thought about the question for a moment. He raised his free hand and pointed up with his index finger. He started to speak but stopped. Bullet sighed, then looked away from the Dalton and everyone else in the room as if searching among the red speckled tiles for an answer.

"That will have to wait," Bullet finally decided. "Before that, I have something else in store for your wife. I'd prefer to do it to you, but I think you'll appreciate it more if she gets to experience it herself."

"What? No! What are you going to do?" Dalton asked. Fear shot into Lenore's still bloodshot eyes.

"Be patient, my *friend*," Bullet answered him.

Friend, Dalton thought. Anger sprouted to his hands. He balled his fists tightly but caught himself. He expanded his fingers and sighed. *How can he even say that?*

The boy turned and retrieved one of the small trick-or-treat bags they had brought along. He reached inside and rummaged around, searching for something. Moments later, a grin stretched across his lips behind the thin slit in the white mask. Slowly he retracted his hand and revealed a small curved piece of metal. There was an almost invisible strand of what appeared to be fishing string attached to one end and a sharp point at the other. *A needle.*

"I'm going to shut the bitch up permanently for you, Dalton," Bullet growled. His gravelly tone seemed more menacing. "You won't have to hear her complain anymore."

As Bullet moved toward Lenore, he dropped the trick-or-treat bag to the floor. Dalton jumped to his feet. The knives against Mara and Lenore's necks tightened. Dalton almost failed to stop, but he steeled his feet. It was all he could do to stop. He *needed* to stop them, he *needed* to intervene. But he couldn't, not without putting them in more danger. *Or should I?*

He battled his own mind. How much longer could he sit still

while they hurt the two most important women in his life, even though he had not realized that until a few hours ago? How would he know when to act? Could he deal with the consequences?

"Don't, Dalton. Just sit back and watch," Bullet directed. "You so much as make me feel uncomfortable and I won't hesitate to have my friend here slit Mara's throat while I stab your wife straight through the chest."

Dalton felt the blood run from his face. He looked to Mara and saw the fear in her eyes, the dark tear-stained circles under them. His baby was scared to death. Still on his feet, he moved his gaze to Lenore and saw the same fear. He longed to do something, to prevent any more pain, any more suffering, but what could he do? He could not just sit by and watch. He couldn't. But if he made one false move, one of them would pay for his mistake. Completely.

As he stared into Lenore's saddened but beautiful green eyes, she shook her head, silently pleading with him to sit down. His mind raced. She was pleading not for her own life, but Mara's, her daughter's. If he sat down, if he just let it happen, he could only faintly imagine the pain Lenore would be forced to endure. If he refused to sit or moved into action and attacked, at least one of them would die, maybe both.

Maybe he could intervene. Act quick and put himself between them and these psychotic monsters. Maybe he could gain control of one of the knives, or maybe even the pistol stashed at Bullet's back. But the best he could do was fight off one monster at a time. The other two would be free to attack, to kill. Lenore was right, it was logical to sit back down. It didn't seem logical to let Lenore suffer, but what was logical about tonight?

Finally, he sat. A tear of shame streamed down his face as he locked eyes with Lenore. "I love you. I'm so sorry."

"I…it's okay," Lenore stuttered as she tried to steel herself to the coming pain.

"All right, enough of that shit. Let's get to the real fun." Bullet stepped around the couch and took up Skull-face's place behind Lenore. The skinny boy moved to the arm of the couch beside her. Carelessly, Skull-face grasped Lenore's chin with his left hand and wrenched her head back before placing his right hand on her forehead. He forced her to look up into the ceiling. Then Bullet hovered over her and grinned behind his mask.

"Screw you," Lenore muttered.

With an ever widening grin, Bullet lowered the needle into position at the edge of her lower lip and laughed lightly at her comment with a raised brow. "So kinky, Mrs. Summers, your husband's watching. But...that could be arranged."

Before the words could sink in, before Dalton could react, Bullet thrust the needle into her skin.

Lenore screamed. Her body shook violently despite Skull-face's grip around her jaw and chest. Dalton quaked at both the sight and sound of his wife. The sight of the needle disappearing behind her lip, the ear piercing wail.

Dalton dared a look at Mara who was bawling at her mom's side. *She's doing this for Mara. She's doing this for Mara.* He repeated the words over and over in his head, trying to rationalize the scene in front of him, yet there was no sense in any of it.

The glinting of stars against the black night sky disappeared under a headlight lit canopy of sparsely populated branches. An older rock anthem vibrated the car as Aiden guided it on the path home.

I finally did it. I finally talked to her, Aiden thought.

"I actually kissed her," he said aloud. An involuntary smile spread from cheek to cheek and he bit his lip gingerly as he replayed the memory. Her soft strawberry lips. The moment they touched. That brief pause and rush down his spine.

He sighed, releasing a pent up breath.

Usually he would sing away as he drove down the road. He'd belt out the verses and chorus like no one could see him in his glass cathedral. Tonight was different, though. His mind would not allow him to concentrate on the lyrics playing through the speakers. Instead, his thoughts were consumed by the flavor and shape of Faith's lips and the feeling that had surged through his body.

He wondered if she had really wanted him to talk to her before tonight. Why had she not said something? It didn't matter. He had finally made the move and things were beginning to kick off. He imagined taking her out on a date at some restaurant. Sitting across from her, lost at sea in her emerald green eyes. Refusing the desire to let his leg wander over to hers under the table. Then his thoughts shifted to the movie theater, watching some movie, any movie. Her hand cupped within his. His arm eventually draped around her neck once he finally mustered the courage to make the movie move.

He simply could not erase the grin on his face.

As his thoughts flew, the music suddenly ceased on the speakers. An automated female voice replaced the music to announce an incoming text message from none other than the girl on his mind, Faith Moreno. He had thought he could not grin any larger. He was wrong.

Aiden accepted the message and the same voice transcribed the text in surprising clarity.

"Hey Aiden! I had a great night. See you soon," came Faith's words in a cool synthetic voice. The message ended and the music resumed.

The canopy of trees lightened as Aiden turned onto Rankin Road and accelerated forward. He glanced back up at the night sky. It seemed like each one of the countless shining dots shone for him tonight, their beauty rivaled only by the one and only Faith Moreno.

Up ahead, the driveway came into view. The stone columns stood erect and resolute on either edge of the entrance and trees lined the hard top. As he made the turn and continued down the cement drive, excitement took over again. He could not wait to tell his mom and dad of tonight's adventures, of Faith. Maybe not the kiss, though, not yet. He'd tell Dad soon. It killed him that he'd likely have to wait till morning, though, unless on the off chance one of them was still up at this late hour. He checked the digital clock on his radio. *11:37 PM.*

Around the bend in the drive, the house came into view. Immediately Aiden noted that the lights in the living room were on. A gentle golden hue painted the front windows. The Halloween lantern was still lit by the front door. His spirits lifted, but he still crinkled his brow.

That's odd, seems a little late for them to still be up.

Then he caught sight of two unfamiliar vehicles parked in the driveway. They almost blocked his usual spot next to Mara's car. There was an older Camry and something he did not recognize. He squinted, but it did little to dissuade the grin on his lips. That was likely to be a permanent side effect, he thought.

Maybe they had friends over for a party of their own. Aiden laughed at the thought.

CHAPTER 15

"Hold still and it'll hurt less," Bullet argued with Lenore as she jerked and writhed beneath Skull-face's firm grip. She had made such a ruckus that Skull-face had fully mounted her body. He pressed his weight down onto her while Bullet prepared to make the next loop around her lips.

"Stop! I'm begging you, please stop!" Dalton yelled. His insides churned as the unsanitary needle pierced into his wife's lip again. The soft gentle skin around her mouth retracted in toward the thin piece of metal until finally the skin gave way and the needle pierced through reddened flesh. His cries for mercy dwindled to a stuttered whimper. "Please stop!"

Inches away from Lenore's tortured frame sat Mara, her eyes clamped shut, hands clasped tightly between her firmly braced legs. Streams of water trailed from her eyes like the strong supports of a dam had snapped behind those youthful blues. The blade at her neck glistened with those same tears. Right now that blade was all that held Dalton back. He wanted to jump up, to wrap his hands around one of their necks and squeeze and squeeze until their body stopped kicking.

"I think I might sew your mouth shut next after all," Bullet said angrily. "Would you just shut up? It's only going to get worse for her the more you blubber over there."

He pulled the needle from her upper lip and let the strong clear string fish through the tiny piercing in her lip. Dalton tried to look away but he couldn't. His body clenched and writhed as he watched the string glide through her lips and then come to a jarring halt when the ungainly knot at the end met her lower lip at the needle's initial entry point. He quivered, his stomach becoming queasy.

Lenore screamed. She tugged at the new wound with each shriek. Her body jerked and quaked as the pain and realization set in.

"If you'll just sit still," Bullet said again before plunging the needle in her lip and then reeled up and out her upper lip, quicker this time. "See there, I'm getting the hang of it."

"You sick basta —," Dalton groaned angrily before being cut off.

"Shut up," Skull-face yelled shrilly.

"Why?" Dalton began to rail. "Why should I shut up? It doesn't matter what I do, you're still going to do whatever the f—"

The familiar chime sounded through the living room. Everyone froze, and except for Lenore and Mara, their eyes darted upward to the ceiling. Lenore yelped as her head was wrenched to the side by the fish string sewn through her lip when Bullet's attention had shot toward the entrance. They kept staring into the ceiling as if it would produce some answer to the melody's forewarning. They all knew what it meant, though.

"What other piece of worthless human flesh do I have to deal with tonight?" Bullet huffed angrily. He looked at Dalton and posed a question, "Why the *hell* do people show up to your house so late?"

Dalton gave no answer. He sat there praying that whoever it was would just leave, turn around and go away for their own sake. He was not sure he could bear to see another human's blood spilled on his doorstep. And for what? He still had no answer to that burning question. Why had they chosen his family? The question nagged at him again.

A few moments passed with everyone in suspended animation, staring along the ceiling. Then the sound of the approaching car's engine reached them. Its deep throaty rumble increased as it drew closer and then went silent outside. Dalton's eyes widened.

Bullet's gaze shot to the front door and then back to Freddie. He nodded toward Mara and Freddie quickly cupped the palm of his hand firmly over her mouth. His attention cracked back to the entrance, waiting.

No! Dalton's mind screamed. He looked to Lenore and saw the same horror in her tortured eyes. *No, A—*

The garage door creaked open. Bullet shuffled on his feet behind Lenore, her eyes were wide, pleading.

"Y'all having a party or—" Aiden began before he turned the bend and his eyes locked onto the horror of the living room. He froze, a look of absolute terror overtaking his features.

"Run, Aiden! Run!" Dalton screamed with all the might he had left.

Aiden's eyes darted between Dalton, the masked strangers, his distraught sister, his mother. Aiden stood in place like a stone column, unable to move even though his mind begged him to place one foot in front of the other.

"Run, Aiden! Get out of here! Now!" Dalton continued to yell for what felt like minutes while his son stood dumbfounded.

Breaking the stalemate, Skull-face rebounded and jumped to his feet. It was the motivation Aiden needed. His mind and limbs finally synced and he tore back toward the garage. Skull-face turned back toward Bullet who was still locked in place, needle held high above Lenore, staring where Aiden had just stood.

"We've got to stop him!" Skull-face yelled frantically.

Bullet finally jolted out of his trance and shook his head. He nodded desperately. He let the needle drop onto Lenore's chest and reached behind his back, retrieving the pistol.

"Scare him. *Don't* harm him," Bullet ordered sternly, though there was a certain reservation in his tone as he handed Skull-face the pistol.

"Whatever," Skull-face chided as he grabbed the weapon and bolted out the door.

The doorframe, his parents' cars, the exit from the garage, all of it passed by like a blur, like some untouchable nightmare. He just ran, terrified of the scene inside. Had it been real? Aiden's mind began to second guess what he had seen inside. Three masked intruders. His dad yelling at him to run. His sister broken down in tears on the couch with a knife to her throat. His mother's eyes crying for him to run with...with her lips half sewn shut. It had all seared into his memory with such vivid clarity. The disgusting Freddie Krueger mask. The red skull and the eerie white mask with a singular hole in the forehead. Real or a nightmare? *Real.*

The door slammed behind him and the starry sky came into view. As he had feared, the sound of rushing footsteps followed him from inside the house. He kept running. *Just get to the car.*

Aiden veered around the rear of the Camry in the dark before the floodlight flickered on. For a second he was blind. Everything was a searing white, but he didn't stop. He kept moving. He knew where he was going. Finally, shades of black and grey came back into view and the outline of his Camaro appeared, a bit closer than he'd expected it. He altered course, skidded around the other side of the car and dashed for the driver's door. As his hand made contact with the handle, a voice shouted behind him.

"Stop right there, Aiden!" the thin voice railed angrily. It pierced through the darkness, through the cold air and caused his body to shiver. "You get in that car and they all die."

Aiden's hand clasped the handle, keys held in the opposite hand. His mind begged him to just wrench the door open and make a run for it. His heart had other plans. He closed his eyes and huffed, making a small mist across the lamp light cast over him by the floodlight. Without letting go of the door handle, Aiden turned to face the voice. It was the intruder with the red skull on his mask.

"And believe me, we'll do it. Can you imagine it, slicing open your dad's belly, letting him bleed out while his intestines fall out," Skull-face taunted him. "Or maybe Mommy. Just come back with me and they'll be all right. That's all you have to do."

His body quivered. *What type of monsters are they?*

Aiden released his grip on the door handle as he contemplated his options. He stared down the intruder, the boy that had been sent to fetch him, to stop him from leaving. The red mask, some indistinguishable graphic on his black t-shirt and dark blue jeans all shrouded in shadow, out of reach of the blaring glare of the floodlight. He could make a run for it and let his family suffer or stay and maybe, just maybe, keep them from that fate. His mind wrestled with his options even though the answer was clear to him. He fidgeted with the door handle. He wanted so badly to open the car door.

A faint glow reached out to him from inside the Camaro through the tinted glass. He dared not turn his head to look, but he didn't need to. It was his phone. Some notification had apparently woke the screen briefly enough to merit his attention. He had left it in the car in all his excitement. His excitement. Now his horror. Without taking his eyes off the skull mask, he continued to mull his decision over and over again through his mind.

Finally, Aiden let his gloved hand let go of the handle and stepped from behind the car. He stepped out into the glare of the floodlight, out into open territory, his decision made. He started to walk toward Skull-face despite every instinct that told him he should bolt in the opposite direction. His hands shook not only from the cold, but from the fear that was building exponentially under his skin. The cold did not help matters any as it seeped under the thin fabric of his costume.

Skull-face cocked his head as Aiden approached. "Are you serious? You're dressed up like Spiderman?" There was something familiar in that high taunting voice, but his tensed mind could not decipher the connection. "It is Halloween, though, I guess."

Aiden took his steps slow and careful. He moved closer to masked man, trying to ignore the question. He had not changed before coming home because he figured his mom would complain if he didn't let her get one last Halloween costume picture, that was if she had stayed up. That was sure to be the last thing on her mind right now.

A glint of light sparked around the masked boy's shadow as he came more into the floodlight. Aiden saw the gun form in Skull-face's hand and stopped in his tracks. His breathing became more labored and his eyes glued to the black piece of metal.

"Come on now, Aiden, I don't have all night," Skull-face urged.

Who are these people? Aiden wondered. He forced his right foot to move and managed another short step forward. Suddenly he was not as sure about his decision. He had to, he knew he couldn't run, but the thought of a bullet colliding with his chest gave a new reason to take a step backward. He willed his left foot to move and then the other, finally moving again, his eyes moving back to the red skull.

Then he made his move. Without a second thought, he veered to his left and sprinted behind the garage. He had committed. He ran.

"Stop!" Skull-face screamed after him, waving the gun frantically after his fleeing target.

Aiden tensed his body as he ran, waiting for his skin to split open where the bullet would smash into him. Waiting for it to exit out his chest in a spray of red and meaty chunks. The impact never came, but he couldn't loosen his body as he ran.

The patting of rushing footsteps chased after him. He hoped the darkness around this edge of the house would make it more difficult for Skull-face, throw him off and provide him with more time. As Aiden's eyes adjusted, the blackness gave way to a border of trees. A combination of red maples, prickly hollies and sycamores. The trees gave way to the calm ripples of the lake and the family boat dock a good twenty yards away from the rear face of the house.

"Aiden!" the boy, yes, the boy, Aiden was sure, yelled after him.

Refusing to stop, Aiden made the bend around the northwestern corner of the house. He immediately stole away under the upper deck which served up a grand view of the lake on a nice summer evening. He reached out for the door leading into the small shed under the house. Aiden wrenched the door open and quietly rushed in. He yanked the door back into its frame without a sound.

Inside, he took up a spot in the corner next to a green-shafted weed eater. A push mower and a set of empty round paint drums sat to his right. A series of shelves lined the opposite wall occupied by a slew of varied items. A clear Tupperware box of Christmas lights, garland and what Aiden was nearly positive was the family Christmas tree. An old cardboard box with some knick-knacks from his Paw Jensen, his mom's dad who he saw maybe twice a year at best. A bright red toolbox, the same one he had rummaged through on numerous occasions.

The sound of footsteps increased in volume, Aiden's eyes shot to the shed door. The lock. He rushed forward and twisted the small protrusion on the door, earning a faint *click*. It sounded like thunder to him. He shrunk back into the corner. The footsteps grew closer.

"Aiden." The voice was muffled through the door. It was nearby, maybe a few feet from the door, hovering somewhere under the deck checking in the shadows. Aiden imagined the pistol waving in a horizontal arch searching him out. Involuntarily, he shook.

Suddenly, the door handle shook. Aiden froze and held his breath. The brushed silver knob jiggled, "Aiden? You in there?"

The knob shook again, but Skull-face did not call out again, instead he listened. Aiden held his breath, his eyes locked on the small lock in the center of knob. Finally, the sound of footsteps started up again, moving away from the door.

The boy yelled his name a few more times, each time the sound becoming quieter as Skull-face continued his search, moving further away. Aiden finally let go of the breath he was holding. He looked down at his shaking hands. He gripped them together, trying to stop them, trying to calm his nerves.

As the voice faded away, Aiden looked around the room for a weapon. He knew what he had to do now. First he needed a weapon, though. He needed something that could give him a chance on his way back up to his car. He surveyed the small tack board. His eyes settled on a long screwdriver. He reached up and pulled it from its peg. He looked at it carefully, imagined poking at the skull-faced boy with it. He grimaced. Then his eyes caught sight of on old pickaxe. He crinkled his brow in disgust, but found himself laying the screwdriver down onto the clean workbench.

The axe was an old tool, one of the ones handed down from his grandpa. Cautiously, like somehow it might jump up and grab him, he reached down and lifted it by the long wooden handle. He felt the small imperfections in the wood, the roughness in its texture. He gripped tighter and raised the metal end up to his eyes, measuring up his new tool, his weapon. He slid his keys between the costume bottoms and his bare skin and then he gulped and bit at his lip nervously. He took one last glance at the axe before letting its business end arch down and hang lightly at his side.

* * *

The boom of the door slamming against its frame sent an unexpected shudder through Dalton. He had lured himself into the false belief that the night could not get any worse, that it wouldn't be long before this nightmare was over. Now, as Skull-face made pursuit of his Aiden, he saw how frail a hope it truly was.

Was it possible that there was no bottom to how badly events could turn? Was the spiral down infinite, unknown? Maybe death was the lighter option. Nothingness. An ending.

No, Dalton! Stop acting like that, he chided himself

For the first time since their hell bound trio had graced his home's doors, Bullet's demeanor had changed substantially. His body swayed back and forth in quick short pumps. It looked like a nervous movement, erratic, involuntary. The boy held his hand up by his face. Dalton glimpsed his fingers fidgeting around and under that horrid white mask.

Something has him worried, Dalton thought, bewildered by the sudden exhibition of nervousness in the boy.

The knife was down by Bullet's left thigh. It seemed that the boy's mind and hand were disconnected as it hung limply, barely gripping the blade's handle. To his right, Freddie had relinquished his position behind Mara. Instead, he stood a foot away from Bullet, whispering quietly to him.

On the couch, Lenore and Mara sat covered in tears. Their combined visage mirrored their vexed bodies. They shivered not from the cold night air outside, but the shock of mental anguish. Lenore attempted to open her mouth but recanted quickly as the three stitches drew tight around her lips. She quivered and drove her mouth shut, closing her eyes, sobbing.

Heat gathered in Dalton's head as his fists clenched and unclenched, then came to a close as solid balls of flesh and bone. Their captors were off balance, and something had their leader spooked.

Dalton knew that now was the time to act, if there ever would be a
time.

He jumped from the recliner and closed the five feet between him
and the two boys before either had time to react. He arched both arms
out wide and wrapped an arm around each as he came at them hard.
They fell to the ground as one mass with a loud crack of tile.

There was a moan, a slow noise to his left, Bullet, and then
movement to his right. Before Dalton could react to the incoming vision, a gloved fist found purchase under his jaw. He grunted in pain,
but was still able to get to his hands and knees. Dalton jerked back as
another fist attempted to lay a bruise along his cheek, barely missing.
He took the opportunity and brought his own clenched fist up under
Freddie and dug into his gut. He earned a deep grunt followed by a
spattering of saliva. A flash of light glinted off a blade as one of the
boys resumed their attack. Barely thinking, Dalton grappled for the
wrist behind the small hunting knife and gripped on tight. Freddie
pulled and yanked, trying to get free from Dalton's firm grip.

Freddie punched out with his free arm but Dalton caught him by
the wrist and pushed both arms up into the air, applying all the pressure he could to the wrist just beyond the shining blade. Dalton
pushed hard, grunting. To his left, Bullet was getting his bearings. Dalton squeezed Freddie's hands and finally the boy's hand gave way
and the knife toppled to the ground. It clanked to the tile and skittered
a few feet away. Dalton shoved backward, realizing that he could
overpower the boy.

As he forced Freddie backward, his back flared like fire. His chest
jutted painfully forward as a fist had buried itself into the most vulnerable part of Dalton's lower back. He stumbled and then suddenly his
feet were swooped out from under him. He fell to the ground, cracking his ear and forehead against the cold tile.

Everything went fuzzy, spinning in circles. Someone was talking, about what he couldn't quite make out, it sounded like gibberish a hundred miles away. He stared out, squinting and stretching his eyelids open. As his vision cleared, his eyes settled on the corpses that occupied the corner of the room. Tamieka's glassy cold eyes stared back at him. He shivered and jerked back.

Before Dalton could get his hands underneath himself, a hand gripped under his armpit and wrenched him up with a strength that Freddie did not possess. His body was yanked around to face Bullet. The boy's empty eyes were only inches from Dalton's own terrified eyes.

"I thought I had made it plenty clear that you were to cooperate," the boy stated slowly, his raspy tone chopping up the words to drive the point home. The boy's warm breath was dank and soggy against Dalton's lips and nose. The words were cold and angry, they sent a chill up Dalton's spine. Then the chill of metal against his throat grabbed his attention. Bullet's blade.

Dalton swallowed though he had no spit to drown.

"Now you're going to sit down like a good little boy, aren't you?"

Dalton only nodded without even thinking about what he was doing. Fear had him on autopilot, making the decisions for him. Guided by Bullet's firm grip under his armpit, Dalton walked a semi-circle around the boy, his face never moving more than an inch from the white mask. Abruptly Dalton found himself thrust back. He landed hard on the recliner, its cushy leather felt bare and firm as his body slammed against the cushion. It rocked to and fro, but Dalton did not dare move.

Breathing heavily, Dalton ripped his gaze from the masked boy, still surprised by the strength that had wrenched him off the ground. His eyes settled on his wife and then his daughter, not knowing what to say, not knowing what to do.

"Now I'm pissed." The voice behind the white mask was angry, livid. "You just keep screwing up my evening! *My* evening!"

Confused and scared, Dalton watched the boy pace briskly by him and around the couch before stopping behind Lenore. His hands moved quickly. He gripped his fingers under Lenore's chin and wrenched her head backward. In the same instant, his blood-stained blade appeared over the crook in her neck. There was a bloodlust in those dark eyes. His lips pursed and writhed between the small slit, his breathing becoming heavy and labored.

"No—" Dalton yelled.

"Shut the fuck up!" the boy bellowed. The knife shimmied. Dalton was shaking. Bullet was shaking too, not in fear, but in rage. Dalton's eyes widened.

"Now, Dalton, tell your darling little wife that you *love so much* that it's going to be okay," Bullet instructed in a deliberate and menacing tone. "Tell her that everything is *going* to be fine."

"What?" Dalton asked, though somehow he knew what it meant. He could not bring himself to acknowledge it. Not now, not after all they had been through and survived. Not after how much he realized he had missed her, mistreated her. *No.*

"*Tell* her it's all going to be okay," he repeated.

"I…uh…" The words would not come to him.

"I *said* tell her it will be okay," he screamed madly. The knife jerked back and forth. Lenore yelped as the blade made a paper thin cut across her neck. "Oh, now look what you made me do, Dalton."

"No…."

"*Tell her!*" Bullet screamed. It split through the room. Dalton squinted at the sheer volume and the suddenness of it.

Dalton's body shook. A tear carved a path down his cheek as he locked eyes with his wife. With only a look, he conveyed to her all the sorrow and shame he felt before he finally opened his lips.

"It's…it's going to be okay, honey," he nearly wept. He sniffled, trying to stay strong, if only for her.

A saddened grin broke onto Lenore's lips for the faintest of seconds, restrained by the cruel bands of fishing string. Beside her Mara whimpered, confused and scared, rocking back and forth.

"See, that wasn't so hard," the boy's voice was calm again, almost kind. He lifted the blade from Lenore's neck and pursed his lips, blowing a small rush of air through the small opening in his mask. He looked down at the back of Lenore's head and massaged her shoulder with his free hand. "Not hard at all."

Dalton let a relieved sigh escape his lips.

Without warning, Bullet raised the bloody blade in the air and then plummeted down with all his might. The curved silver sunk between Lenore's breasts. Her body caved backwards as the cold metal pierced through her organs. She gasped, mouth open wide, eyes shocked, gleaming a brilliant horrified green.

"*No!*" Dalton yelled. The single word seemed to stretch on for minutes as his eyes reached out to his wife. She stared back in pain and agony. Mara screamed. He went to move, but Freddie quickly reminded him of the knife under Mara's neck. "No…"

Bullet wrenched the blade from side-to-side, earning grunts and screams from Lenore. Dalton let his eyes well up as he begged, "Please! Stop! Please, just stop! You're a monster!"

"A monster?" Bullet chided him. "It's your fault, Dalton, don't blame me."

Then he tugged on the knife and pulled it from Lenore's flesh, out of its sheath of meat and bone. He smiled at Dalton as the blood dripped freely down onto Lenore's cheek and clothes. Then he leaned down and kissed her on the cheek. He stood up erect again, never losing the wicked grin that tore at Dalton's soul.

As Lenore's breathing became fitful, Bullet raised the knife above his head ceremoniously and sighed. Dalton squinted his eyes between sobs. Then he brought the blade down again. It hacked into her chest, buried deep. Then it was torn back out, blood and meat trailing the blade. Dalton could not look away. The boy brought the blade down a third time, and then a fourth. Over and over and over again. Blood flung across the room, splattering onto Dalton's shirt and his hand.

Dalton never broke eye contact, staring into those scared green eyes. He cried to her one last time, "I'm sorry. I love you *so* much."

Then her eyes went cold and glassy, and she slumped over. Dalton shuddered at the sight of his wife's limp body, a bloody cavity where once a baby bump had been. Helpless, damn helpless.

The air was stale in the small work closet. The smell had always afflicted Aiden's senses but he ignored the scent of old tools and leaned an ear against the door. Outside, on the other side of the door, every few seconds he heard his name called in a quiet but high tone. The boy in the skull mask. The calls had moved further away from him, becoming faint echoes.

The pickaxe rested at his side. He held on to the tool with a determined grip, squeezing and relaxing his palm around the wooden handle. The thought of using the axe in his own defense had yet to enter his mind, but its simple presence gave Aiden courage.

He recounted his plan in his head again. *Get to the car. Get the phone. Call 911. Simple. Right?* He rolled his eyes.

Why did you have to forget it in the car, dipshit?! Aiden chided himself. *This would be so much easier if you hadn't.*

The skull-faced boy's calls for him had faded. Aiden waited a moment longer, pressing his ear against the door, listening. Nothing. No footsteps, no calls or cackles. With his free hand, Aiden reached for the lock. He twisted the small device on the knob and carefully cracked it open. Peeking through the small opening, he saw nothing but trees to his left and the lake to his right. The sound of crickets and cicadas met in the opening along with frigid air. The immediate area seemed to be clear, but the forest beyond the trees was a mess of pure black.

Aiden took a deep breath and raised the sharp end of the pickaxe level with his eyes. He held it firmly in both hands. Cautiously, he stepped out of the closet, leaving behind the safety of his locked hide-away. To his right, the back yard stretched out until it ended by the lake. The family pontoon rocked gently next to the dock, its Charlotte green cloth roof appeared a drab grey as did the cylinders that kept it afloat. The stars overhead were beginning to disappear behind wispy gray clouds. He could see thicker more ominous puffs of gray and black moving in behind them. Still no sign of his tracker.

Axe still raised, he stepped lightly through the grass at a quick walk. His eyes jerked back and forth at every shadow that jumped near or far. He made the bend around the house, cautious to check the corner before proceeding. There was nothing but empty space between him and the woods. He kept moving up the hill by the house. His heart pounded with such ferocity that it felt as though it might burst through his chest, ending him before even his skull-faced foe would have a chance.

Crack.

Aiden froze and then backed up against the stone wall of the house, trying to conceal himself in the slight overhanging shadow. He squinted, peering out into the woods for the source of the noise. Beyond the rustling of a few leaves in the gentle breeze, the woods were quiet. He felt like they were laughing back at him, at his predicament. He saw nothing. No more movement, and no more noises.

Determined that he imagined the noise, or that it had been some forest critter, Aiden turned. Immediately he wished he'd paid more attention to the totality of his surroundings instead of staring out into the woods.

A crack of pain shot up his nose as a fist collided with his face. Aiden stumbled back and lost his grip on the only thing that stood between him and getting away. The pickaxe dropped to the ground with little more than a quiet thud on the compacted dirt. Realizing his mistake, Aiden jerked around to retrieve the weapon.

"Don't even think about it," Skull-face commanded. The pistol in his hand gave him an authority that his voice would not ordinarily command.

Aiden froze in place, eyes glued to his salvation. Just within reach, but a bullet was faster, far faster.

"All right now, you're going to cooperate now or I swear I'll blow your fucking brains out right here. They'll just hear a boom and it'll all be over. *All over.*"

Aiden nodded and redirected his eyes to follow Skull-face after he let out the breath he had been holding in.

"Now, you're going to lead the way back up to the house and we're going to go in through the front door, all right?" Skull-face explained. Aiden nodded.

Walking the precarious yards past the skull-faced boy felt like walking on hot embers, but Aiden forced himself to keep moving. He kept his eyes straight ahead, refusing to look back at the menacing mask and continued up the grassy hill. As he made the turn around the front of the house by the garage, the boy poked the barrel of the pistol into his lower back.

"Hey, change of plans. Give me your keys."

Aiden turned and looked at him quizzically.

"It wasn't a request. *Give* me your keys."

Aiden withdrew his keys and was about to toss them to Skull-face before the boy threw his hands up.

"No, no! We're not playing that." Skull-face laid his left hand out flat, palm up, in front of Aiden. "Just lay them in my hand."

Restraining his frustration, Aiden placed the keys in the boy's outspread hand and immediately stepped back as if he were afraid that the black plague of old might seep out of those God-forsaken palms and carry him away. He pursed his lips angrily.

Skull-face grinned. With the pistol never losing sight of Aiden, the boy walked around the passenger side of Aiden's Camaro like he was ready for a midnight joy ride. Then he looked back to Aiden.

"You all think so much of yourselves in your big house," the disgust in his voice was evident. "Hundred and fifty dollar shoes, condescending looks and expensive cars."

Aiden's brow crinkled at the sudden diatribe. Then a harsh screeching of metal against metal weighed on his ears. Aiden cringed, inwardly fuming, as the key dug into the paint along the passenger door, leaving a long jagged line behind it.

"Okay," Skull-face sighed like a significant weight had lifted from his shoulders. "Now that that's done, we'll get you back inside. Let's go."

Aiden turned and made his way for the front porch. Knowledge of the pistol somewhere behind him motivated him to keep moving. At the entrance, Aiden stopped and looked back to Skull-face. He nodded and Aiden opened the door.

There was movement inside as the door swung slowly inward. For the most part, everyone was as he remembered them minutes ago. Except now the white-masked figure was standing behind his mother, who he couldn't see from his current vantage point. Everyone turned to see him, except her.

"What took you so long?" Bullet's words bit at Aiden's captor. Then Aiden saw the blood all over Bullet. His brow crinkled.

"The little prick hid," Skull-face explained.

A hint of surprise in his movements, Bullet turned slightly, "Why is he bleeding?"

"He tried to stab me with an axe. I punched him in the face," Skull-face said. "Thanks for caring."

Dalton's eyes met Aiden's. They were sad, torn. Aiden frowned in confusion. It was not simple fear in his dad's eyes, there was something more.

"Come on in, Aiden," Bullet invited the boy.

Confused and scared, Aiden stepped slowly over the threshold and then down into the living room. He circled around the couch and froze.

"Mom…"

CHAPTER 16

The frosty air sent a chill up Deputy Ashton Keating's spine as he walked down the broken sidewalk back to his patrol car. Sprigs of dead grass and weeds poked up between the barely illuminated cracked slabs of concrete under his thick legs.

It was the second call he had responded to in the past hour and the second call of the night over an overly zealous Halloween prankster. The elderly occupant of the bland apartment unit, a Peggy Church, had not appreciated the teenage boys' idea of a fun night out at her expense. When Ashton arrived at the complex, he had found the elderly Church keeping the two teens under the small overhang beyond her front door with a short-barreled shotgun.

At first it had worried him, but as he swung open the door of the brown squad car with the Cabarrus County Sheriff's Office logo on the side and slid in, he let himself laugh quietly. Those kids got what they deserved, a good scare for bothering their elder. Hopefully two less troublesome teens for next Halloween.

He called in to let the station know that everything was good and started the car's engine. Overhead the clear sky was beginning to give way in the east to a swath of tall, ominous gray clouds. Cold and wet, it was not the combination that the Deputy desired on the job. As if it being Halloween was not enough already. At least there would be no snow, that would be a few more months out, if they even got any this year.

"Please hold off 'til eight," Deputy Keating pleaded with the clouds. If it was going to rain, he wanted to be home cuddled up against his wife under a heap of thick comforters with the sound of the tiny droplets pinging off the tin roof, not stuck in his squad car with only his jacket and heater to comfort him. He sighed, from the look of the sky he gave himself roughly a five percent chance of getting his way. That was being generous.

He cut the blue lights. The complex descended back into the same shades of greys it had been painted in before he arrived. Then he put the Charger into drive and pulled out onto Bethpage Road. Tonight he was covering the northeastern quarter of the county, Kannapolis and the Concord Mills area. Fortunately most of his calls for the night had come from the rural parts of the county, which was most of it. Keating was guiding the cruiser down the small road when his radio squawked.

"Charlie 270, I've got a well-check in north Kannapolis. Subject is a black female, average height, black hair, stocky build. Name's Tamieka Dula. Her daughter called it in. Said she was heading for the residence of Lenore Summers off Rankin Road a few hours ago and she's been unable to contact her."

Deputy Keating huffed and gripped the walkie attached to his uniform.

"10-4. On my way."

He made a quick U-turn and got back up to speed. *At least it wasn't another stupid kid causing problems.*

CHAPTER 17

The faint glow of moonlight had all but disappeared as dark storm clouds rolled in over the lake. Within the walls of the Summers' home, it felt as though darkness had ruled for far longer.

"Got it," Freddie assured Bullet, dropping the kerosene can against the door trim of the entrance with a hollow metallic ring. "I emptied the entire thing out. All around the porch, up on the walls, everywhere, just like you said."

"Good." Bullet stood with his hands crossed at his waist, blood still dripping from the blade in his right hand and splattered across his shirt and white mask, Lenore's blood. Deep hues of it mottled the pale earthen brown of the floor tiles. A path of crimson from the foyer over to the stack of three bodies etched the path where Tamieka had been drug to her resting place.

On the couch, Aiden sat shoulder-to-shoulder with Mara. He rocked rhythmically, his moistened honey brown eyes locked on his mother's body. Her eyes were blank, her form only a crumpled shell next to two other bodies, Nathan and a black woman he did not recognize. All in a bloody mound. In his home.

Mara hugged him tightly, trying to register the impossible reality before her. It was as much for him as it was for her. Guilt washed over her. She could never take back the mean things she had said, how she had locked her mother out of her room. There were so many choices that she regretted.

Feet away, Dalton leaned forward with his face in his hands. The tears had finally stopped. He felt sure his body was incapable of producing anymore. Bullet, Skull-face and Freddie stood huddled in a circle, Bullet's back to the couch while the other two also kept an eye on their captives. Bullet did not seem happy. He shook his head vigorously, mumbling too quietly for Dalton to make out anything he said.

Finally, Bullet nodded and turned back to face them, followed immediately by his two sheep. He took a step forward, tilting his head to the side and back again as he surveyed his prizes. First Dalton, then Aiden, his lips curled angrily, and then to Mara. He cleared his throat and Dalton knew that something was wrong, something was nagging at the monster. Dalton looked over to his son, confused.

"All right," Bullet opened his mouth. "Before we continue, Aiden, you have to change. It's too distracting having you sit down here dressed like Spiderman. It seems like you're laughing at me. I swear no one is taking me seriously."

Dalton's eyes widened at the statement. *No one is taking you seriously?* A fire burned in his chest. It raged and roiled, begging to break free. How could this boy, this coward behind a mask, think he wasn't being taken seriously?

"You're going to lead my friend here to your room, change into something less distracting and then come back," Bullet explained, nodding at Skull-face. "I don't want any trouble."

The last sentence almost sounded genuine. Dalton's brow wrinkled in confusion as he met his son's worried gaze. Yet, he could find no malice in the boy's voice. How had it suddenly changed? Why?

"Let's go," Skull-face ordered.

Aiden stood up warily. He felt numb to everything around him, his mind stuck on the permanent look on his mother's face the moment Skull-face had escorted him back into the house. Her face was contorted in pain, mouth tugging against the crude threads, screaming even after her body had become nothing more than an empty shell. Blood drenched her stomach and poured over onto the leather cushions. Splatters of the crimson liquid dotted the couch and his sister. It was everywhere.

He took a step forward, then another, willing himself to move even though his mind barely registered the pressure of his feet touching the ground or his arms moving slowly at his sides. He looked straight forward and moved past Skull-face.

"Change and back down," Bullet reminded Skull-face, and then emphasized his last command. "Don't hurt him."

Skull-face nodded and then took up a position behind Aiden. "I've got this, man."

Nodding with lips pursed, Bullet returned his attention to Dalton. "It won't be long now."

The staircase rose steeply into absolute darkness. Aiden mindlessly took the first step, then the second, the next. Behind him Skull-face flicked the light switch. The dark fled from the gentle glow of the hall's recessed lighting and then Skull-face mounted the steps behind Aiden.

He poked the tip of his blade between Aiden's shoulders to remind him not to do anything stupid and then let Aiden put a step between them. Aiden was silent. He just kept moving.

They crested the stairs and moved slowly down the hallway. Aiden felt like he was on autopilot, gliding near weightlessly toward his bedroom door. It seemed so far away, distant and empty. The image of his mother's empty eyes haunted him.

Unsure which door to take, Skull-face remained a few

steps behind, ready.

"Come on, move it," he complained, pressing Aiden to quicken his pace without any evident response. He shook his head and huffed. His eyes drilled into the back of Aiden's head impatiently. Then his gaze drifted south, tracing the contours of Aiden's shoulders beneath the blue and red fabric under the subtle light. His eyes continued steadily downward. The skin-tight Spidey suit left very little to the imagination as the boy walked. Skull-face grinned. He stepped quicker to close the gap between them and reached out, planting his palm fully against Aiden's butt, and squeezed.

Aiden jumped. He snapped back to reality as the unwelcomed hand found purchase, wrenching away from Skull-face. He looked back at the masked boy, fear and confusion in his eyes. What the boy had done had still yet to fully register. His brown eyes looked at the horrid crimson mask. Blood. He grimaced.

"Oh, come on, can you blame me? That costume is *so* tight," Skull-face jeered and then changed course. "Whatever, let's get this over with. Move."

His trance-like state broken, Aiden turned and walked the remaining distance at a brisk pace. Fear poured through his mind now that the shock had dissipated. It was as if the reality of his situation, his family's situation, had just dawned on him. The blood, the knives, the gun, the bodies, the masks. All of it in his house. All so close and ready to snap life out of his grasp at any moment.

I've got to do something. I can't just go back down there without a plan. And what the hell *is wrong with this guy?*

Aiden pushed open the door and stepped in to his bedroom. His mind now unshackled by the bounds of shock, he took to scanning the room. There had to be something he could use as a weapon. Anything. A red cup with the NC State Wolfpack mascot splashed across the front sat on his desk with a slew of pens, he hated pencils, too primitive he would tell his mom. His computer monitor, keyboard, mouse. All useless. The mesh metal trash can that weighed all of a quarter of a pound if he was lucky. A pile of unfolded clean clothes laid on the floor next to his obviously slept in bed. Junk scattered the floor, but nothing sturdier than a small pen or heavier than his computer's CPU, which he doubted he could wield ably.

"All right," Skull-face said before shoving him forward. "Change."

He turned to face his captor and pursed his lips, angry at being pushed around like this, at how helpless he was. He took a quick glance behind Skull-face for anything he could make use of. More of the same.

He let go of any chance of a real weapon, there would be no pickaxe under the bed or in his closet. He turned around and rummaged through the pile of clothes next to his bed, silently trying to find both a set of clothes, and maybe a weapon.

What am I going to do, beat him to death with the trash can? He's got a freaking knife.

Aiden pillaged through the mound of clothes. He took his time and acted as though he could not find what he needed. Skull-face waited behind him. Then out of the corner of his eye, something beautiful came into view. His baseball bat. The same wooden contraption he'd used maybe a handful of times during middle school. His eyes brightened and he had to force back the grin that wanted to shoot across his lips. Despite the discovery, he was still at a disadvantage. The bat was out of reach. It would be too obvious a move to get his hands around

it. A frown burrowed its way back in as he picked up the closest shirt, a plain black tee, and a pair of faded blue jeans. He
threw the clothes onto the bed and then remembered, he needed one more item.

"Come on now, I don't have all night," Skull-face complained.

Aiden reached back into the disheveled pile, searching for
one last item. Finally, he pulled his arms back and placed a
pair of black boxer briefs on top of the shirt and pants.

"Can you at least turn around?" Aiden asked.

"Uh. No."

"Seriously, man?" His request was met with a brick wall.
The masked boy simply stood there, his expression unreadable
behind the red skull. "Come on, man, I'm not...I'm not wearing anything under this."

"And the problem is?" the boy's voice jeered at him.

A chill ran down Aiden's spine at the sounds that had
come from Skull-face. He swallowed. He stared at the mask
for what felt like minutes.

"I don't have all day, Aiden," the boy said. He huffed as if
he was the one being inconvenienced.

Aiden squeezed his eyes shut and took a deep breath. Fear
began to coarse through his veins. Slowly he turned to face
away from the masked figure. He looked down at the set of
clothes on his bed and took a deep breath. *Just undress, Aiden,
and get dressed again. It's going to be just fine.*

Cautiously, he reached down to his waist and lifted the
upper half of the costume. For a moment his head turned
shades of red and blue as the top passed over his head. He
could feel Skull-face's eyes boring down on him. He took in
another deep breath and closed his eyes. It had nothing to with

being naked in front of the boy, PE in a public high school had rid him of that fear. It was the voice behind the mask's tone that scared him and the unwelcome groping hand in the hallway.

"Come on," Skull-face jeered. "Hurry up or I'm gonna help you."

The words jarred him to action. He grasped the costume bottoms and forced himself to push them downward. He stopped, gulped and then pushed the rest of the way in one quick motion. Rapidly, he lifted his legs out of the pant legs and threw the bottoms to the ground. He grabbed for the briefs laid out on the bed and stepped into them.

"Not so fast," Skull-face spoke.

The briefs snagged on something just above his knees. Aiden looked down to find a hand gripping around the fabric. Skull-face's hand. He swallowed and tried to calm his breathing, frozen in place. Aiden tried to go against the boy and yanked up on the briefs, but they didn't budge.

"Back off!" There was an anger in Aiden's voice combined with the fear that coursed through his body.

"Shut up," Skull-face bit back. "I'm going to enjoy this."

Aiden shivered at the unwelcome sensation of a finger lightly caressing his shoulder. He pulled away, but a hand gripped onto his other shoulder. A finger brushed his shoulder again and moved lazily along his arm. A tremor shot up his spine and he tried to pull away but there was little use.

Then a thought jarred into Aiden's mind. Both of the boy's hands were occupied. One held the long curved blade braced against his shoulder while the other...while the other lingered along his bare waist. Aiden took in another breath and then wrenched his briefs upward, a sudden relief swelling through him. Before he could move, his body was shoved forward, face first onto the bed. He yelped in surprise.

A hand grasped the stretchy band of his briefs and yanked harshly. He felt a chill as he was exposed again. Skull-face's hand clutched brashly onto his backside and then the full weight of the boy fell on top of him. Aiden writhed under the boy's grip.

"Get off—" Aiden yelled, but the sound became nothing more than a muffled grumbling as Skull-face wrapped a hand around the boy's face and covered his mouth. He continued to mumble, trying to scream. He shook and writhed, doing everything he could to get out from under the boy's weight, out from under the dirty wandering hands. A zipping sound sent Aiden's mind and body into a frenzy of motion.

"Lie still. Everything's going to be just fine, Aiden," Skull-face said quietly as his lips reached Aiden's neck.

The bat!

He thrashed from side-to-side frantically, trying to rip his body from the boy's grasp. He managed an inch to the right. An inch closer to the bat. He could see the butt of the bat leaning against the end table at the head of his bed. He reached out, fingers outstretched. It was only a few more inches. He jerked his body again, managing to move up a fraction of an inch. Still too far.

"Ah, you like that?" Skull-face chided him as his hands and lips moved feverishly.

Aiden clenched his teeth as his body quaked under the foreign skin. His eyes found the bat again. He reached out again. *Come on!*

Finally, the tips of his fingers found the glossy surface of the little-used bat. He scratched, begging for a grip on the wooden stick as he felt a hand attempting to reach around his waist. Frantic, his mind changed directions. He flailed the other direction, throwing Skull-face off target, and nearly off of him.

"Playing hard to get," Skull-face sounded giddy. "I like it."

While the boy enjoyed his moment, Aiden slid forward another inch and grasped the bat in his hand. "How about this, bitch?"

With all the strength he could muster, Aiden yanked the bat from its perch and slung it around, only hoping he would connect. In the second before impact, Skull-face saw what his inattention had wrought and began to move, but it was too late. The thick wooden stick railed into his shoulder. He toppled over, off Aiden's naked form and onto the floor with a high-pitched yelp.

Planting a hand on the bed, Aiden lifted himself and peered over the edge at his handiwork. The freak was on his side cradling his left shoulder. A glint of metal caught Aiden's attention. The knife. It was lying on the opposite side of the bed. In all the commotion, Aiden had not realized that the silvery object had taken a backseat to Skull-face's preferred venture. Aiden glanced back to Skull-face whose eyes went wide, realizing his mistake.

The slim boy in the skull-covered mask lurched forward, but his tight jeans bunched around his ankles kept him off balance. Aiden angled forward and snatched up the long blade as Skull-face shuffled forward, trying desperately to get the blade. Aiden raised the long blade before his captor, his former captor, its length glinting in the room's singular overhead light. He let the bat fall back to the floor.

"Stay down," Aiden ordered angrily. Adrenaline pumped through his veins but he still felt dirty, violated. Skull-face retreated back to the floor, his expression unreadable behind the mask. Aiden wished he could see the person's eyes. He wanted to know that whoever was behind that mask was scared as hell, just like he was right now.

He reached down and tugged his briefs up his legs. Then, without taking his eyes off of Skull-face, he gathered the disheveled stack of clothes he had laid out on the bed and began to dress. Skull-face twitched forward, but Aiden thrashed and waved the knife wildly at the boy. He moved back but didn't speak a word. Finally dressed, Aiden sighed in relief, if nothing else he was clothed.

"You're not going to hurt me," the young voice wrapped around the mask and hit Aiden's ears like an evil spirit. "You don't have it in you."

Defiantly, Skull-face raised to his feet, nonchalantly zipping his pants back up. "Come on, stab me. Shove it through my heart. Kill me. Slit my throat, let me bleed out all over your carpet. Come on! Can't you do it?"

The demented voice chided him from behind the cold mask. Aiden blinked, his breathing quickened. He wanted to. He wanted to lash out, to spear the knife through the boy's chest with all the force he could mobilize, to watch the boy's eyes go blank like his mother's had. He could see the blood gushing from the boy's chest in his mind. He wanted to watch him suffer. But…but he couldn't do it. His hands trembled at the thoughts that ran through his mind.

"Just put it down, you know you want to."

Aiden shivered. He did want to put it down, it was the only thing that stood between him and death, or worse.

"Hey! Everything okay up there?" a muffled voice echoed into the room. It was one of the masked intruders downstairs, but Aiden wasn't sure which.

"Yeah, everything's fine. He's just taking forever," Skull-face lied. He cocked his head and put his hand out for the knife. More quietly, he spoke to Aiden. "Come on, put it down and step away from it."

The knife shook in his grasp but he held tightly, refusing to give in but unsure what to do next.

"Man, just put it down. I swear I won't touch you... I'm done, I swear." Even though the voice seemed calm, Aiden could imagine the wicked grin behind that ugly mask. "If you don't hurry up and put it down, I can't even begin to explain what they're going to do to your sister and dad. Do you really want them to end up like your mom?"

"Shut up!" Aiden growled back. Skull-face was on the defense now. His words almost sounded like he was pleading.

"I'm telling you, Aiden, if I don't show up down there with you in a few minutes and they come up here and find me dead, they're just going to put a bullet through your head and then kill the rest of your family." The words sounded more scared as Skull-face kept speaking. "Put down the knife and we'll go downstairs, but I have to be in control or it won't be good for them."

Thoughts shot through Aiden's mind. *What do I do? If I give him the knife that means I lost, that I can't do anything to protect Mara or Dad. But if I don't maybe they will just kill us all anyway. Oh hell!*

"You don't have much time, come on, Aiden," Skull-face pled with him. "Put it down."

Aiden stared at the cold red mask. In his hand he held the blade, he gripped it tightly, not wanting to ever let it go. A minute passed in silence. Just the two boys, staring each other down, hoping the other would make a move. He had to. Now he knew it. He didn't know why but something told Aiden that his only way out of this was at the tip of Skull-face's blade. He grimaced at the thought and then, without uttering a word, he dropped the knife on the mattress and stepped back. Skull-face jumped forward and grabbed up the knife and took a few steps back, holding the blade down at his side.

"All right, let's go." The confidence in the boy's voice had returned. He no longer pled or begged.

Aiden dropped his head, looking down at the carpet in defeat. What else was he to do? How could he condemn his sister, his dad? He moved forward and Skull-face matched his step, the knife hanging somewhere behind him.

Shaking less now, Aiden continued forward. He curled his lips angrily. His face burned as he beat himself up mentally. He was doing the right thing. Somehow he knew it, somehow it would work out.

Then a sharp pain spiked through Aiden's back. It shot through his chest. Suddenly it became hard to breathe and each labored breath stung like hell. Shaking, Aiden lowered his eyes. The blade was painted in thick crimson, jutting out below his stomach. He wrapped his fingers around it and stared in horror. His breaths came in short gasps, then he felt moist hot breath on his ear.

"You didn't think I'd *really* make it that easy, did you?" Skull-face whispered in his ear, lips brushing against the soft flesh. "I mean you denied me what I wanted. That was a bad boy."

The blade twisted in his stomach, pain searing through his body, but Skull-face's words seemed to haunt him more than anything. Abruptly, Skull-face wrenched the blade back with a churning squishing sound. Aiden opened his hands, staring at the bloodied cuts along his fingers where he had held tightly to it a second earlier. His body jarred back against Skull-face as the blade tore out from his back, lacing every fragment of his body in tendrils of pain. Then Skull-face spun Aiden around to face him, but before his eyes could meet the crimson skull mask, he felt the knife slice through him again.

He gasped for air, but found it hard to swallow it down into his lungs. His chest was on fire.

"Plea... Please," Aiden stuttered between breaths.

The monster tugged Aiden's body back toward the bed, using the blade still stuck in his chest like the ring in a bull's nose. The sharp edge nicked and sliced through Aiden's insides. Aiden gulped and groaned as the pain become unbearable.

The bed at Aiden's back, Skull-face jerked the knife out of his chest with a wry smile. Blood splattered across Skull-face's shirt and something thick and grisly fell from the bloodstained blade. He lifted his thin leg and kicked Aiden in the chest where he had just impaled him. Aiden yelped in pain as his body was flung backward onto the bed.

Pain surged up and down every inch of his body, the edges of his vision beginning to go in and out of focus. He blinked. His eyes became heavy, trying both to see and stay awake.

"Now I'll get what I wanted," the monster fumed as he climbed over Aiden's body. Aiden felt suddenly claustrophobic, but he did not have the energy to move or to fight back. It felt like the blade had stolen the fight from his bones as it had been ripped from his chest. He could barely muster the strength to put his hand up, which was quickly swatted away.

"No…" Aiden tried, but the word seemed to fade into nothingness just like his vision. It blurred then cleared and then blurred again.

"Now, since you're about to die, I want you to know who did this to you," Skull-face said defiantly. He spoke the words like they meant nothing at all, like death was just another day. "It's going to be a shock for sure. But you're such a bitchy prep, so rich with your nice clothes, car and popularity. Your perfect little pathetic family."

Aiden wrinkled his brow, trying to understand what the boy was saying. Who was he? Aiden struggled to keep his eyes open. The horrid red skull hovered over his face, staring down into his fading brown eyes.

"Ready?" the boy teased. Aiden could barely make out the fingers reaching behind the mask and then a blur as it lifted.

"Wha…" Aiden stuttered.

A flurry of pale red shoulder-length hair fell down and brushed Aiden's sweaty cheek. The skin was pale, not un-healthy, but white. Familiar forest green eyes shone down on him in a hateful and lustful glee.

"Olly?" Aiden finally managed to get the name out as his vision blurred again, but failed to clear. The pain around his chest lightened just slightly as his breathing became harder. He gasped. Blood choked him and gurgled over his lips. "Oll…"

"Yes, Aiden. It's me."

The faint sensation of a hand moving lightly down his chest made him shudder as his vision darkened. He felt a dis-tant tug on his jeans and then the world around him went black and the pain stopped.

CHAPTER 18

It all felt like the world was bearing down on him. The crushing weight of guilt, regret piled atop the loss. Dalton was lost in Lenore's cold empty eyes. The beautiful sea green circles seemed paler than just moments ago, their vibrancy sinking below the milky depths.

He diverted his gaze to Mara. She looked lost as she looked down into her lap. She rocked gently back and forth with her hands clasping and unclasping, fidgeting. Finally she looked up at him, the fear in her eyes stung in Dalton's chest.

What have I done?

Dalton didn't bother to give her a doleful grin. He refused to lie to her with some false sense of hope. It sure as hell felt like there would be none of that tonight. Instead he let the frown on his lips, the tears and his sodden cheeks tell her he was sorry. He was sorry for not being home tonight sooner, for not keeping these monsters out of their house. He was sorry for letting it get this far, no matter how little control he had. He was sorry for not being strong enough to stop them, for letting them hurt her. And, he was sorry for not loving her mother, his love, like he should have. The guilt he felt in his heart sent a chill up his spine, one of the many tonight and one he was sure he would relieve daily.

But still he didn't know why it was all happening. And now Aiden was here and in danger like the rest of them. How Dalton wished he would have stayed at Mason's tonight, avoided all of this. He didn't want to think about what the boy behind the bullet mask had in store for him, or Mara.

I've got to do something. But what?

He looked back up just in time for Bullet's slim figure to pass between him and Lenore's body. The boy was pacing the floor anxiously. His posture had become stiff and rigid, his words angrier, and Dalton was sure it had something to do with Aiden. That single thought worried him.

"If you came here to hurt us, to hurt me, you've succeeded. Why stay?" Dalton begged, his voice coming out pathetic and weak.

The boy continued to pace. Freddie stood stoically just two foot from the sofa arm by Mara. Their demeanors could not be more different.

"Why don't you just leave?" Dalton asked again.

Freddie took a single step forward, "We'll leave when we're ready to leave."

"But why? What more do…" Dalton started before Bullet cut him off, the rough quality of his voice pushed to the brink by the anger that spat out.

"Shut up!" he yelled. "Shut the *fuck* up!"

Dalton sat back, more alert, scared by the boy's outburst.

"How many times do I have to tell you?" Bullet paused. He seemed to be gathering his thoughts, sorting out what he would say. "We're here to have a little fun and then leave with a bunch of money. But, you're beginning to make this no fun at all since you can't seem to keep your damn mouth closed. It's a simple request really, shut up!"

"No! You've had enough *fun*. Take whatever you want and leave us alone!" Dalton bellowed back. He was surprised at the strength behind his voice. He felt anything but strong, horrified even of his own words.

Bullet's black eyes widened behind the lonely holes of his white, and now red-splotched, mask. His lips curled hatefully as he began to shake. Dalton felt the anger building behind that mask. Bullet lurched forward, his curved blade leading the way. Dalton flinched backward, twisting his head to look away.

A hand grabbed his shoulder and squeezed tight. He felt the boy's clammy breath on his ear, the blood-coated blade coming to rest on the side of his neck. Dalton refused to turn, to meet his gaze.

"You know, Dalton," his voice was quieter, the anger more subtle, but it still lingered under the slow and deliberate warning. "I don't think you're in any place to be making any *fucking* demands."

Dalton let out a breath he was unaware he had been holding, and it came out in a stutter.

Who is this monster?

Satisfied, Bullet stood up and let the knife rest at his side before stepping back. This time he did not pace. The confidence that had defined him just hours before seemed to have returned.

A thumping noise distracted Dalton from his stupor. He looked upward as did everyone else in the room. *Aiden!*

Bullet tilted his head to listen just as another thud echoed from upstairs.

"Hey! Everything okay up there?" Bullet yelled, pushing his voice to reach through the walls and ceiling to the next level. A second later the reply came.

"Yeah, everything's fine. He's just taking forever." Skull-face's treble voice came muffled through ceiling. Dalton imagined the thin-framed kid, the freak that had squealed with joy as he water-boarded Lenore. He imagined breaking the boy, cracking his back, letting him writhe on the floor in pain. *No.* Dalton shook his head. He tried to wipe the image from his mind, hating himself for the desire that had crept up in him. Yet, he could not help but revisit the image. Who could blame him, these kids deserved it.

The alpha male cocked his head sideways. Dalton could see the irritation in his eyes. The boy huffed before speaking under his breath, "He better hurry up."

An excruciating five minutes passed before the sound of footsteps reached them from the upstairs hallway. Dalton let out a reserved sigh. At least Aiden would be with them again, instead of alone with some stranger.

What took so long, dammit? What had that noise been?

Bullet's attention shot toward the kitchen where his comrade and Dalton's son would soon appear. His brow lifted in anticipation. Dalton could not help but wonder about the boy's interest in his son. Why did Aiden's entrance seem to cause him such apprehension?

The footsteps quickened as they came to the stairs. Dalton and Mara mimicked Bullet's gaze. Waiting, worried about the same person as their masked captor.

The sound of the footsteps changed from the tap of shoes on wood to the lighter clinking of shoes on the rough textured tile floor. They were in the kitchen. The footsteps continued and then Dalton saw a boy come around the corner, but it was not Aiden and he wore no mask.

Dalton's stomach dropped as his eyes were magnetized to a broad sanguine smear that ran across the right side of the boy's thin face, framed by shoulder-length red hair. It contrasted with his pale complexion. His eyes followed the crimson trail down in stuttered streaks and smears along his neck that changed into nothing more than a dark black stain that covered most of the boy's black t-shirt. Dalton's body shook before he could pull his eyes from the stains. He looked back to the boy's face, the same face that had been covered by a demonic red skull just minutes ago, the face that had reveled in torturing his wife and now stood at the precipice of the living room with a wicked grin across his small blood-speckled face. But there was no sight of Aiden.

"Where's Aiden?" Dalton screamed at the unmasked Skull-face. "What have you done to him?" His body shook in horror and rage as he began to come off of the seat.

"What did you do, Olly?" Bullet yelled, for the first time that night using the boy's name. He took a step forward and then moved quicker with each step as he bound toward the smiling boy. The smile quickly died to a frown, a nervous glare.

Mara broke down into tears, knowing exactly what the blood meant, who it belonged to. She knew just like everyone else in the room did, even though they refused to come to terms with it. Freddy stepped forward and poked his knife carefully at Dalton's chest to make him sit back down. He obeyed, but his eyes never left the blood stains.

Bullet reached Olly in a matter of seconds. He gripped his hands tightly around the boy's small arms and wrenched him off the kitchen platform and up against the beige wall. He smashed Olly's head into a picture frame. Glass cracked and fell to the floor in sharp pieces while the frame and picture of the Summers family from two years back at the beach remained pinned between the wall and Olly's shoulder.

"What the *hell* did you do, Olly?" Bullet bellowed at the boy.

As Bullet railed on Olly, on Skull-face, Dalton found himself wishing that Bullet would ram his knife through the boy. He imagined Aiden's body crumpled on the floor in blood, but quickly pushed the image aside.

"Calm down, calm down, man," Olly pled, his feet dangling several inches above the ground. "I just did what we were here to do. Have a little fun and kill them all, right?"

Kill them all, right? The words ran through Dalton's mind. It shot back and forth, blinked on and off like some neon sign affixed to a building out in Vegas. *Aiden!* He had known from the moment the boy had turned the corner and his eyes had caught sight of the blood, his son's blood. He had known, but was unwilling to accept its finality, until now. His son was dead, Aiden was dead. He slumped back into his chair, helpless. His body felt heavy, like a leaden weight, useless and doomed to nothing but torment and loss.

"You killed Aiden?" Bullet's voice shook with rage.

"Yeah," Olly shrugged. "Right after I had a little fun with him, you know."

"I told you not to hurt him!" Bullet let his grip on Olly's arms go and the boy dropped to his feet. The picture frame crashed to the floor, more glass shards sprinkling the tile as the wooden frame cracked and broke into several pieces. Pieces scattered the floor. Bullet punched the wall just an inch beside Olly's head with a scream. He punched again, and again. Olly jerked and squinted his eyes shut with each blow next to his head.

"Calm down, man, that's what we came here to do. I can't help you had a soft spot for the kid. I mean, yeah, he was a good looking boy, but he was nothing special," Olly tried again.

Bullet punched out one more time, but this time his fist connected with the side of Olly's face. The boy stumbled back against the wall. He groaned and cradled his cheek.

"What the—" Olly began before Bullet raised the business end of the pistol in line with Olly's temple.

"Don't tempt me right now," Bullet bored his black eyes into Olly's, his voice quieter but the rage evident. There was more he wanted to say, Dalton could tell it from the sound of his voice, but he stopped.

Lowering the weapon, fully expecting Olly to keep his mouth shut, Bullet spun around. He eyed Joe first and then faced his remaining two captives. His eyes burnt with rage, his lips quivered.

"What..." Dalton began to ask, his voice quieter than he'd expected, straining to hold back the tears.

"Shut up! Shut up! *Shut up!*" Bullet screamed, swinging his hands back and forth furiously. He pressed the thin digits against the sides of his temple and closed his eyes. "Agh!"

Between the holes in the white mask, Dalton watched Bullet's eyes dart back and forth between him and his daughter. Dalton looked over to Mara, frowning. "I love you, darling. I'm so sorry."

She simply nodded. It was enough.

Biting his lip angrily, Bullet groaned. "You should be sorry, this is all your *fucking* fault. All of it."

The gruff voiced boy started to pace the room, repeating a small path about two yards in length in front of Dalton and Mara. He kept his eyes on Dalton, beaming with rage.

"This is all your fault," he repeated. He stopped and looked down to the ground, then up to Dalton. "I never wanted to hurt Aiden, I promise you that. Aiden was one of the few good people I knew. He cared. He wasn't selfish and pompous. He wasn't just some piece of meat, either." Bullet's gaze shot angrily at Olly. The boy shrank back and eyed the floor. Then he retrained his attention onto Dalton.

"He was what's right in this world." Bullet paused, and then spoke his next few words slowly. "You're what's wrong with it."

"Who are you?" Dalton asked weakly, fear and rage shooting through his veins.

"Oh, we've met, Dalton," Bullet said. "We've met."

Scrunching his brow, Dalton let himself try to place the boy in his memory, the voice, the eyes, anything. Nothing came to the forefront.

"I'll help you remember, Dalton." Bullet let what might've been a grin cross his lips through the rage. Then he reached a finger behind his head and hooked the strap holding his mask on.

"What are you doing?" Freddie asked.

"Shut up, Joe," Bullet began, using Freddie's real name. "This was the plan all along, *except* for Aiden."

"What? You said we'd keep the masks on. That no one would ever know who we are and we'd leave!" Freddie, or Joe, railed back.

"Stop being so damn naïve, Joe," Bullet blasted back. "Do

you really think the cops won't figure it out anyway? Serious-ly? I came here for one purpose, and I'm not leaving until I'm done and you best go along."

Joe took a step back, grunted, but nodded.

Bullet turned to look at Olly to let him know that stood for him, too. The pale faced kid nodded irritably.

Reaching behind his head again, he pulled up on the strap the held the white mask with the singular bullet hole in the middle. The mask began to droop down and then fell from his face and clattered to the floor.

His face was white and untanned, his full lips giving way to a broad chin and sloping neck. His nose was a gentle slope between those coal black eyes and thin cheeks. There was something familiar in that face, something Dalton could not place.

"Remember me now?" Bullet asked with a mischievous grin.

Straining to find the boy's young face in some memory, Dalton shook his head slowly.

Bullet sighed. "Three years ago, *this* very night, you looked right in my eyes just like now. The same fear. The same cowardice. And it was raining."

Suddenly, an image surfaced in Dalton's mind. The same eyes, the same face, only younger.

CHAPTER 19

He was outside, stumbling in a heavy rain. He lost his footing and almost dropped to the wet grass before he caught himself. His head felt light as the rain pounded against his face.

Suddenly, a bright light seared his vision and for a brief moment it seemed that the night had vanished and the sun had decided to shine for just a second. Then it was gone. The shadows of night and the storm covered every inch of the country road. Dalton stumbled again, one drink too many, maybe two, or three. He wasn't sure how many he had consumed at the bar. All he was sure about was that someone had wrecked. Had he caused it?

He shook his head, trying to clear the murky thoughts that were slowly running around up there. He stumbled again, his foot stuck in a fresh rut of mud. It must have been where the car's front end had buried into the ground before flipping end over end on the edge of the road into this small field.

Dalton regained his footing. Then he heard something. He turned to look back toward the road where his Beemer sat on the side of the road still running, headlights cutting through the rain and shadows. It came again, a voice, muffled but obviously scared. It was coming from the wrecked car. He pivoted around slower than he thought. He shook his head, trying to clear his vision again. Dalton stumbled forward a few more steps. The voice kept screaming.

"Help!" It was a small voice, a boy's he thought.

Dalton stepped quicker, trying to keep his balance despite the amount of alcohol running through his system. Closer now, he got a better look at the car. It was an older model Camry, silver, the door panel was banged in pretty badly and it had come to its final resting place upside down. The passenger window frame was half the size it should have been. Dalton placed a hand on the undercarriage of the car which was facing the sky, half to validate to himself that this was real and half to keep his balance. His head continued to spin, his limbs jerking to keep their balance. He dropped to his knees. Water jumped up onto his trousers and he could feel the wetness of the mud seeping in through his jeans around the knees.

"Hurry!" the young voice called out. There was a gentle raspy tone in that voice, young and undeveloped, but it was there.

He leaned over, willing his head to calm down as he tried to peer into the vehicle, to find the owner of the voice. At first he saw nothing, it was so dark and the rain made it hard to keep his eyes open.

"Please help!" the boy begged. "The door won't open. My brother's hurt."

Hurt. The word ran through Dalton's mind. Without thinking, he reached for the door handle and began to pull on the door, yanking and wrenching back and forth. It didn't budge. Dalton looked back into the car, still he only saw faint shadows. Then a bright show of lightning lit up the sky. There he was. Pale white skin, dark black hair and black eyes. Dalton shivered, he wasn't sure if it was the eyes or the fact that the boy was stuck in this wreck that shook him most. In the same instant, he saw an older man hanging upside down and limp from the driver's seat.

"Is he alive?" Dalton slurred, his body unsteady. The mud seemed to be encasing his knees, the water growing higher as he sank in the mud.

"No," the boy said matter-of-factly.

Dalton's eyes went wide. Water poured onto his pupils but he *didn't care.*

"Oh no! No, no. No. No. No." It was all Dalton could think to say as the alcohol swam through his system. He fell back onto his hindquarters and then crawled away from the vehicle like some demonic spirit laid within it.

"Wait!

Dalton shook the images from his mind. His eyes went wide. He stared up at the boy, into those baleful eyes.

"You remember me now, don't you?" Bullet said. Dalton felt like the boy had reached into his mind and drew out the memory. He had done a lot to repress it, to forget it. Bullet smiled.

"No." Dalton tried to lie, hoping that somehow it would help.

"Don't insult me! You killed my dad and my brother!" Bullet screamed viscously, spit flying from his mouth. Freddie removed his mask revealing the black-faced boy Dalton had witnessed earlier.

As the words shot from his mouth, Mara's eyes glistened with recognition. She looked to her father, confused. Dalton met her gaze, frowned and tried to think of what to say. He couldn't lie anymore.

"Honey, no," Dalton began, trying to keep his voice from stuttering. "I didn't kill them, I promise. I... I..."

"Come on, Dalton, tell your precious little girl how you screwed up my life," Bullet continued to scream. "Tell her how you took everything from me. *Everything!*"

"I..." Dalton began to stutter. *How do I explain? Why?* "I... I was drunk."

"Drunk or sober, who gives a shit? You were there, you caused my dad to run off the road. You came all the way to the car. You even spoke to me. And then you ran like a fucking coward. You left us to die."

"I'm sorry," Dalton stammered. "I was scared, I was..."

"And you left us to die, like dogs. I held my little brother in my arms and watched him die. I lied to him, told him it would be okay, and you left us there. You left us to die."

"I'm sorry. I wasn't myself... Chase." Dalton stopped after speaking the boy's name. He had run from that day for so long. Three years. *Had it really been three years?* The authorities had ruled the accident the driver's fault, the boy's dad. They said it was a cut-and-dry case of drunk driving and bad weather from the amount of vodka in the man's system. Chase, the kid who screamed for help, the owner of those deep black eyes, the mad teenager that stood in front of him now wielding a menacing black pistol in one hand and a large curved knife stashed between his pant and belt.

He remembered watching the news clip online the day after. He'd taken a sick day and drove to another bar where he drank away his guilt. He knew it was stupid, he had been drunk the night before, when *it* had all happened. Now the only way he could imagine to cope was to return to the same bottle that had put him in that precarious situation. He had imagined the authorities showing up at his door. Cuffing him and taking him away. He'd watched the news religiously for days, waiting, knowing it wouldn't be long before they came for him. But they never came.

He had memorized the facts of the crime, knew them better than anyone else but Chase. Eric Miller had been thirty-four years old, the father of three boys, Reily, Chase and Dusty Miller. Reily had died of a drug overdose two years earlier at the age of sixteen. Chase had been thirteen at the time of the accident and his younger brother was only nine. The news station said their mother had died in child birth with their youngest. Chase was all alone now, except for a few relatives, and it was all his fault.

"So you know my name," Chase stated, the anger settling but still on reserve. "And that's all you have to say? Did you know that after the wreck, after my brother..." the boy stuttered. He fought back a tear, it was a scene Dalton had thought impossible just minutes before. "...after he died, and my dad. Did you realize that I had no one left? No one that really cared at least? Sure, they packed me up and sent me to live with my uncle and aunt."

Bullet, or Chase, stopped for a second. He dropped his eyes to the floor and then locked eyes again with Dalton. "Do you know what that was like? Do you *know*?"

"No —" Dalton tried before Chase cut him off.

"Of course you don't!" Chase bellowed, the anger boiling over now. He swung the pistol precariously back and forth. "Of course you don't! How could you know? It's not like you gave a damn about me. You didn't care that you sent me to live with them. To a bunch of sick-os, druggies." He nearly spat his words. "Worthless pieces of shit. Do you know what they did to me?" he asked, but he didn't stop long enough for Dalton to answer. "They said I was costing them too much money, that I was dragging them down, that I had to be useful."

The boy stopped for a moment and wiped the spit from his lips. When he continued, he spoke quieter, slower. "Do you know how many times they beat me? Every week, sometimes every day! For the last three years. And it's all your fault!"

Dalton jerked back in his seat as Chase screamed those last five words.

"I'm sorry. I didn't know. I didn't mean for all this to happen. I promise. You don't understand how —" Dalton pled before the boy cut him off. Tears of guilt and fear trailed down his face. Mara sat half in shock on the couch, trying to take it all in.

"Of course you didn't *mean* for it to happen," Chase agreed. "But it *did* and you just acted like it would all go away while I suffered. Eve-ry. Single. Day. Because of you."

"Is that what this is all about?" Dalton asked, realizing how stupid a question it was but needing to hear the answer. "Was this all to punish me?"

"Ding, ding, ding. We have a winner," Chase jeered, mimicking the voice of some prize announcer as if none of the mayhem, the blood and bodies, laid piled up around them. Then his face went sober, his eyes narrowed and he stepped forward. He placed his free hand on the head of the leather recliner Dalton sat in. He dropped down and let his forehead make contact with the crown of Dalton's head and brought the pistol up to Dalton's temple. "And I'm not done yet."

His whole body shook as the barrel of the gun rested at his temple. All it would take was one little squeeze and it would all be over. But would it be that bad? It would be over. All of the past he was running from would be over, everything that had gotten between him and his family, the pain that he'd suffered the past three years. It would end. *No.* Suddenly he hated himself for the thought, the selfishness that had pulled him in. *Mara. I have to be here for Mara!*

"Well, it looks like it's time for the next person to die," Chase said calmly. He was no longer mincing words, or at least he was no longer hiding the truth. The boy stood up and moved between Olly and Joe. He huffed and pursed his lips like the thought vexed him. The pistol moved in Mara's direction.

"Please no. Let her live," Dalton pleaded. "She has nothing to do with this. She isn't to blame! I am! Me!"

"Yes, you are. But she's a lot like you," Chase said, nodding apologetically. "I see how she is in school, and she's just too much like you. Plus, it'll hurt you."

"Please!"

Without warning, Chase redirected the pistol, his arm outstretched to his right. *Bang!* A quick flash of flame exited the barrel before the side of Olly's head blew open. Blood and bits of brain splattered onto the floor, the wall. His body crashed to the floor. He hadn't even known what hit him.

"What the —" Joe yelled, confused and scared.

"Shut up!" Chase screamed at Joe and then looked at the boy soberly. "He disobeyed."

It felt like a warning, as much as it did payback for a slight. Joe swallowed and stared back at Chase, horror written on his face. He nodded slowly.

"Aiden was supposed to survive. He was good, a friend. Not like this piece of trash," Chase pointed his gun carelessly at Dalton and then looked down to Olly's corpse. "And this idiot screwed it all up!"

A friend? Aiden?

Chase seemed to catch the question in Dalton's eyes, though his statement felt out of place. "We go to school with your kids."

"Oh." It was all that would come to Dalton's mouth.

At his feet, Olly's body was strewn over the floor. Blood coalesced about his head, turning his already red hair a darker shade as it soaked in the pungent liquid. Then Dalton saw a chance. The kid's knife. The long bloodied weapon laid only a few feet from Dalton's feet and it seemed that neither Chase nor Joe were worried about picking it up.

Dalton catalogued the location of the knife away in his memory and looked back up at the angry alpha male. He met eyes with the boy whose life he had ruined, and who was bent on ruining his. Chase moved, slowly and deliberately, across the room to where Mara sat and stopped beside her. In the blink of an eye, he had his blade over her neck. He bent down and whispered in her ear just loud enough for Dalton to hear while his eyes dug into Dalton's red-veined sky blues.

"Are you ready to die, Mara?"

"No! Please no," Mara begged, sobbing uncontrollably. "Daddy, help, please!"

"That's right, beg him to save you, Mara. *Oh Daddy, please save me,*"

Chase mocked her.

"Stop it! Let her go! It's me you want! Let her live!" Dalton begged, groveled. He leaned forward, keeping his hand low and ready for when the moment arrived. "Please let her go! Baby, just look at me. It's going to be all right."

The blade moved, but it didn't touch her. Chase grinned. Unexpectedly, Joe stepped forward, "I thought we were taking her with us?"

"Change of plans, Joe... Well, not really," he said matter-of-factly. Dalton wondered how much Chase had been using these two, how much he had manipulated them to get them to go along. It didn't matter. All that did was keeping Mara alive.

"Come on, man," Joe tried. "But she was supposed to be our reward for helping you. You keep changing the plan!"

"It is my plan," Chase countered. "It's her time."

Suddenly, Joe shoved his hands into Chase's chest and plowed him to the ground, pushing the blade aside. The boys fell to the floor by the couch, tussling in the floor. The blade clashed against the tile and Dalton heard a fist find purchase.

It was now or never. Dalton jumped from his seat and scooped up the long curved knife, trying to ignore the blood on its handle, Aiden's blood.

"Run, Mara! Run!" Dalton yelled. "Go for help!"

She hesitated, scared to move, scared to leave her dad. He yelled for her to go one more time and she came to, lifted herself from the couch and bolted for the kitchen.

The scuffle on the other side of the room went silent and both boy's popped up over the arm of the couch. By the time they looked, Mara was half-way across the living room and Dalton was on his feet with a knife in hand.

"Dammit! You fool!" Chase yelled at Joe. "Get her! Do whatever you want with her, but make sure she ends up dead! Go! Dalton's mine."

Chase flipped the pistol around in his hand and passed it to Joe. "Finish her off."

CHAPTER 20

Her feet pounded up the stairs, struggling to keep up with the beat of her heart. It felt like it might burst under all the pressure, the loss.

Joe had not said a word yet, but Mara knew he was hot on her heels, and there was no telling how that would end if he caught her. Mara pushed the thought from her mind and instead focused on getting up the stairs. Her foot left the last step and she sprinted down the short hallway. She careened into her room and slammed the door shut behind her.

She breathed heavily, more out of fear than exhaustion, as she locked the door and came to a rest against it. *Bang!* The door shook violently under her back. Mara jumped forward as if propelled by the shaking of the door.

"Open up!" Joe yelled through the door as he pummeled the hard wooden panel. It shook and creaked, but stood strong.

Facing the door, Mara realized her mistake. *What am I doing? Why did I come here? I'm trapped!*

Panic began to set in as she tried to decide what to do next. She was certain the door would not hold for much longer under such a constant barrage. It was strong, but it wasn't built for the task. She scanned the room for anything that could be used to keep the deviant at bay, that might give her a chance. Her eyes found the row of stiletto heels at the edge of her bed, then her vanity, makeup and co—

"Ah!" She let out a shrill scream as the door jolted with a loud bang, louder than before. It shimmied. "No."

She returned her attention to looking for some hope, some object that could make her something better than defenseless. Mara stepped up to her vanity and picked up a comb with a long pointed handle and examined the edge as Joe continued to hammer the door.

"Open up, bitch! I'm coming in one way or another," he called after her. She could hear the irritation in his voice, the pent up rage, but it only motivated her to do something. She wasn't stopping, not now.

Mara grimaced but put down the comb. It was useless. *Useless.* Maybe more than the comb was useless, maybe it was useless to try to defend herself. But it didn't matter, she wouldn't just go down without a fight, not after all that she had witnessed tonight, after all she'd been through.

She spun around and canvased the room again. It was all so familiar but suddenly felt so confusing and different. She couldn't explain the feeling. Nothing she laid eyes on seemed useful anymore. Not a single item seemed to be a suitable instrument to give her a chance against the monster about to break through her door.

Then her eyes locked on the partially open window as the light drapes floated in a small gust of cool fall wind. The same one that Nathan had slipped in through just hours ago. Her heartbeat slowed as the thought of Nathan entered her head. It was stupid to think about him right now, but she couldn't help herself. It had really been just hours ago that he had been in her room, with her. It seemed so distant now. A tear escaped her eye.

A renewed effort at the door brought her back to reality. Her mind began to process a plan. Just outside the window was a large red maple, its branches networked up around the rear of the house, close enough to her window for Nathan to have climbed in the window on numerous occasions. That was her hope.

Mara spun around and raced to the vanity where her car keys sat on the edge of the table next to a variety of eyeliners. The door jerked again as another fist rammed home. It creaked, ready to let loose at the hinges. Mara about faced and made for the window. She pulled back the drapes and peered outside toward the shadow-covered ground at least twelve feet below and then up the tree branches. The lake sat calm in the background. The cold autumn air bit her exposed skin lightly.

She took in a deep breath and extended her leg out the window. She hung there for a moment, swaying her leg gently, working to find the branch without turning to look out the window. Her shoe hit something solid, she applied some pressure and found purchase on a large branch. Mara took in another breath and then carefully slid the rest of the way out, placing her full weight and trust in the old maple.

She closed her eyes and clung tightly to the branch. The task of moving seemed Herculean, impossible. She tried to slip further down the tree but the fear of falling overwhelmed her. Then a massive bang and the shattering of wood echoed out from the window. She dared a look back into the house and saw the outline of light behind the drapes where the door now stood open.

"Where'd you go?" Joe called. "You can't hide forever."

Mara held her breath and stilled herself. Her gaze remained steady on the window. Maybe if she didn't speak, if she kept quiet, he'd just go back downstairs, consider her gone.

"Hello there, Mara," Joe burst between the drapes, hanging half way out the window.

She screamed and let go of her grip on the branch. Her body began to slip. Her heart jumped up her throat as she flung her arms out for the branch. She was falling. Then her arm caught the branch and wove tightly around it. She breathed heavily as she hugged the branch and then glared up at Joe.

"Come on back in now," Joe said. "Come on back and let's get this over with. Or would you prefer I knock your ass off that tree?"

Mara refused to go back inside the house. She would not willingly give herself to Joe, not after what he did to her, how he used her. Her insides churned. She frowned, but then redirected the disgust and useless guilt into anger toward the beast, toward escaping. Mara took hold of the anger and used it to move. She slid one foot first, then another, slowly moving down the large branch. Rough bark scraped against her bare legs and threatened to cut through her thin blouse as she moved down inch by inch.

The boy stared on in confusion, somehow unsure why Mara would choose to go down the tree rather back into his "caring" arms. Mara kept moving, she increased her climb down the branch.

Suddenly the branch shook. Mara came close to losing her grip again. She looked up to find Joe climbing over the window sill. He was getting his grip on the branch, he was coming after her. Mara took a deep breath and quickened her descent. Only eight more feet. Seven. Six. Five. She squinted and let her body drop the remaining distance. Her feet hit the ground hard, sending her down onto her side. She grunted, but the adrenaline running through her veins pushed her to get up.

Mara shoved her hands into the grass and lifted herself back up to her feet. She took a quick glance back up the tree. Joe was still at least ten feet above. *Jump. I dare you,* Mara thought before she bolted off and around the corner of the house.

As she made the bend, Mara heard a quiet grunt and then the sound of quick footsteps in the grass behind her. Joe had made it down. She pushed her legs to work harder, pumping with everything she had, begging all that volleyball practice to pay off now, when it counted most.

Finally up ahead, she saw her silver Z4 in the driveway. She started to grin when a deafening boom blasted out behind her and a plum of grass and dirt jettisoned from the ground just a yard ahead of her. Mara's hands flung into the air as she screamed. She dared a look back to find Joe running with the pistol at the ready.

It only pushed her harder. Mara put every ounce of her being into her legs and pushed forward, trying to move in a quick zig-zag pattern to throw of the boy's aim. At last the car was in reach. She grabbed the door handle and yanked it open. Taking one last look behind her, she saw Joe's dark outline a good ten yards behind, struggling to keep up. He raised the pistol again. Mara ducked down and slid into the sports car's bucket seat and pressed the *Start* button. The engine roared to life as a bullet ricocheted off the door.

Mara screamed and slammed the shifter into reverse, not bothering to check behind her. She spun the car out into the grass and then rammed the shifter all the way back into drive and sent the accelerator to the floor. Grass and dirt flew everywhere and the car burst forward.

"*Dammit!*" Joe yelled after the escaping BMW. He couldn't let her get away. Chase would cut his throat.

Suddenly he remembered the gorgeous BMW M4 in the Summers' garage. A mischievous smile broke his face and he jolted back for the house. Weaving between the car he and his friends had arrived in and another that had arrived later, he stomped up onto the porch, past the tall columns and wrenched the front door open. The force of the door knocked the dying candle off its perch and onto the porch. Joe didn't see the flame blaze as it found the kerosene he had poured earlier.

Joe flew past the foyer, catching the house's only two occupants off guard. He thought he heard Chase say something but he couldn't make it out as he bound around into the kitchen. He found

Dalton's keys right where the man had left them on the kitchen counter. Joe snatched them up and darted out into the garage without a word to Chase.

Not wasting time, he bolted over to the M4 and swung the door open. It slammed against the van sitting next to it with a crack. Joe grimaced but jumped into the sporty bucket seat and searched for the ignition. He raised a brow, there wasn't one. Then it hit him when he saw the *Start* button. He smiled in aggravation and pressed the button. The throaty roar of the car's engine blossomed and his grin only grew. He shifted the car into reverse. *Too bad it's not a manual.*

Mara had too much of a head start for him to wait any longer. He let go of the brake and floored the accelerator. The Beemer's front end lowered as the tires catapulted the car backwards. He torqued the wheel to the right as the car cleared the garage door and the car spun to the side and jerked to an abrupt stop. Metal crunched against metal, the tail of the BMW caving in the driver's door of a black Camaro.

"Ouch," Joe quipped as he shoved the shifter into drive and pinned the accelerator the floor. The car lurched forward, pinning him to the back of his seat. He swerved to miss the cars sitting in the driveway and then floored it again. *This bitch isn't getting away tonight.*

The sports car sailed down the concrete path and swerved out onto the road. There was only one way she would have went, the other direction was a dead end at the end of this small inland peninsula. Joe kept the pedal to the floor as he guided the machine down the road faster and faster.

Mara had a good half-minute start on him but a limited number of routes. More importantly to Joe was that her car's speed and handling could not hope to match the horsepower and turbochargers under the M4's hood. It was a machine meant for speed and he was catching up.

Up ahead and around a sharp curve, as his tires cried out, he caught sight of taillights. Mara's taillights. He was lucky, she had just pulled onto the adjoining road, right. Joe let go of the accelerator as he came to the intersection and spun the car's tail end out onto the small two-lane road. His tires protested loudly before catching traction again and pushing him forward.

He locked his eyes on the Z4's taillights as they got closer. Joe looked down at the instrument panel to the circular speed gauge, 70 and climbing. Mara's taillights brightened as she braked for an up-coming curve. Joe refused to brake. He closed the distance between them, hovering only feet from her bumper.

You're not getting away tonight, Mara.

Light glared off the side mirrors threatening to blind Mara. She squinted. He was close. Too close.

She couldn't see the car hidden behind the headlamps, but who else would be in hot pursuit? Only Freddie, only Joe. She floored the accelerator as the car made it around the curve, trying to lose him. She groaned, he stuck close, only a second or two delay and he matched her speed.

Mara swerved into the opposite lane and then back again. Joe mimicked her move. Then his engine roared harder. Joe began to over-take her, eking closer to the rear passenger quarter panel. Mara yanked the wheel back to the right to cut him off. Brakes screeched and his headlights dipped as the distance between them increased.

How am I going to lose him out here?

The road was curvy and empty. It was too late for much traffic, maybe none, and the dark made it more difficult to navigate at such high speeds. She could only see as far her headlights could cast their glow and the faster she accelerated, the shorter that distance felt.

The light blanket of colored leaves shuffled at the edge of the road and then was tossed into the air in whirling patterns as she pushed the car down a small straight stretch. Joe was gaining on her again, the gap growing smaller and smaller. She pressed the accelerator harder, willing the speedometer past 80. Still he gained, then abruptly the entire car shook. Her head jerked forward and then backward, landing uncomfortably against the stiff leather headrest.

You've got to be kidding me!

She swerved again. She had to lose him, but how? A thought hit her. Mara assumed outrunning him was not an option, but she could potentially stall just long enough to get into a higher traffic area. She buried the brake pedal to the floor. Her tires screamed and the front end bowed to the pavement.

Another set of squeals joined hers. Immediately she released the brake and slammed the gas. The car jolted forward. She could not outrun him, but maybe the split second it took for him to react would be enough to gain some ground.

Or not. In a matter of seconds Joe rebounded fully from the ruse. His headlights grew in the rearview mirror and then began to disappear, covered by the rear end of her own vehicle. Her attention torn between the road and the mirror, she spotted something up ahead.

Headlights. Another car was coming. Mara stopped swerving from lane to lane and kept the car steady in the right lane. She earned a not-so-gentle nudge from Joe that threatened to push her back into the opposite lane.

The headlights up ahead grew rapidly, forming finally into a car. As if brought on by the new vehicle, tiny drops of rain began to splatter on her windshield. The car zoomed by in the opposite direction just as Joe's bumper rammed her again. Her hands were wrenched from the steering wheel and the car began to turn on its own accord. Mara screamed as she fought to regain control of the steering wheel. She gripped tight and jerked the wheel back to the right, earning a screech from her overworked tires. The car shimmied before Mara got it steady again and then jammed the brake down again. Her head jerked forward as Joe slammed into her car. She shook away the pain in her neck and shoved the accelerator to the floor again. The car lurched forward, gaining a few yards between her and Joe. She switched on the wiper blades to clear the water pellets from her view.

In the distance she heard screeching, waning into oblivion, then the headlights of the car that had just passed by reappeared. They were in pursuit. Mara squinted in confusion until the familiar blue and yellow lights began to flash atop the car and along the front grill. Mara grinned for the first time that night and a well of hope swelled up inside her.

The police!

Her joy was cut short as her body was driven back into her seat. The sound of metal against metal screeched in her ears as the car was pushed to the left. She worked to compensate. Her tires screeched and screamed as she tried to maintain control. She swerved into the opposite lane, hoping to catch him off guard. Instead, he took advantage of the move and throttled forward. When Mara turned the wheel to move back into the right lane, Joe wrenched the wheel hard to the left, clipping her rear bumper just behind the wheel well.

"Ah!" Mara screamed as her Z4 spun sideways. The car continued to spin, tires burning against the pavement, squealing in protest. The smell of burnt rubber stung her nostrils as the world turned around her. For a second she could see Joe sitting behind the wheel of her dad's BMW.

He stole Dad's car! It was a stupid thought with the car spinning wildly out of control, but it was the first thing to enter her mind.

The car dropped and hit the dirt shoulder and then slammed into the small roadside ditch. Mara lost her breath as the passenger side of the car lifted from the ground. It had to be going fast but it all felt so slow at first. Joe's headlights disappeared under the door replaced by dark storm clouds and the bare limbs of trees. Then time spun forward.

The car flipped onto its roof. The thin cloth headliner slammed into Mara's skull with tremendous force. Glass shattered. Metal screeched violently, splitting in her ears. She felt as if her head had been bashed open. Then her body was wrenched back as the airbag deployed. Her nose cracked. Pain surged up through her face.

The car continued to flip, end over end. Mara's body slammed against the door panel. She felt her waist cave under the pressure. Then it all suddenly stopped with another crunch against her skull.

Mara grunted and shook her head lightly. She immediately regretted it as a sharp pain burrowed between her eyes and deep into her head. She tried to move but only succeeded in discovering a painful spark in her side. She reached up to the throbbing in her head and felt something wet. She found blood streaked across her hand, the smell of copper under the overbearing stink of burnt rubber. Mara groaned. She was pressed against the door. Earth and grass poked through the broken glass at her side, buried in the ground. She peered out of what was left of the windshield. Everything seemed like it was propped on its side, out of place. The patches of leaf-covered grass and then the forest giving way to blackness beyond her headlight's reach. Mara groaned again and forced herself to look up, out the squashed passenger window. A scattered assortment of half-naked branches and dark storm clouds painted the opening. She squinted as rain drops landed on her cheek.

Rubber crunched to a halt on dirt somewhere nearby. In the distance a siren yelled through the rain, but she didn't see the blue lights yet. Instead she heard the sound of a car door slamming shut and quick footsteps. As the footsteps grew in volume, the faint flashing of blue among the trees grew into strong strobes and the siren screamed louder.

Suddenly, she realized it was cold. She shivered as the cool air enveloped her and the persistent rain sullied her clothes. Why did it matter? She groaned as the faint movement of her leg sent a sting up her waist and spine. More tires screeched and a door clanked open. The footsteps slowed and then Joe came into view. He was grinning. The headlights made his dark skin seem almost pale for just a moment, just before he began to move closer.

"Stop right there!" another voice commanded. It had come from behind.

The police! Please! Please stop him! she begged.

Joe stopped, confused. Then rolled his eyes before stepping forward. "You think he can help you?" Joe chided and laughed. "Not tonight, honey."

With that, Joe lifted his pistol. Mara watched as the barrel aligned with her eyes. She refused to look away.

"Freeze! Put the gun down now!" the voice yelled, a new authority booming forth. "I said put the gun down!"

Joe cocked his head and grinned, "Bye bye." Then he pulled the trigger. *Bang! Bang!*

It felt like someone had rammed a sledgehammer into her chest at a few hundred miles an hour. "Ah!" Mara yelped. She looked down to see blood seeping from her chest. Then she let her eyes move back up to Joe. He was doubled over, his free hand covering a spot on his lower shoulder. He pulled his hand away to reveal a grisly mass of red streaming down his chest. He looked at Mara in confusion, almost shock, then he turned around just as the officer came around the front of the car.

"Freeze!" the police officer yelled again, gun drawn and ready.

Mara gasped. It suddenly felt hard to breathe. Her vision began to blur. Fear rushed in. *I don't want to die this way. No! Not like this!*

With what strength she had left, she watched the scene before her.

She heard the loud thunder of Joe's gun going off as he turned toward the cop. She thought he had missed, but she couldn't see well. In the same instant, another shot rang off and Joe's body flew back and hit the ground. Then another. Joe's blurred body jerked and then suddenly ceased to move.

Mara sighed. Everything felt distant, even the pain, though it was excruciating, seemed to be farther away, less intrusive. Then she heard a voice, the police officer.

"Are you ok—" he stopped abruptly. He was handsome. *Young*…she thought, she couldn't tell for certain, his features were blurred.

Deputy Ashton Keating tried to smile for the girl. He would make her comfortable, but that was all he could do. EMS would never arrive in time and there was no way he could get her out of the car on his own, not without harming her more.

"You're going to be fine," Ashton assured her, rain water dripping from his nose and soaking his shirt. It beaded down through the window and splashed against her legs. "What's your name, darling?"

She was too young for this. So was the dead black kid on the road's shoulder for that matter. He had done what he had to. He had taken action. He tried to smile for the girl as he asked her for her name again, "Darling, what's your name?"

"Ma… Mara," she spoke in a slow stutter. She was looking up at him, but then she wasn't, not really. She was already distant, like she was there and not there at the same time.

"Mara? Well, Mara, help is on its way," he said. It was on its way, but it would be too late, of that he was certain. He reached through the shards of glass that used to constitute the windshield and took her hand, trying not to introduce any new pain. Her fingers where small, and cold. They felt fragile and soft in his grip. An image of his own teenage daughter, Kindred, superimposed itself in his mind. She was grinning happily. He was certain that Mara had done the same, often probably. The thought of his daughter in the same position as this poor child tore at his soul, but he held back a tear that threatened to break the surface.

"Da... D... Dad," Mara spoke.

Deputy Keating grinned sadly, "No, Mara, I'm Deputy Keating. I'm here—"

"No...Dad. Dad is in dan...in danger. He nee... He needs help," she slowly got out between stuttered breaths, "at home."

"Your dad needs help at home?"

Mara nodded vigorously, fighting off the pain. Her vision blurred more. Suddenly her body convulsed and she coughed violently. Blood spurted between her lips. The deputy looked down at her caringly.

At least I'm not alone, Mara thought.

"Is he in danger? Just nod, you don't have to talk." Deputy Keating tried to understand without pressing her too hard.

Mara nodded, and swallowed. He could tell that it hurt her.

"Is there someone else there? Someone trying to hurt him?" Ashton tried one more question. He knew there was little time left for more.

She nodded weakly, "Hel... Help him."

"I will," he promised her.

Deputy Keating frowned as the girl's thin fingers went limp in his hand. He squeezed tightly and watched as her eyes became distant, glassy.

"I promise." He sighed to hold back the emotions building inside him. He looked away from the girl and tried to focus on what he had to do next. He needed to know where *home* was.

CHAPTER 21

Chase grinned, baring his healthy white teeth. Dalton had always expected something less pristine to reside within the jaws of a monster. He held the knife at waist level out in front, ready to strike.

"This isn't how I envisioned our little night ending, Dalton," Chase, Bullet, the boy who had lost everything at Dalton's hands jeered. "A fight to the death."

He chuckled like only someone with nothing to lose could. Dark, menacing. Almost demonic.

"No, I had envisioned you dying slowly and painfully," the boy continued as he got to his feet and moved in slow and carefully, blade at the ready. "Mmmm. I thought about it a lot. Stabbing you over and over and over again. Not fatally at first. Oh no, that would be too easy. First somewhere that would just hurt a lot. Maybe your thigh, your calf. Wouldn't want you die too quickly on me. Then of course I'd work my way up."

He closed his eyes in a demented fantasy, groaning. It was as good a moment as any other. Dalton dove forward and stabbed out at the boy's midriff. Chase moved to the side and sliced out, connecting with Dalton's shoulder.

Dalton yelped as the blade carved a shallow red path along his deltoid. Instinctively, he reached for the wound. The boy was fast. The boy reared backward, driving his elbow into Dalton's face. Spit and blood flew from a new split along Dalton's chin. He stumbled back, lost his footing and fell to the floor with a loud thud.

Chase dropped to his knees and flung his body over Dalton. He grabbed for Dalton's knife-wielding hand. "This isn't going to end well for you, Dalton," Chase growled as he wrapped his fingers around Dalton's wrist.

He gripped tight and pressed Dalton's hand to the ground. At the same time, he lifted his body up just enough to make his own knife useful. He raised the knife and jabbed down.

With his free hand, Dalton punched out. He connected with the boy's jaw, earning a dull thunk. He did not notice the pain throbbing in his fingers as the adrenaline began to kick in, unaccustomed to the brutal nature of fist fighting. Chase reeled back in pain and loosened his grip on Dalton's hand.

Dalton used the moment to push back against the hand that held him down while he sent another fist square into Chase's nose. A small shower of blood and a grunt were his reward. The boy's grip loosened from his wrist and Dalton reeled back. He lashed out aimlessly at whatever resided directly above him with the blade.

The boy let out a pained yell and wrenched back. The scream had been accompanied by the sickening sound of metal slashing through skin. Dalton punched out again and Chase tumbled onto the tile with another grunt. Dalton shuffled frantically up to a standing position as Chase worked to do the same. The boy cupped his stomach. The pitch black pigment in his t-shirt contrasted heavily against the pale white skin underneath where the shirt was sliced open. A thin line of red seeped slowly over his stomach.

Dalton didn't grin like Chase would have. Instead he grimaced, and tried to steel his nerves as his hands almost vibrated with adrenaline. Then out of the corner of his eye, he saw something off. A bright reflection of orange and yellow danced outside the windows.

Then a tall flame breached the entrance where the lantern had been sitting earlier that night. *Dammit!*

"You'll have to do better than that, Dalton," Chase chided and abruptly jumped forward.

Dalton pulled himself from his trance just in time to sidestep the blade by a mere inch. He slashed out with his own massive curved blade. Its red-soaked edge glinted as it arched toward the boy's neck, the blade inches from its target, but Chase dipped down with cunning speed. He slipped his hand over Dalton's knife-wielding wrist and continued the motion down and around. He kept a tight grip as he wrenched Dalton's arms around and behind his back, rendering the blade useless in Dalton's hand. Dalton screamed and his fingers sprang open.

The knife clanked to the floor.

Expecting what was to come, Dalton tried to ignore the pain. As he expected, Chase brought his arm up from below, swinging wide, attempting to stab Dalton in the chest, gut him.

Dalton knew it was either his life or a bad cut. He chose a bad cut. He willed his body to move against the boy's grip, his shackled hand seared as he stepped to the side and brought his other arm around. With a shred of luck, Dalton managed to get his free hand pressed against Chase's incoming hand. He shoved away as hard as he could manage and closed his eyes. Pain bloomed up his upper arm.

"Ah! Dammit!" Dalton yelled between gritted teeth.

He opened his eyes to find the long blade pinning Chase's arm to his like a shish kabob. *Not what I had planned!*

"Argh!" Chase screamed louder than he had all night. He almost mimicked Dalton, mouth wide in pain, eyes crooked.

Before Dalton could react, Chase yanked the knife down and out. It stung like hell as the blade made a new path out, carving the old cut further. Crimson spewed on the carpet as the blade exited the skin and their arms separated. Dalton wanted to pull away from the boy and cradle his arm, comfort himself. Instead he reached out with his free arm while Chase still reeled from the pain and gripped the fresh wound on the boy's arm. He pressed his fingers into to ripe opening. He gritted his teeth and pushed back against his stomach as it went to churning.

Chase screamed. His body shuddered under the intense wave of pain that swept through him. Overtaken by the agony that coursed up his arm, his fingers fumbled their grip on the large knife. It plopped to the leather sofa, painting erratic streaks of iron-infused red as it clambered down to the floor.

"This ends now!" Dalton growled, then released the boy's arm and brought his fist around again, finding purchase just under Chase's nose. The boy stumbled back.

In the seconds since Dalton had last saw the flames building at the front door, the hellish display of red, orange and yellow had ravaged a path into the foyer and kitchen. The heat from the fire now encompassed him, threatening to reach out and singe his skin. The cabinetry in the kitchen was ablaze and the grey fog was forming along the tall ceiling. He coughed as he inhaled a large breath of the dangerous smog.

Dalton jumped on Chase, tackling him to the ground well out of reach of his weapon. He was at a disadvantage, with or without a knife. The boy had clearly prepared for this moment. Dalton had sat in his comfy chair and took the elevator every chance he got.

He took another swing, driving his fist into Chase's abdomen. He was rewarded with the sound of air rushing from the boy's mouth. Chase lashed out with his good arm, hooking it harshly against Dalton's temple. Dalton's world fuzzed out and then back in. When his vision cleared again, the boy was in his face, and he found a surge of heavy pain break through his stomach as the boy upper-cutted him.

Dalton grunted with each blow.

"Just. Give. Up!" Chase yelled after each blow.

"No," Dalton grunted between gritted teeth.

The flame reached closer. The temperature was blooming, becoming unbearable. Sweat trickled down Dalton's body from both exhaustion and the heat building up around them. The blaze had already consumed the kitchen, the foyer and was now encroaching fast on the living room where Dalton was making his last stand. Smoke billowed around them, making it hard to see. A fist he had not expected smacked him under the nose. His head jarred upward, more blood sprinkling the floor.

Dalton groaned and returned the blow aimlessly. He found his mark, his fist connecting with the boy's waist. He coughed hard after swallowing another lung full of smoke. Chase did the same in the middle of a swing that ended abruptly as his body shook from the cough.

With only a moment to spare, Dalton stole a quick glance around the room. There was only one clear exit that didn't involve jumping through a searing wall of flames. The door leading onto the back deck with the view of the lake. As he searched, his eyes hit another door. A small closet next to a heavy curio covered in glass. It was framed in black walnut and held an assortment of Lenore's china and other knick-knacks. *Lenore's.*

In the corner of his vision he saw one of the knives just a foot or so to his right and then Chase rearing back for another swing. Dalton ducked and the fist careened over him by an inch in a long arch. The boy's momentum carried past Dalton, his swings becoming erratic. Dalton shoved past and scooped up the blade. He spun around and jousted forward as Chase turned around.

He met Chase's stunned gaze as the blade pierced into his soft skin just above his waist and below his stomach. The boy groaned and blinked in confusion. He gasped and then snarled his lips angrily.

"It's not going to end...like this," Chase told him, fighting off the pain. Dalton gritted his teeth, hating every second that the blade remained grafted into the boy's body.

But he had wanted this. He had wanted to watch the boy die, watch him pay for what he had done. Yet, now that he had the opportunity, now that he had the ability to pull out the knife and strike again, he suddenly didn't want to. His body shivered, anger fighting with the thought of ending another person's life. Then his wife's face replaced Chase's. He stared into those empty green eyes, dead and gone. Then it was Aiden, his eyes glassy and cold. Dalton gritted his teeth again as a rage built inside his chest. His gaze shot to the closet.

The closet.

Dalton shoved the knife hard against Chase's skin and wrenched him to the side. He threw his injured arm around Chase and held on as best he could, ignoring the pain that surged up his limb. Chase must have been in shock. He didn't punch out or fight. Dalton shoved him toward the closet door. Only two more feet. The flames seemed to lick at his body now. Sweat poured and the smoke choked.

He reached for the door and turned the knob. Pain surged up his arm as the torn muscle flexed. He grunted and started to push Chase toward the opening. Suddenly, Chase was lucid again. He saw what was happening and lashed out. Dalton's head jerked back as a fist haphazardly made contact with his skull. Then another feeble blow. Dalton yanked the blade out of the boy's body and seared his eyes into the boy's black pits.

"Fuck you!" Then he put his entire body behind the knife and thrust it back into Chase's stomach. The roar of the flames drowned out the sound of the metal blade slicing through soft flesh. It covered his garbled scream. He lashed out aimlessly.

The monster that had plagued him with high words and demented games. The boy who had commanded the brutalization of his daughter and had slaughtered his son and wife. The freak behind a simple mask, that hurt teenager, now whimpered and groaned, gasped as the knife moved in his stomach. Dalton grinded his teeth and then pushed Chase fully into the large closet. He yanked the knife from the boy's stomach, stepped back and slammed the door shut.

Screams echoed from behind the door, quickly followed by panicked thumping on the wooden slab. Dalton coughed as the smoke took up most the room in his lungs. He lunged to the side and put all his strength into pushing the massive curio cabinet. It began to lift, but came back to the floor. He heaved again and the cabinet toppled over and crashed onto the floor. Glass shattered all over the tile floor reflecting the red and orange of the approaching flames about the dark room. Dalton leaned his back into the cabinet and shoved it against the wall just as Chase got his wits to use the handle. The door slammed shut in his face.

The monster tried again to open the door, but it wouldn't budge, held tight by the heavy cabinet. Dalton coughed again, his head feeling light from the smoke. He turned to run out the back door but his feet were slow, heavy. Flames burst around him. The couch and recliner became a blazing wildfire. The ceiling above was coated in what appeared to be liquid as the hues of orange, blue and red consumed the room.

Dalton stumbled forward. The back door was within reach, only another three yards from where he stood. The distance seemed to elongate as his vision narrowed and his head began to spin. He stepped forward and lost his balance. He squinted, trying to clear his vision, trying to peer through the heavy smoke. Ahead, the world seemed to stretch out. He reached out with his good arm and lifted his chest from the floor. He started to crawl.

Smoke billowed around him. A horrid noise pierced through the roar of the flames. Something crashed behind him. He didn't care, he had to get out. He had to live for Mara. Then a shrill but muffled scream rose above the howl of the flame. Then there was another and another. Dalton tried to bury the noise as he pushed forward, but it dug into his skull. He coughed again, this time over and over again. The flames were only feet behind him. His vision blurred as his head began to spin. Then his world faded away.

The vendor hall was a buzz of activity. Suits and conservative skirts danced from one booth to the next in search of that next business contact or art purchase. Dalton had his eyes set on one piece of art in particular. She was beautiful, slender but not too so, long legs, soft brown hair with just a little wave that hung inches below her shoulders. She used her hand to push a stray lock back behind her shoulder. Perfect pink lips and beautiful sea green eyes, so intelligent and unwittingly seductive.

Dalton stood across the aisle watching her talk to some kid, probably a college intern for some Ivy League school from the looks of his suit. They were eagerly discussing her newest book. Dalton's chest was thumping, his breathing coming harder than usual. Her name was Lenore and he was about to ask her out on a date.

With a sudden gasp, Dalton jerked upright. His left arm tore back from its ill-chosen perch on the sodden grass. It protested against the strain on his fresh open wound. Pellets of cold liquid peppered his exposed skin. It felt good against his overheated body. Beyond the droplets, the sky was dark and the cold air bristled against his skin. He reached around his body toward the bloody mass on his other arm.

"Careful now," a man's voice urged him. A strong hand helped him sit up and stayed against his back to support him. "Take it easy."

Dalton squinted in the rain and found the man knelt beside him.

An officer, his entire uniform was sodden, his face soaked, water beading off his chin and down to the ground. An officer. The sight of the lawman sent a small calm over his body. Finally, Dalton could not hold back his surprise. He was alive.

"I'm Deputy Ashton Keating. Is there anyone left in the house?" Deputy Keating asked.

Dalton didn't answer right away. He managed to angle his face toward the burning structure. Even a generous fifteen yards away, he could still feel the heat beating off the mammoth flames. They rose up toward the midnight sky, daring Mother Nature to try to quench its raw power.

No.

"No," Dalton said. He had no way of knowing whether Chase, or Bullet, was still among the living or a charred mass of melting flesh. He had trapped the boy in the closet. For a brief moment he felt a twinge of guilt before the rain washed it away. The calm of his next words chilled him. "No. They're all dead."

Suddenly, his mind spun around on him.

"Mara!" Dalton flung his eyes back toward the deputy. "Mara! Did you find Mara?"

It was an unlikely chance, but he had to ask. He needed to know if she was all right. She had to be all right. Had to be. He needed her to be all right.

"Are you Dalton Summers?" Deputy Keating asked, trying to maintain a professional detachment.

Dalton nodded, "Yes. I'm her dad. Is she okay? Is she with you?"

For a moment, the only sounds came from the growing deluge and the dwindling blaze as it fought against the rain. The two men looked at each other for a horrible moment. Ashton shot his eyes down and then back up to Dalton, and swallowed.

"No, sir," The deputy said. "She's uh…she's dead. She was shot."

He paused. "She told me to come here, that you were in danger."

Words would not come to Dalton. Only pain, gut wrenching, agonizing pain, not of the physical variety but of the mind and heart. His body went numb and he almost fell back to the ground but Deputy Keating kept a firm handle on him. Dalton wailed. It was a horrible sound. Grief, guilt, pain. His tears mixed with the cold rain, pouring down his face in equal measure. She was all he had left, and now she was gone, too. Gone. Forever.

The officer pulled Dalton in and wrapped an arm around him. He looked out onto the roiling lake over Dalton's head, trying to be strong for the man. He had no idea what he was going through and he would not lie to the man to comfort him. He just held him and let the man grieve.

In the distance, Dalton heard the sound of sirens. Then the flash of blue lights reflected in the hundreds of raindrops and broke through the dark. Seconds later, two more officers jogged around the corner. They stopped when they saw the Deputy cradled over Dalton.

Mara. Aiden. Lenore. Nathan. Why? Why?

The simple question ran over and over through his mind. There was no answer. Yes, he had made a mistake, a horrible mistake, but his family had not deserved to pay for it. Not his precious Mara. Not his little buddy, Aiden. And not his loving to a fault wife...Lenore.

It was his price to pay, not theirs. His weeping turned to anger, he rocked back and forth as the tears kept flowing. He couldn't live like this. He couldn't.

Inches from his face, through the pouring rain, he saw the Deputy's standard issue pistol. He didn't give himself time to rethink. He reached around with his good arm and snatched the weapon from the officer's holster and jerked away from the man's embrace. Then he shoved the barrel to his temple.

"Whoa! No, no!" Deputy Keating rushed back with his hands out.

His next words were calm and deliberate. "Put the gun down, Dalton. Just put it down."

"No. I can't. I can't live like this. Without...without them," Dalton said. The tears were hard to see through the thick downpour, but they poured down his cheeks nonetheless. "They weren't supposed to suffer. Not like this. No, not like this. It's my fault. I can't live like this. I just can't."

The other deputies drew their weapons. Dalton heard the click of the safeties disengaging as they took aim. Ashton waved them down, urging them to lower their pistols. Reluctantly, they obeyed.

"Dalton, this isn't your fault," he said. He didn't know the whole situation, he didn't even know half of it, but he knew the man was grieving. He reached his hand out. "Just put down the gun. It doesn't have to end this way. They wouldn't want you to do this."

"You don't know shit!" Dalton yelled angrily. Angry at himself, at the boys that had hurt his family, at Chase, at the man who was trying to help him. He had to pay for what he had done. Dalton tightened his grip on the trigger. He began to squeeze, but he couldn't do it. His finger refused to move. He closed his eyes and tried again, but he couldn't make himself pull the trigger. *Coward,* he thought.

"Please, Dalton, put the gun down." The deputy's tone became more commanding.

Dalton opened his eyes and without thinking, he pulled the pistol from his own head and aimed for Deputy Keating. "Shoot me!"

Ashton Keating stumbled a few feet back at the sight of the hollow barrel staring him down. He held his hands up with fingers outspread. "Hold on there, Dalton. You don't want to do this."

The two deputies to Keating's right raised their weapons again. This time Keating did not stop them.

"Think about what you're doing. You're in pain, Dalton. You're hurting. I don't know what you're going through and I'm not going to act like I do, but you can't end it like this," Deputy Keating tried to explain between strained breaths, keeping his voice calm. "You're not going to shoot me, Dalton. You're going to put down the gun and we're going to walk away from this. You're going to come with me and we're going to help you."

The chill of the rain suddenly made Dalton shiver. Then the realization of what he was doing broke through like a raging avalanche. His hands began to shake and he released his grip. The gun dropped to the ground, splashing against the sodden soil. His whole body was shaking. Deputy Keating rushed in and grabbed Dalton's arm before he fell to the ground, ignoring the weapon. He pulled Dalton over his shoulder and took in a rain-soaked breath.

Dalton began to sob. His body was racked with guilt, pulsing with each tear. He had to *live* with this.

CHAPTER 22

It was raining again.

It was a light rain, but it seemed to press down unsympathetically against the array of black umbrellas. Arms struggled to support the light constructs that kept the rain from pelting their skin and clothes, against their heavy hearts.

Dalton's bloodshot eyes moved from casket to casket. Each was sparkling white with an arrangement of roses atop the sorrowful box. A bouquet of beautiful white roses capped Aiden and Mara's caskets. Dalton couldn't stop his tears as the realization hit him again, as it had a hundred times over the past days. He would never see them again, not here. A set of red roses crowned the coffin in the center, Lenore's.

He wanted to rush up and drop his head against the smooth finish of the dreaded boxes, to cry, to mourn without restraint. But he couldn't, not now.

"This is not the end. Not the conclusion of a life, but the beginning of something greater," the pastor continued. The elderly man was dressed in a black suit and pants, a white button-up and black tie. He looked back down at his Bible contemplatively and then returned his attention to those gathered around the three boxes. Dalton's parents and Lenore's. Old faces, worn with time and stricken with grief. So many friends and other relatives also gathered behind them. Then the pastor turned to Dalton as he spoke not to the crowd, but to Dalton specifically.

"Mourn our lost loved ones…" he paused again. "But remember, death is but a passing on to a greater place. Rejoice for them."

Dalton bit his lip. A subtle anger rose from his chest. *Rejoice? How can I rejoice? They're gone, dead. I'm left here to remember.* He closed his eyes and tried to calm himself. *No. He's right.*

The acceptance of the pastor's words did little to assuage Dalton's grief, his guilt, but it gave him something to hold on to, something to move forward with. He took in a deep breath and blinked the tears from his lashes as friends began to file by, placing singular yellow roses on each casket.

There were so many faces that Dalton didn't know. Lenore's work associates in the publishing world. Classmates, coaches and teachers who knew Aiden and Mara. He saw Faith Moreno step up to Aiden's casket, tears streaming down her face. Dalton knew they had been the best of friends and that his boy had always had a thing for the girl. It had brought him to tears when she told him just days ago that Aiden had finally got the nerve up to talk to her again. A surge of pride had ran through his veins, then sorrow at the love his son would never know, the life he'd never have. He wiped another tear away as the line dwindled and disappeared.

Dalton stepped forward and placed a hand on Aiden's casket, the tears began to pour, his heart hurt. There was so much he wanted to say as Aiden's face entered his mind. The boy hadn't liked sports, but he always loved a good movie or book. He was his mother's son. The phrase hurt. Dalton dropped his cheek to the casket. He was so proud of the kid, he only hoped Aiden had known. "I love you, Aiden."

A comforting hand found Dalton's shoulder. He looked back with a grief-stricken frown. It was his mother. In what world did it make sense for Dalton, a middle-aged man, to be standing in the presence of his elderly mother when his teenage son lay lifeless in a wooden box about to be buried six feet under?

He let his hand slide off the casket as he moved to the foot of Mara's resting place. He again placed his hand on the cold wet box. He wished it was warmer for her, hoped it was comfortable. Dalton pushed aside the inane thought as the tears blurred his vision. He wished he could attend just one more of her volleyball games, watch her spike a winning ball. She had loved the sport so much. He wanted to hear her call him *Daddy* one more time. Dalton turned his face from casket and closed his eyes, but he was met with her gorgeous blue eyes.

"I love you, darling." He opened his eyes again, and again he let his hand drop away from the sleek box.

Then he stared up at the red roses that decorated the head of the horrid box. He imagined the strong beautiful woman that laid inside, lifeless and cold. Dalton knew at that moment that nothing could hurt him worse than this, nothing could tear apart his heart, his world, more than had already been accomplished. His eyes shifted to Mara's casket for a second and then back to Lenore's. His kids had known he loved them, he'd shown them, been there for them. But Lenore. Lenore he had neglected and wronged in about every way he could, and why? For a moment he didn't know the answer, but then it came rushing in. He pushed his own faults onto her, he had pushed her away, he had pushed away the most loving and selfless person he'd ever known. And now?

Dalton let his mind linger back twenty-one years earlier, to the day he met Lenore at the art conference in Georgia. He had been a junior associate at a Charlotte architectural firm and she was attending to promote her first book. He had stumbled all over himself when he'd first spoken to her.

Dalton smiled briefly at the memory before the guilt of how he had treated Lenore the past years crept back in. He would never know if she had forgiven him. How could she? Could he?

"I love you, Lenore…" He stared down at the white casket, a symbol of purity, the red roses, love. But all he found was his own guilt, the wracking grief and realization of what his actions had caused. Dalton's knees shook and then went numb. He dropped to the ground by the cold box, oblivious to the rain. Water soaked through his slacks and around his knees. His hand still gripped the gloss-coated box. Through tears and stuttered breaths he apologized, as he would continue to do from that day forward.

"I'm sorry… I'm so…sorry. I'm sorry."

CHAPTER 23

The small office smelt of old cologne. It was musky but not overbearing. Books lined the wall to Dalton's left and three narrow windows crowned the wall to his right. In front of him sat a short stocky man of about fifty. The man's grey hair formed a crown around the dark skin of his head. A thin mustache and goatee outlined his small lips just under a pair of rimless glasses.

"So how are you feeling, Mr. Summers?" Doctor Kapil Prashad asked in a nasally tone, his attention confidently locked onto Dalton.

"I'm hanging in there," Dalton responded, trying not to focus on the fact that he was talking to a psychiatrist. The police had felt he needed to work out his feelings. Something about his "outburst" after he'd been drug from his burning home. They weren't pressing charges, though, not after they had found all the dead bodies and his home's security feed.

"It's all right to talk to me about how you're feeling, Mr. Summers. Dalton. Can I call you Dalton?" Doctor Prashad asked.

"Yes, of course, Doctor," Dalton agreed.

"And you may call me Kapil."

Dalton nodded. He licked his lips nervously and crisscrossed his fingers. *Let's just get this over with, please.*

"I'd like to begin our sessions with a few questions, Dalton," he started in, it was his first session with Dalton. "Some of these may not be easy for you to answer right now, but I want you to be as honest with me as you can. All right?"

Dalton nodded again, "Yeah. I'll try."

"Good, that's all I ask. Hopefully this will become easier after a few visits."

Doctor Prashad looked down to his desk where a notepad sat. He scribbled down something. Dalton pursed his lips, wondering what it was. The doctor looked back up with a gentle smile.

Half an hour later, Dalton was walking out of the office and to his car. He stepped up into a new Jeep. After the incident, that's what he was calling it now, he'd sold the BMW, and the other cars. Then he'd bought an apartment in Charlotte in one of the high rises. Everything about his home, the land, the cars, Kannapolis, it all reminded him of that night. He had to get rid of it, though he had a feeling that Doctor Prashad would have disagreed with his logic had he the opportunity.

He shifted the SUV into drive and pulled out of the parking lot. As much as he hated going to the psychiatrist, he secretly hoped it would help. He knew that he'd live with what happened that night every day of his life, but he wasn't coping well himself. He hated to admit it but he needed the help.

With time he hoped it would pay off, that he could move on, that he could live with what happened. No matter what the doctors said, though, it was his fault, he knew it.

The Jeep glided under a stoplight surrounded on all four sides by massive glass-faced buildings that reached higher than he could see, much higher. People walked the sidewalks. Some were in conversation with fellow walkers, others were absorbed in their phones, but they all seemed happy or unreadable. A woman with a little toddler crossed the adjacent street as he stopped at the next light. The little blond-haired girl smiled brilliantly as they stepped up onto the side-walk. For a brief moment her bright green eyes met Dalton's. He smiled.

Then the light turned green and Dalton guided the Jeep forward. Ahead, an outcropping of trees and decorative shrubs dominated the next square, hollowing out a space of reds, yellows, oranges and browns amidst the glassed towers. Dalton let his gaze drift to the serenity of the gently flowing water lapping over the edge of a pool behind an almost bare tree. Children played and lovers sat wrapped together in long coats on the wrought iron benches enjoying the trickle of the water.

He let himself smile just a bit. The light turned red and he came to a stop by the oasis. He watched the people walking to and fro, sitting, talking. A young couple, or maybe business associates, walked through the sparse crowd. Another man in a suit rushed by, completely bypassing the calm scene. Another sat on a bench and pulled out a lunch. Then in the background, just at the edge of the pool of glimmering water, a man stood. No, a boy. He stood in a black t-shirt and jeans, his face pale and thin, and dark eyes shone into Dalton's soul as he glared back.

Dalton's heart pounded, his pulse jumped. *What? No!* He clasped his eyes closed, not wanting to open them again, but did immediately. There was no one there. His eyes darted back and forth among the crowd. He was nowhere. Dalton looked down and slowed his breathing. Then the light changed. It was time to move on.

ABOUT THE AUTHOR

Jordon Greene is the author of the Amazon Bestselling conspiracy thriller *They'll Call It Treason*. A graduate of UNC Charlotte, Jordon works as a full stack web developer for the nation's largest privately owned shoe retailer and spends his spare moments keeping up with the next big action movie, listening to hard rock music and writing his next novel. He lives in Concord, NC just close enough and just far enough away from Charlotte.

Visit Jordon Online
www.JordonGreene.com

If you enjoyed this book, please consider reviewing it and telling others about it.